DISCARDED

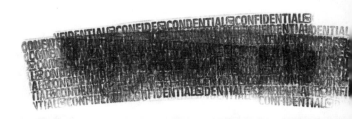

CAREER
DISCOVERY
ENCYCLOPEDIA

2

CIT

FAS

FERGUSON PUBLISHING COMPANY
CHICAGO, ILLINOIS

Career discovery encyclopedia / Holli Cosgrove [editor-in-chief].
         p.   cm.
    Includes indexes.
    Contents: v. 1. A-Circus performers -- v. 2. City managers-Fas -- v. 3. FBI-Lawyers --
v. 4. Layout workers-Pac -- v. 5. Paint industry workers-Rom -- v. 6. Roofers-Zoo.
    Summary: Six volumes with over 500 articles on all categories of occupations present
such information as job descriptions, salaries, educational and training requirements,
sources of further information, and other pertinent facts.
    ISBN 0-89434-184-7 (set)
    1. Vocational guidance—Dictionaries—Juvenile literature.
    [1. Vocational guidance—Dictionaries. 2. Occupations.]
I. Cosgrove, Holli, 1964–
HF5381.2.C37   1997
331.7'02—dc21   96–52611
                                                                    CIP
                                                                    AC

Printed in the United States of America.
U-2

CONTENTS

VOLUME 2

CITY MANAGERS

WHAT CITY MANAGERS DO

City managers direct the day-to-day operations of a city. They appoint department heads to manage the various areas of city government, and they oversee their work. They also make long-range plans for the city's needs as it grows larger. One important job of a city manager is to prepare a yearly budget for the city. The budget outlines the amount of money the city plans to spend on law enforcement, public health, recreation, economic development, and other services such as garbage pickup and street improvements.

City managers are usually appointed by the city council. They may, in some areas, be elected to the office which means they have to campaign for the job. They may also be hired by the mayor.

The manager presents plans to the council members and reports on ongoing projects. These plans and projects involve housing, city transportation, crime prevention, street repairs, and water and sewer systems.

City managers may be responsible for appointing department heads and a staff to coordinate the various activities of the government. These people have supervisory duties over tax collection, public health, public buildings, law enforcement, and all the other details of keeping a city or town working smoothly. In addition, the city manager will coordinate, and compile reports received from the department heads and distribute them to the city council.

City managers need to be decisive, problem-solvers with a knack for communicating with a variety of people and groups.

EDUCATION AND TRAINING

City managers must have a bachelor's degree. With a master's degree, a person has a better chance of getting a city manager job. The most useful college degrees for city managers are business management and public administration. Some city managers have a master's or other advanced degree in political science, urban planning, or law. Some degree programs in public administration include part-time work in a city manager's office. To be eligible for city management jobs, people are usually required to take a civil service examination. Recent college graduates may begin as assistants in a city manager's office. There they learn to solve various city management problems. After perhaps five years' experience, they may become qualified to be city managers themselves.

OUTLOOK AND EARNINGS

Because city managers tend to remain at their jobs, few job openings are expected to appear in the near future. Applicants who have advanced degrees and complex management and financial skills have the best chance of getting a job.

City managers earn average salaries of $57,000 a year. Their salaries vary according to their education and experience and the size of their city. A city manager of a small community with fewer than 2,500 people may earn $33,000, while a manager of a big city with 500,000 to 1 million residents may earn $125,000. Members of the city council decide what the city manager's salary will be. If city managers do their job well, they may be paid a higher salary to keep them from moving to another job.

WAYS OF GETTING MORE INFORMATION

Young people interested in becoming city managers can take part in their school's student government. During vacations they may be able to get jobs in their city's local government offices.

For more information write to:

International City/County Management Association.
*777 North Capitol Street NE, Suite 500
Washington, DC 20002-4201*

National Association of Schools of Public Affairs and Administration
*1120 G Street NW, Suite 520
Washington, DC 20005*

Organizational Skills

People Skills

Social Sciences

The city manager works closely with the mayor so that they can better plan the city's future.

CITY PLANNERS

SCHOOL SUBJECTS:
CIVICS/GOVERNMENT, GEOGRAPHY/SOCIAL STUDIES

PERSONAL INTERESTS:
BUILDING THINGS, THE ENVIRONMENT

OUTLOOK:
FASTER THAN THE AVERAGE

OTHER ARTICLES TO LOOK AT:
Architects
City Managers
Civil Engineers
Landscape Architects
Surveyors

WHAT CITY PLANNERS DO

City planners develop plans for making cities as efficient and attractive as possible. City planners must be concerned with the economic life of the city, its cultural life, and with environmental factors such as water pollution and trash disposal. They work closely with city officials and citizens.

Planners begin their work by becoming familiar with the existing buildings, transportation routes such as bus, subway and railroad lines, geographical features such as hills and rivers, and other important elements of the city, including schools, parks and airports. They pay special attention to stores and factories, studying their needs for services such as water and electric power, and how people can travel to and from them. Churches, recreational areas, residential districts, and other parts of the city are also studied. In addition, city planners are involved in figuring out how and where to provide shelters for the homeless, space and facilities for drug treatment centers, and low-cost housing and nursing homes for senior citizens.

Once the city planner understands the needs and goals of the city, he or she draws up a plan showing how land could be used for housing, business, and other purposes. The plan should provide information about the types of industry that can be expected, their location, and how these industries will benefit the city as well as the problems they may create in terms of water, sewage, and transportation. To do their job well, city planners have to see two sides of the coin: what's best for the city as well as what's best for the businesses and industries they want to attract to the city.

The plan will also include ideas about zoning to regulate the use of land. If redevelopment of rundown areas is required, the plan will suggest ideas for remodeling or replacing old buildings. They also are responsible for determining the cost of a specific project as well as ways it might be paid for.

EDUCATION AND TRAINING

A college education, with a major in planning, architecture, landscape architecture, civil engineering, or public administration, is the minimum requirement for a trainee job involved with city planning. Courses in economics, demography, and health administration are also highly recommended. For a career in city planning, however, a master's degree in city or regional planning is normally essential. The last part of the master's program usually includes a period of practical experience called an internship. This is accomplished by taking regular paid (sometimes not paid) employment during the summer in a planning office approved by the college.

OUTLOOK AND EARNINGS

The employment outlook for city planners is expected to be faster than the average in the next decade. Cities will continue to face important concerns having to do with economic development, environmental problems, transportation needs, and energy production. Also, planners will be needed to help determine how undeveloped land along coastal and rural areas should be zoned and used. Demand for planners will be especially high in areas experiencing rapid growth, such as California and northern Virginia, and in areas that have placed a strict priority on planning, such as Maine and parts of Florida. Small towns and cities in older parts of the country, particularly the Northeast, will need planners to work on preservation and redevelopment projects. In addition, as older public facilities from bridges to highways to tunnels wear out, planners are needed to help design new ones.

Salaries received by city planners vary depending on who employs them, how much education and experience they have, and their level of responsibility. The overall average is about $45,000 a year. Planners with more than ten years of experience can make from $52,000 to over $63,000, with those working in heavily populated areas making the most. Qualified job seekers who are flexible about where they can live and who are willing to work in small towns or rural areas will have the best prospects.

WAYS OF GETTING MORE INFORMATION

Students interested in becoming city planners can learn more about this career by finding a summer or part-time job in the office of an architect or civil engineer.

For more information write to:

American Planning Association
1776 Massachusetts Avenue, NW
Washington, DC 20036-1904

Researching areas for potential development, a city planner studies maps of city districts.

CIVIL ENGINEERING TECHNICIANS

SCHOOL SUBJECTS:
MATHEMATICS, PHYSICS

PERSONAL INTERESTS:
BUILDING THINGS, COMPUTERS

OUTLOOK:
FASTER THAN THE AVERAGE

OTHER ARTICLES TO LOOK AT:
Architects
Construction Inspectors
Operating Engineers

WHAT CIVIL ENGINEERING TECHNICIANS DO

Civil engineering technicians help engineers design, plan, and build highways, airports, tunnels, bridges, and other structures. They help engineers in all areas of work, from estimating costs of a construction project to assisting in the preparation of drawings, maps, and charts. Technicians also often order the building materials that will be used on a project. Some technicians may inspect water treatment systems to make sure that they are not polluting the environment.

Civil engineering technicians work under the direction of engineers and carry out different jobs depending on what is needed at the time. One of their responsibilities is to make sure that each step of the construction process is completed before the next stage is started. The variety of job responsibilities requires that a technician have a basic knowledge of civil engineering and be able to do work at the construction site.

Although civil engineering technicians participate in all stages of the construction process, some may specialize. Some techni-

cians, for instance, focus their work primarily on building materials. They run tests on rock, soil, cement, steel, and other substances and then report back to the engineers on which materials would be best suited to a particular building site. Other specialists within the field include *research engineering technicians,* who test and develop new construction equipment, and *sales engineering technicians,* who sell building materials and construction equipment.

EDUCATION AND TRAINING

Civil engineering technicians must be able to draw and understand blueprints and sketches and follow directions carefully and completely. They must be good at organizing projects and paying close attention to details; a small error could completely stop a building project and cost thousands of dollars to fix.

The best way to become a civil engineering technician is to complete a two-year civil engineering technology program at a technical or vocational school. To be accepted into one of these programs, high school graduates should have a strong background in mathematics (algebra and geometry), physics, and the other sciences. These programs will include courses in mechanical drawing, advanced physics and mathematics, surveying, and computer programming. Students will also take courses in such specialty areas as heavy construction, construction technology, and bridge construction. Some technicians may get their training at a four-year college while majoring in engineering.

OUTLOOK AND EARNINGS

The future is bright for civil engineering technicians throughout the year 2005. This results from a continual need for new bridges, highways, and other public works. However, slowdown in construction might limit opportunities.

The average salary for civil engineering technicians is about $30,000 per year. Those who work for the government should make somewhat less than those employed at private construction companies.

WAYS OF GETTING MORE INFORMATION

A good way to find out about being a civil engineering technician is to get a part-time job on a construction site, often as an assistant to a technician. Taking shop courses in high school is another good way of finding out about this career.

9

In addition, call or write to:

American Congress on Surveying and Mapping
5410 Grosvenor Lane
Bethesda, MD 20814-2122
Tel: 301-493-0200

American Society for Engineering Education
11 Dupont Circle, Suite 200
Washington, DC 20036
Tel: 202-331-3500

American Society of Certified Engineering Technicians
PO Box 1348
Flowery Branch, GA 30542
Tel: 404-967-9173

American Society of Civil Engineers
345 E. 47th Street
New York, NY 10017
Tel: 212-705-7496

Manual Skills

Organizational Skills

Sciences and Mathematics

A civil engineering technician confirms that road construction follows the engineer's blueprint.

CIVIL ENGINEERS

OTHER ARTICLES TO LOOK AT:

Civil Engineering Technicians

Construction Inspectors

SCHOOL SUBJECTS:
MATHEMATICS, PHYSICS

PERSONAL INTERESTS:
BUILDING THINGS, FIXING THINGS

OUTLOOK:
FASTER THAN THE AVERAGE

WHAT CIVIL ENGINEERS DO

Civil engineers design and supervise the construction of a variety of structures, including bridges, dams, tunnels, buildings, highways, airstrips, and water-supply and sewage systems. Some civil engineers specialize in a particular category, such as railroads, irrigation, sanitation or public health, airports, transportation, waterworks, and even forests.

Like all engineers, civil engineers apply scientific knowledge to practical, everyday problems. In designing structures, they often must do a great deal of research and testing. They may have to change a design many times before it is considered acceptable.

Once a design has been completed, civil engineers supervise the building of the structure. They purchase materials, choose the equipment that is to be used,and assign the work crews. They must consider the time and cost involved in completing each part of the project. They must also try to solve any problems that occur. Civil engineers spend a lot of their time on construction sites. Many of these are in or near major cities and commercial developments, while others may be in very remote areas. Some engineers travel from place to place to work on different projects, spending two or three years at one site and then moving on to the next.

More than 40 percent of civil engineers work for government agencies—federal, state, county, and city. About 35 percent work for companies that provide engineering consulting services, such as developing designs for new construction projects. Others work for construction firms, public utilities, railroads, and manufacturers.

EDUCATION AND TRAINING

Most civil engineering jobs require a bachelor's degree in engineering. A large number of schools offer this degree, as well as master's degrees and doctorates. While a bachelor's degree is sufficient for an entry-level engineering job, students who wish to teach engineering or learn a new technology will improve their chances for promotion by getting an advanced degree. Since there are many other related types of engineers—petroleum, mining, nuclear, industrial, aeronautical, metallurgical and chemical, to name a few—it is sometimes possible to switch to another field of engineering without having to start at the beginning.

Students interested in becoming civil engineers should begin preparing while in high school. Important courses include algebra, geometry, physics, and chemistry. Courses in mechanical drawing are valuable. Because civil engineers must be able to communicate well with others, both in speech and in writing, English is also important.

The work of civil engineers often affects the public health and welfare. In such cases, many states require that they be licensed or registered.

OUTLOOK AND EARNINGS

The employment outlook for civil engineers looks good through the year 2000. Their skills will be needed for the design and building of new transportation systems, factories, and office buildings. They will also be needed to help repair or replace roads, bridges, and public buildings.

In the 1990s, civil engineers with a bachelor's degree start at about $28,000 a year in private industry. Those with a master's degree start at about $35,000 per year. Those with a doctorate begin at about $47,000.

Civil engineers working for the federal government earn slightly less. The salaries of all civil engineers increase with experience. The average salary for a mid-level engineer is $46,000 in private industry and $42,000 in the government. Senior-level engineers who manage others may earn $88,000 or more.

WAYS OF GETTING MORE INFORMATION

Schools and public libraries have many books on engineering and construction. Ask a librarian to help select a group of books. In high school, you can join a group such as the Junior Engineering Technical Society or attend a summer camp such as the Worcester Polytechnic Institute's 12-day program.

For more information write to:

American Society of Civil Engineers
345 East 47th Street
New York, NY 10017
Tel: 212-705-7496
Email: marketing@ny.asce.org

Institute of Transportation Engineers
525 School Street, SW, Suite 410
Washington, DC 20024
Tel: 202-554-8050
WWW: http://www.io.com/~itehq/

Junior Engineering Technical Society
1420 King Street, Suite 405
Alexandria, VA 22314
Tel: 703-548-5387
WWW: http://www.asee.org/external/jets

Frontiers in Science, Mathematics and Engineering
Worcester Polytechnic Institute
100 Institute Road
Worcester, MA 01609
Tel: 508-831-5000
WWW: http://cs.wpi.edu

A civil engineer verifies that the building under construction conforms to the blueprints designed by the architect.

CLERKS

OTHER ARTICLES TO LOOK AT:

Bank Services Occupations

Bookkeepers

Insurance Policy Processing Occupations

Receptionists

Retail Sales Workers

Secretaries

WHAT CLERKS DO

Clerks are the support workers found in every office, business, and store. They perform a wide variety of tasks, from greeting customers and seeing to their needs, to typing and filing, to operating computers, phones, cash registers and other machinery.

There are many types of clerks. *Billing clerks* keep track of a company's business transactions. They send out bills and check for payments received by the company. *Car rental agents* are clerks who act as salespersons. When a customer needs to rent a car from the airport or the company's local office, the agent writes a rental contract and answers questions about such things as the size of the car, air-conditioning, mileage, and extra insurance the client may need. *Counter and retail clerks* also work directly with customers, in supermarkets, department stores, laundries, bicycle repair shops, and any business that sells goods and is open to the public. They receive payments and answer customer questions.

Data entry clerks work in stores, insurance and manufacturing companies, hospitals, schools, banks, government agencies, and utility companies. They enter information into a computer system, which the computer then processes to produce such documents as bills and mailing lists. *File clerks* are responsible for keeping business records accurate, up to date, and properly stored, either in folders inside file cabinets or on computers. *General office clerks* perform a variety of tasks to help an office run smoothly, including typing, filing, answering telephones, delivering messages, and operating office machines.

Hotel clerks are employed by hotels, motels, and inns to greet and register guests, assign rooms, issue keys, answer questions about the hotel and the area, and take care of guests' bills when they check out. *Railroad clerks* keep track of all transactions of a railroad company. Their duties include selling tickets, keeping books, and recording the time each train arrives or leaves a station. If the train is off schedule, the clerk must note any reason for the delay. *Shipping and receiving clerks* make sure that their company's products are shipped properly and that the products they receive from other companies arrive in good condition.

Statistical clerks collect and organize information that businesses and governments need to make smart decisions. *Stock clerks* receive, sort, store, and give out supplies used by businesses, industries, and institutions. They work in stockrooms and warehouses. *Traffic agents* are concerned with the movement of cargo (goods) by air, water, truck, or rail. They handle the booking, billing, claims, and related paperwork for the movement of goods.

EDUCATION AND TRAINING

Some businesses will hire high school students as counter and retail clerks and as stock clerks. Most other clerk jobs require a minimum of a high school diploma. Courses in English, business, mathematics, typing, and bookkeeping are helpful. Some car rental agencies, especially in Florida and the Southwest, prefer agents who speak Spanish as well as English. Companies looking for traffic agents prefer candidates with one or two years of college, and many hotels prefer clerks with a college degree. In hotels where foreign travelers stay, clerks may be required to speak a foreign language.

OUTLOOK AND EARNINGS

There will always be job opportunities for clerks because of the wide variety of businesses needing them. The average salary for full-time clerks ranges from about $11,300 per year to $25,000, though starting wages may be lower and will depend on the employee's skills as well as the size and location of the company. Experienced clerks may make $32,000 per year. Wages tend to be highest in public utilities and mining companies, and they tend to be lower in companies involved in construction, finance, insurance, and real estate.

WAYS OF GETTING MORE INFORMATION

Students who wish to learn more about a clerk's job may seek a part-time or summer job in a local office or business, store, or car rental agency.

For further information, write to the following:

Association of American Railroads
50 F Street, NW
Washington, DC 20001
Tel: 202-639-2100

National Retail Federation
701 Pennsylvania Avenue, NW
Washington, DC 20004-2608

The Educational Institute of the American Hotel and Motel Association
PO Box 1240
East Lansing, MI 48826-1240

Manual Skills

People Skills

Organizational Skills

A railroad clerk checks train schedules and arrival times.

CLINICAL CHEMISTS

SCHOOL SUBJECTS:
BIOLOGY, CHEMISTRY

PERSONAL INTERESTS:
HEALTH, SCIENCE

OUTLOOK:
ABOUT AS FAST AS THE AVERAGE

OTHER ARTICLES TO LOOK AT:

Biomedical Engineers

Chemists

Because of their advanced education and training, clinical chemists handle more sophisticated equipment and testing. They may be responsible for ordering, purchasing, maintaining, and repairing the specialized equipment and instruments required for the laboratory tests. They design new laboratory procedures, and establish or continue training and supervision of other employees in laboratory procedures and skills.

Clinical chemists work most often in hospitals, clinics, commercial laboratories, and even for manufacturers of home diagnostic testing kits to work on product development.

WHAT CLINICAL CHEMISTS DO

Clinical chemists perform laboratory tests. These tests are an important way for physicians and patients to detect, diagnose, and treat disease. For example, tests can determine the level of medication in the blood to see whether a patient is taking the proper dosage, and whether the body is responding to the treatment.

Clinical chemists are specialized lab technologists who prepare specimens and analyze the chemicals and hormones found in body fluids (blood, urine, spinal fluid, and gastric juices). The clinical chemist's exact duties depend on the test being performed. If the test is automated, the chemist is responsible for calibrating (setting), loading specimens, and monitoring the instruments to make sure all goes correctly. After the results are ready, the chemist verifies their accuracy and sends them out or reports them to the attending physician. A test that is more involved, such as identifying cell types in leukemia, requires very different procedures, including special stains and chromosome studies.

EDUCATION AND TRAINING

Clinical chemists need at least a bachelor's degree with a major in medical technology or one of the life sciences, but most have advanced degrees: a master's, Ph.D. or even an M.D. degree. Although the emphasis is placed on courses in chemistry, biological sciences, microbiology, and mathematics, the curriculum may also include courses in management, business, and computers.

Most states require clinical chemists to be licensed or registered. In addition, most employers require certification by such organizations as the American Medical Technologists and the Credentialing Commission of the International Society for Clinical Laboratory Technology.

OUTLOOK AND EARNINGS

Because of the increased volume of medical testing, the outlook for clinical chemistry jobs is good through the year 2000. However, greater use of automation and specialized instruments may eliminate some jobs for clinical chemists.

Usually, openings occur when clinical chemists leave the field. Career advancement means becoming a sales representative, consultant, or teacher, or moving into administrative positions.

Those entering the career earn between $21,000 and $28,000 a year. Clinical chemists with a master's degree and experience can easily earn over $40,000 a year. Senior administrators earn still more.

WAYS OF GETTING MORE INFORMATION

High school students may do volunteer work in hospitals or medical facilities, often as a nurse's aide or candy striper. This is a good way to find out if working in a hospital environment is right for you.

For more information write to:

American Association for Clinical Chemistry
2101 L St. NW, Suite 202
Washington, DC 20037-1526

American Society for Clinical Laboratory Science
2021 L Street NW
Washington, DC 20036

Maintaining and monitoring complex laboratory equipment is part of the daily routine for a clinical chemist.

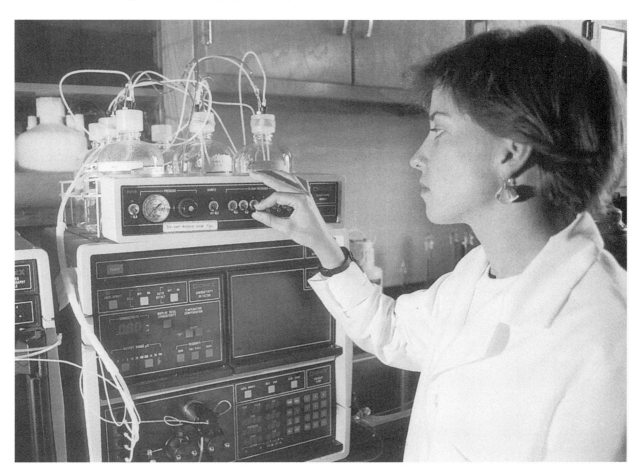

CLOWNS

OTHER ARTICLES TO LOOK AT:

Actors and Actresses

Circus Performers

Magicians

WHAT CLOWNS DO

Clowns work in circuses, in movies, on television, in musical plays, at birthday parties and other events, or in fairgrounds or amusement parks. Their job is to divert and entertain audiences. They perform comical routines often while wearing unusual makeup and costumes. They juggle, dance, or display other technical skills, and make people laugh with their lithe-bodied antics.

Some clowns perform in large groups. Circus clowns often perform routines while the rings are being prepared for other acts. They might sing songs, tell jokes, or do acrobatic stunts. Some of the routines they perform are written specifically for particular clowns. Others are stock comedy routines. Clowns must have a good sense of timing and balance, and must be able to adjust their performance to the audience.

The makeup and costumes vary for different kinds of clowns. *Whiteface clowns* wear white makeup and caps that make them appear to be bald. They are the elegant clowns and are usually in charge of a routine. *Auguste clowns* wear baggy clothes and seem clumsy or silly. They trip over objects on the stage or drop things other clowns were juggling. *Tramp clowns* look unshaven and wear tattered clothes. They often appear sad or forlorn. *Character clowns*, like Charlie Chaplin, have unique routines, and usually perform alone. In some performances, different kinds of clowns work together to create a more balanced or entertaining show.

Clowns must be willing to travel to find work. The work is performed under many different kinds of conditions. They work outdoors or indoors depending on the job. If they get a circus job, they must be willing to travel for much of the year. Circus clowns may perform in a large tent outdoors or in a large indoor arena. While the arena may be large and comfortable in one city, the next city's circus site may be smaller or be more difficult to perform in. Clowns who work in amusement parks may do other work at the park as well. They may help sell balloons or souvenirs, or welcome people to the park. Clowns must be flexible and patient. Other clowns work at birthday parties, shopping malls, business conventions, and on television and video programs.

EDUCATION AND TRAINING

Training in dance and pantomime is very helpful for would-be clowns. Clowns who can move well and can use their bodies to communicate with an audience will have more success. Dance academies, schools for dramatic arts, and colleges and universities offer classes in pantomime and dance. Many high schools also have drama or dance classes for students. Experience acting or performing in plays is very important. Shows are put on regularly by high schools and community centers. There are also a number of "clown colleges" that train clowns for circus work.

Clowns should also be able to project their voices. Any debate or public speaking clubs can help develop this skill. Clowns need to have good voice control as well as poise before an audience. Like other actors, clowns benefit from a solid education. A high school diploma is not required by most circuses, but a diploma and a college education certainly help a clown's job prospects. Employers in the motion-picture and television industry also prefer to hire performers who have diplomas.

OUTLOOK AND EARNINGS

The outlook for people who want to work as clowns is not very promising. There is a tremendous amount of competition, and the field is overcrowded, as it is in other careers in the entertainment industry. It can take more than a year to find a job working as a clown. Wages are often controlled by unions. Like most performing artists, most clowns are not permanently employed and must repeatedly audition for positions.

With perseverance, a clown can find a first job that is outside the circus. Amusement parks might be easier places for new clowns to get work. Many clowns begin by performing for private parties.

Circus clowns can earn $200 to $400 a week. Outside the circus, a clown can earn $50 to $400 or more per performance.

WAYS OF GETTING MORE INFORMATION

Any experience acting in plays or musicals will be helpful for someone aspiring to be a clown. Besides school performances, many traveling repertory groups and theatrical companies have young performers. Some

communities have summer stock programs that are open to nonprofessionals.

For more information about a career as a clown, write to:

American Guild of Variety Artists
184 Fifth Avenue
New York, NY 10019

Associated Actors and Artists of America
165 West 46th Street
New York, NY 10036

Clowns entertain with unusual make-up and costumes combined with silly pantomimes.

COAL MINING TECHNICIANS

SCHOOL SUBJECTS:
CHEMISTRY, GEOLOGY

PERSONAL INTERESTS:
THE ENVIRONMENT, SCIENCE

OUTLOOK:
DECLINE

OTHER ARTICLES TO LOOK AT:
Energy Conservation and Use Technicians
Geologists
Mining Engineers
Surveying and Mapping Technicians
Surveyors

WHAT COAL MINING TECHNICIANS DO

Coal mining technicians assist other mining workers in the digging out, preparation, and transportation of coal. They help survey, map, and plan the mining of a coal field; they drill test holes and analyze samples; they prepare reports on how mining for coal will affect the environment. Once a coal mine or field is established, the technicians manage safe mining operations and train other workers in safety techniques; they plan the most economical and efficient way of removing the coal; they test for coal quality and air impurities; they dispose of mine waste; they select, operate, and maintain the special machinery used; and they figure out how to reclaim strip mining areas after the coal has been removed.

Coal mining can be hazardous work, and coal mining technicians work under unusual and often harsh conditions. Those employed at surface mines work outdoors for long hours and are exposed to all kinds of weather. In underground mines, technicians work in tunnels that may be cramped, dark, dusty, wet, and cold. All mining jobs are physically demanding, and they almost always involve getting dirty; however, technological advances have reduced many of the health hazards.

EDUCATION AND TRAINING

Students interested in becoming coal mining technicians should begin preparing in high school. Their studies should include mathematics, physics, and chemistry, as well as English (paying special attention to reading, writing, and communication skills). Additional high school courses in computers and mechanical drawing or drafting would also prove helpful.

After high school, interested students should enroll in one of the 20 or so schools around the country that offer two-year coal mining technology programs. Many of these schools offer summer intern programs which allow students to work in actual coal mines. This gives students a clear picture of the coal mining industry in general, and helps them choose the work area that best fits their abilities.

Coal mining technicians are usually hired by company recruiters before they complete their last year of technical or vocational school. After a few years of experience, technicians may advance to such positions as supervisors, production superintendents, or mine managers, or possibly even go into business for themselves as private consultants or contractors.

OUTLOOK AND EARNINGS

Employment levels for coal mining technicians will depend on the demand for coal, which may decrease or increase according to how much oil and natural gas are available. Also, safety regulations and environmental quality controls may lead to lower employment levels for the mining industry in general. Still, jobs will be available for people who are prepared to meet the challenge of producing more coal more efficiently, while at the same time protecting the environment and making sure of mine safety.

It is hard to determine what coal mining technicians earn because they do such a wide variety of jobs. Beginning technicians earn between $21,000 and $27,000 per year. Within five years, technicians hired at $21,000 may earn $35,000 to $44,000, while those who become successful managers or private consultants earn considerably more than $45,000.

School or public librarians can help select books and other publications about the history and nature of coal mining.

For more information, write to the following:

American Coal Foundation
1130 17th Street, NW
Washington, DC 20036

American Institute of Mining, Metallurgical, and Petroleum Engineers
345 East 47th Street
New York, NY 10017

BCR National Laboratory
500 William Pitt Way
Pittsburgh, PA 15238

Masks and other safety devices help protect coal mining technicians as they do their work.

COAL MINING WORKERS

SCHOOL SUBJECTS:
CHEMISTRY, GEOLOGY

PERSONAL INTERESTS:
FIGURING OUT HOW THINGS WORK,
FIXING THINGS

OUTLOOK:
DECLINE

OTHER ARTICLES TO LOOK AT:
Coal Mining Technicians
Geologists
Logging Industry Workers
Mining Engineers

WHAT COAL MINING WORKERS DO

Coal mining workers use large and complex equipment to get coal out of underground and surface mines. The type of machinery they use depends on whether the coal lies near the surface of the earth or deep under the ground.

If the coal is near the earth's surface, the mine is called a surface mine or a strip mine. The first task is to remove the top layer of earth and expose the coal. Workers at a surface mine can either dig the earth away with bulldozers and huge stripping shovels, or blast if off with dynamite. Some of the stripping shovels can remove 3,500 tons of earth per hour. Once the earth cover is gone, mining workers use smaller power shovels to scoop up the coal and load it into trucks.

If the coal lies deep underground, the miners must work in tunnels. Some underground mines use machines that cut into the coal, gather it up, and load it on conveyor belts all at once. The miners who operate these machines must also make sure the machines are working properly, and adjust or repair them when necessary.

Other underground mines get the coal out in several steps. First, they carve out a line around the coal deposit. Then they drill holes in the coal deposit and fill the holes with sticks of dynamite. The dynamite blasts the coal out and workers then drive in with machines that load the loose coal onto conveyor belts or shuttle cars.

Working in mines is physically demanding and dangerous. Both surface and underground mines are noisy and dusty, and underground mines are dark and often cramped. Workers are sometimes exposed to hazardous gases that can seep into underground tunnels. The danger of a cave-in is also possible.

EDUCATION AND TRAINING

Coal mining workers learn on the job; the work does not require a high school diploma. Beginning workers must be at least 18 years old and in good physical shape. They start by doing routine jobs such as shoveling coal onto conveyor belts. After a while, they may assist a machine operator and, gradually, learn how to operate the big machines. Machine operator jobs usually go to those who have the most work experience.

Because coal mining is dangerous work, U.S. law requires all mining workers to have some training in safety and health before they start the job. Mining workers must repeat this training every year. Mining safety depends on teamwork; workers have to cooperate to avoid accidents.

OUTLOOK AND EARNINGS

The number of coal mining workers needed in the 1990s will depend on how busy American industries will be. If industrial production is slow, less coal is needed, and mining slows down, too.

Mining workers generally are paid between $24,000 and $37,000 a year. They can earn somewhat more for working overtime or working nights. Pay varies for different machine operators—more experienced operators in underground mines earn the most. Unskilled workers and trainees at coal preparation plants earn the least. Many coal mining workers belong to a union such as the United Mine Workers of America.

WAYS OF GETTING MORE INFORMATION

School and public librarians can help students find books and articles about coal and coal mining.

For more information about a career as a coal mining worker, write to the following:

American Coal Foundation
1130 17th Street, NW
Washington, DC 20036

International Union, United Mine Workers of America
900 15th Street, NW
Washington, DC 20005

In an underground mine, two coal mining workers operate a power coal cutter.

COLLECTION WORKERS

SCHOOL SUBJECTS:
PSYCHOLOGY, SPEECH

PERSONAL INTERESTS:
COMPUTERS, HELPING PEOPLE:
PERSONAL SERVICE

OUTLOOK:
FASTER THAN THE AVERAGE

OTHER ARTICLES TO LOOK AT:
Bank Services Occupations
Clerks
Insurance Claims Representatives
Insurance Policy Processing Occupations
Telemarketers

WHAT COLLECTION WORKERS DO

Collection workers try to persuade people to pay their overdue bills. They are sometimes called *bill collectors*, *collection correspondents*, or *collection agents*. When a customer fails to pay a bill, the collection worker is given a bad-debt file. This file, contains information about the customer, the amount of the unpaid bill, and the date of the last payment. The collection worker then calls or writes to the customer to find out why the bill has not been paid. The worker tries to get the customer to pay all or part of the bill. If the customer has moved and left no forwarding address, the collector will try to find him or her by checking with the post office, telephone company, credit bureaus, or former neighbors of the customer. In recent years computer databases have been helpful in tracking down information.

Sometimes the customer will say that the bill has not been paid because it is incorrect, or the customer might explain that the item purchased was faulty. In such cases the collection worker suggests that the customer contact the seller of the item. If the problem remains unresolved after these steps are taken, the collector tries again to get payment from the customer.

Some customers are unable to pay a bill because of a financial emergency, such as unemployment. Others have got into debt because they did not manage their money properly. In such cases the collection worker will arrange a new payment schedule. If a customer simply refuses to pay a bill, the worker might suggest that it be turned over to an attorney.

When all efforts to collect a bill fail, the bill is given to a *repossessor*. This collection worker takes back, or repossesses, the item that has not been paid for and returns it to the seller. Items such as furniture or appliances are picked up in a truck. Vehicles are driven to the seller's place of business. If the buyer will not give the key to the repossessor, he or she might use special tools to enter and start the vehicle.

In small offices collection workers sometimes perform clerical duties. They might read and answer mail, file papers, and record amounts paid.

Collectors are employed by banks, finance companies, credit unions, hospitals, department stores, and collection agencies. They also work for wholesale businesses and utility companies.

Collection workers usually work at desks in offices. Most of their work is done by telephone. Customers sometimes become angry and insult the collector or the company. Workers must be able to deal calmly with these insults. At the same time, they must try to persuade customers to pay their bills. Good communication and people skills are required for this line of work.

EDUCATION AND TRAINING

A high school education is usually sufficient for this job. In high school, students should concentrate on courses in business, math, and English. Collection workers are usually trained on the job. This training typically lasts about two months. During the training course workers will learn the company's strategy for getting customers to pay, what language to use, and how to communicate with particularly difficult customers. They will also learn how to use the company's computer and telephone systems. Special courses on becoming a collection worker are also available through the American Collectors Association.

OUTLOOK AND EARNINGS

The employment outlook for collection workers is quite good. More and more people are buying items on credit, an indication that they might not have enough money to pay for them. Thus, more collection workers will be needed to deal with those who do not pay their bills. Many collection workers will leave their jobs because they find the work stressful or because they do not make enough money. This will create additional job openings.

Collection workers receive a salary plus a bonus or commission on the amounts they collect. The average yearly salary of a full-time collector is about $19,000. Those with experience could earn as much as $36,000 a year.

WAYS OF GETTING MORE INFORMATION

For more information about a career as a collection worker, write to:

American Collectors Association
PO Box 39106
Minneapolis, MN 55439
Tel: 612-926-6547

A collection worker talks to a client on a telephone headset.

COLLEGE ADMINISTRATORS

SCHOOL SUBJECTS:
BUSINESS, EDUCATION

PERSONAL INTERESTS:
HELPING PEOPLE: PERSONAL SERVICE, TEACHING

OUTLOOK:
LITTLE CHANGE OR MORE SLOWLY THAN THE AVERAGE

OTHER ARTICLES TO LOOK AT:
Guidance Counselors
School Administrators

WHAT COLLEGE ADMINISTRATORS DO

College administrators develop and manage services for students in colleges and universities. They are responsible for arranging housing, special services for veterans and minority students, and social, cultural, and recreational activities. Specific job titles vary, but the most common are *dean*, *registrar*, and *director of student activities*.

The *dean of students* heads the entire student-affairs program. Associate or assistant deans in this department may be in charge of specific aspects of student life such as housing. *Academic deans* are concerned with such issues as the courses offered or faculty hired in a specific academic division such as the college of nursing. Registrars prepare class schedules, make room assignments, keep records of students and their grades, and assemble data for government and educational agencies. The director of student activities assists student groups in planning and arranging social, cultural, and recreational events. The student activities staff may manage an activities center, help

new students learn about the college, and promote student participation in cultural and recreational events.

Other student-affairs workers are concerned with particular areas of college life. The *director of housing* is responsible for such matters as room assignments and the upkeep of dormitory buildings. *Residence counselors* live in the dormitories and try to help the students live in harmony. Often, these are older students who are there to help new students who may be having problems. The *director of religious activities* coordinates the activities of the various religious groups. *Counselors* provide assistance to students with personal problems, such as loneliness, drug abuse, or worries about their academic work or private life.

Foreign-student advisors work with foreign students and give special help with admissions, housing, financial aid, and English as a second language. *Veterans' coordinators* provide information and services to veterans and potential military enlistees. They advise students on their eligibility for benefits or other forms of assistance and supervise the processing of applications for benefits. The *director of the student health program* hires staff, manages the facilities and equipment, and develops programs and services to meet the students' health care needs. *Athletic directors* are in charge of all intercollegiate athletic activities. They hire coaches, schedule sports events, and direct publicity efforts. There are many other types of college administrators.

EDUCATION AND TRAINING

A bachelor's degree is the minimum requirement for college administrators. Because of the wide range of duties involved with college student affairs, the education and background required varies considerably. In many cases, a master's degree in education, psychology, or divinity may be preferred.

OUTLOOK AND EARNINGS

Leaner budgets are currently making the job market in college administration competitive. However, the number of college-age students is expected to increase by the year 2005, so more jobs may open in the field at that time. Most job openings will be to replace workers who are retiring or leaving their jobs.

Salaries vary greatly for college deans and related workers and depend to a great extent on the part of the country and the size of the institution. In general, most of the jobs described in this article pay salaries that average from $32,000 to $45,000 a year. University presidents make the biggest salaries, followed by deans of students or athletic directors. Some of these positions pay well over $60,000 a year. Registrars, directors of student activities, and housing directors usually make smaller salaries.

WAYS OF GETTING MORE INFORMATION

Participation in student government is a good way to learn more about the variety of administrative needs of a student body. College students can often get part-time jobs on campus that have to do with student affairs.

For more information about a career as a college administrator, write to the following:

College & University Personnel Association
1233 20th St. NW
Washington, DC 20036

A college registrar prepares the class schedules for the next semester.

COLLEGE AND UNIVERSITY FACULTY

SCHOOL SUBJECTS:
EDUCATION, SPEECH

PERSONAL INTERESTS:
BOOKS/READING, TEACHING

OUTLOOK:
LITTLE CHANGE OR MORE SLOWLY
THAN THE AVERAGE

OTHER ARTICLES TO LOOK AT:

Elementary School Teachers

School Administrators

Teacher Aides

WHAT COLLEGE AND UNIVERSITY FACULTY DO

College and university faculty instruct students in specific areas of learning. They teach about nine to twelve hours a week and spend as many as twenty-four hours preparing for their classes.

Some faculty members become student advisers, helping students decide which courses to take and guiding them through difficult problems of college life.

Many college or university teachers conduct research in their field of study and publish the results in textbooks and journals. Eventually, some become heads of departments and take charge of many department activities such as creating new courses, hiring faculty members, and overseeing student activities. They are assisted by graduate students who help them teach and develop materials, conduct research, grade papers, and give tests.

Faculty members who teach classes in the evenings and on weekends, or in places away from the college, are called *extension work instructors*. Sometimes, they even teach classes by mail.

Those who give instruction in typing, filing, shorthand, secretarial procedures, and the use of office machinery at vocational schools and small community colleges are called *business education instructors*.

EDUCATION AND TRAINING

Students interested in teaching in a college or university must have at least a master's degree. A doctorate will be necessary to advance beyond the rank of instructor and earn a better salary. Many states have requirements for certification before faculty members are allowed to teach.

Assistant professor is the entry-level job title for college faculty members with doctorate degrees. Faculty members usually spend no more than six years as assistant professors. During this time, the college will decide whether or not the faculty members' abilities are strong enough for the school. If they are, the teachers will be granted tenure, which is a type of job guarantee. If tenure is denied and assistant professors are not promoted to the level of associate professor, they must either find a job with another college or university or move into another career. An associate professor eventually may be promoted to full professor. Some professors choose to move into administrative work.

OUTLOOK AND EARNINGS

In the 1990's competition has been stiff in the field of college and university teaching. It has been difficult to get and keep jobs.

However, experts are predicting that the field will pick up by the end of this century and into the next.

The amount of money one can earn as a college or university teacher depends on the subject one is teaching, on the level of one's education, and the degree of one's experience. Salaries are also influenced by the type of school, its size, and its geographical location. Those teaching in four-year schools receive higher salaries than those in two-year schools. Full professors average about $63,450 per year; associate professors earn about $47,040; assistant professors earn about $39,050; and instructors about $29,680.

WAYS OF GETTING MORE INFORMATION

Students interested in a teaching career can learn more by observing their own teachers and asking them why they chose their field.

For more information write to:

American Federation of Teachers
555 New Jersey Avenue NW
Washington, DC 20001

Professors may lecture in small classrooms or large auditoria, depending upon the size of the university and the popularity of their courses.

COMEDIANS

SCHOOL SUBJECTS:
ENGLISH (WRITING/LITERATURE),
THEATER/DANCE

PERSONAL INTERESTS:
ENTERTAINING, WRITING

OUTLOOK:
ABOUT AS FAST AS THE AVERAGE

OTHER ARTICLES TO LOOK AT:

Actors and Actresses

Clowns

Radio and Television Announcers

Writers

WHAT COMEDIANS DO

Comedians make people laugh. They do this in many different ways. Some entertain audiences in nightclubs and at concerts. Some perform in comedy shows on television. Some even write the jokes and other material that another comedian will use.

Comedians who work in nightclubs are often called *stand-up comedians*. They try to entertain audiences with stories, jokes, one-liners, and impressions. In comedy clubs in large cities, they may do more than one show a night, and go on either before or after another comedian. Depending on whether they are the opening act or the main act, they perform sets of material that are anywhere from 10 minutes to an hour or longer.

Stand-up comedians spend much of their time traveling from city to city, entertaining different types of audiences and sharpening their acts in the process. To book these out-of-town performances, the comedians may call the club owners themselves or go through a booking agent. In medium- and small-sized cities they will perform only one night and then drive or fly to the next city.

Stand-up comedians entertain at conventions, concerts, hotels, parties, and outdoor festivals—anyplace where they can be paid to entertain an audience.

After a comedian has sharpened his or her act, he or she may be asked to appear on television on a talk show or a comedy special. Some comedians do complete comedy concerts that are videotaped and broadcast. If comedians become well known, they may have a television series developed especially for them.

Many comedians write material for other comedians. While it might seem like fun, it can be very hard to come up with funny material for a weekly television show. Many of the jokes are written and then rejected for various reasons.

Although it can be a glamorous profession, comedians also face many difficulties. They are away from home for most of the year. They are also very vulnerable. Comedians go on stage alone and if they don't make the crowd laugh, they have no one to blame but themselves. But when the audience does laugh, comedians feel richly rewarded.

EDUCATION AND TRAINING

There is no way to become a comedian except to step on a stage and perform. People from all walks of life have become comedians. But it takes a great deal of work and practice to become a good comedian. It takes many hours on stage to know how to deliver a joke, structure the pace of a show, and read an audience to tell what they would enjoy.

While there are no schools for comedians, certain school subjects can be very helpful. English and composition are necessary to write jokes well. Speech and drama classes will help to build a strong presence on stage. Mathematics is also important, since most comedians have to keep track of their own finances.

The most important thing a comedian needs to know is something that cannot be taught: to be funny and be able to make others laugh. While this skill can be improved through practice and hard work, it is most often a skill that a person either has or does not have.

OUTLOOK AND EARNINGS

The pay scale for comedians varies widely. Stand-up comedians only earn money when they are working. They get paid either per show or for a week of performances. The headline performer makes much more than the opening act. In large comedy clubs in the nation's major cities, a headline comedian can earn from $1,000 to $20,000 per week, depending on his or her popularity. The comedian that opens the evening's show can earn from $150 to $300 per week, while the middle comedian can earn from $400 to $800 per week. Those who are just starting out earn very little but can make valuable contacts with club owners, agents, and other comedians. The comedy club usually pays for the comedian's lodging.

For comedy writers, the pay scale is also very wide. Those who write jokes for famous comedians usually get paid around $50 for every joke used. Those who write for television get paid different rates depending on their experience, reputation, and the budget of the show. The writers of a network comedy show can be paid anywhere from $50,000 to $150,000 or more a year.

For more information, write to:

Comedy Writers Association
PO Box 023304
Brooklyn, NY 11202

National Comedians Association
581 Ninth Avenue, Suite 3C
New York, NY 10036

Comedian Eddie Murphy jokes with talk-show host Arsenio Hall while taping The Late Show program.

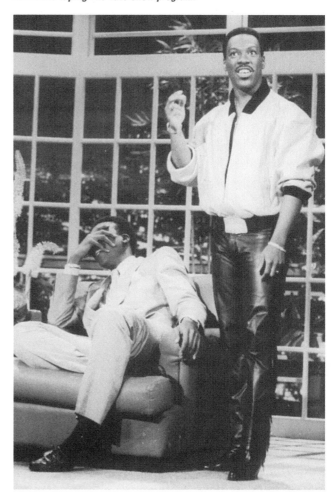

COMMUNICATIONS EQUIPMENT MECHANICS

SCHOOL SUBJECTS:
MATHEMATICS, SHOP (TRADE/VO-TECH EDUCATION)

PERSONAL INTERESTS:
FIGURING OUT HOW THINGS WORK, FIXING THINGS

OUTLOOK:
DECLINE

OTHER ARTICLES TO LOOK AT:

Computer and Office Machine Technicians

Electrical and Electronics Engineers

Electronics Engineering Technicians

Telephone Installers and Repairers

WHAT COMMUNICATIONS EQUIPMENT MECHANICS DO

Communicating is sharing information. Today, much of the communication between individuals, businesses, and governments takes place electronically over standard telephone wires. Telephone wires transmit more than just phone calls. Telegrams are sent over phone wires, as is the information shared by computers located in different cities. Thanks to the facsimile machine, an architect in Chicago can send copies of drawings to a client in New York, again using telephone lines. The telephone system plays a very important role in our ability to communicate with one another. *Communications equipment mechanics* install, maintain, test, and repair telephone communications systems. These mechanics usually work in telephone company offices or in phone company customers' offices.

There are several kinds of communications equipment mechanics. *Central office*

equipment installers work in a telephone company's central office, assembling, installing, and replacing the complex switching and dialing equipment that is headquartered there. Sometimes they will assemble a whole new central office. At other times, they might install equipment to expand a central office or to replace outdated equipment. They also adjust and test the equipment. These installers must be able to read blueprints and use a variety of hand and power tools.

Central office repairers test and repair switches and relays used in telephone circuits. They use switching equipment, hand tools, and electronic testing meters to locate problems and make repairs. *Maintenance administrators* test a customer's lines at the central office to discover where and why problems are occurring. When a problem is found, they direct outside maintenance crews in making repairs. In addition, these workers may contact customers to arrange service calls and then send over repair crews. They must understand the causes of any equipment failure.

PBX systems technicians work on private branch exchanges, which are special telephone systems set up in businesses that bypass phone company lines. *PBX installers* install these systems, which may include customized switchboards. *PBX repairers* maintain and repair these systems. They also may work on mobile radiophones and microwave transmission devices.

EDUCATION AND TRAINING

The training needed to become a communications equipment mechanic begins in high school or vocational school. Useful high school classes include computer courses, algebra, geometry, English, physics, and shop. Knowledge of the major principles of electricity is important. In addition, most telephone companies conduct their own training programs for new employees who have high school or vocational school diplomas.

Many telecommunications companies prefer to hire graduates of two-year technical schools. Programs in telecommunications technology, electronics, or even computer maintenance teach many of the basic skills required for these workers.

OUTLOOK AND EARNINGS

There will be fewer jobs for communications equipment mechanics in the future because of continuing automation and equipment advances. New equipment has fewer mechanical parts that break, wear out, or need to be periodically cleaned and lubricated. In addition, computers can detect problems in equipment automatically and route operations around trouble spots until repairs can be made. Many telephone companies are laying off employees, and it will be hard for new workers to enter this field. Most communications equipment mechanics currently employed have many years of experience. Average annual salaries are around $35,000.

WAYS OF GETTING MORE INFORMATION

A good way to explore the work done by communications equipment mechanics is to take electrical shop classes in high school.

For more information, write to:

Communications Workers of America
501 3rd Street NW
Washington, DC 20001

United States Telephone Association
1401 H Street NW, Suite 600
Washington, DC 20001

A communications equipment mechanic works on an older piece of equipment that is more difficult to fix than modern machines.

COMPOSERS

OTHER ARTICLES TO LOOK AT:

Music Teachers

Musicians

Orchestra Conductors

Singers

SCHOOL SUBJECTS:
MUSIC, THEATER/DANCE

PERSONAL INTERESTS:
ENTERTAINING/PERFORMING, MUSIC

OUTLOOK:
LITTLE CHANGE OR MORE SLOWLY THAN THE AVERAGE

WHAT COMPOSERS DO

Composers write music for musical stage shows, television commercials, movies, ballet and opera companies, orchestras, and other musical performing groups. Composers work in many different ways. Often they begin with a musical idea and write it down using standard music notation. They use their music training and their own personal sense of melody, harmony, rhythm, and structure. Some compose music as they play an instrument and may or may not write it down.

Most composers specialize in one style of music, such as classical, jazz, country, rock, or blues. Some combine features from several styles. Composers who are working on commission or on assignment meet with their clients to discuss their wishes. They will talk about the composition's length, style, and the number and types of performers. After the piece is completed, the composer usually takes part in rehearsals and works with the performers.

Composers work at home or in offices or music studios. Much of the time they need to work alone to plan and build their musical ideas. Some composers work with other musicians to help create a piece of music. Composing can take many long hours of work, and composing jobs may be irregular and low-paying. However, it is extremely satisfying for composers to hear their music performed, and successful commercial music composers can earn a lot of money.

EDUCATION AND TRAINING

There are different requirements for composers of different types of music. All composers need to have a good ear, and almost all composers must be able to notate, or write down, their music. Composers of musicals, symphonies, and other large works must have years of study in a college, conservatory, or other school of music. Composers of popular songs do not need as much training. However, studying music may enable them to develop and express their musical ideas better. Music school courses for those who wish to be composers include music theory, musical form, music history, composition, conducting, and arranging. Composers also play at least one musical instrument, usually piano, and some play several instruments. Most composers of classical music know how to speak, read and write at least one foreign language, often Italian or German.

While in high school, students interested in musical composition should take as many courses in music as are available. These may include vocal technique, choral singing, music theory, and orchestra.

OUTLOOK AND EARNINGS

As long as there are commercials, movies, operas, and orchestras, there will be a need for composers to write music for them. The average earnings of a composer are difficult to determine. Most earn very little and work only part-time, while others may earn a great deal. Some composers work on commission. When a piece of music is commissioned, the composer is paid a lump sum for writing it. Other composers work under contract with a music publishing or recording company. Their compositions become the property of the company. Some composers receive royalties for their compositions. Royalties are payments to the composer for each performance of the piece or each record or sheet-music sale.

Few composers earn a living only by composing. Most have other jobs at the same time, such as teaching or playing an instrument. Composers who write music for commercials, for popular performers, or for movies earn the most money. In the classical music or jazz categories, cash prizes are awarded to some composers by the record industry, universities, and foundations. These awards can make the composer more well known and can lead to further opportunities. For some compositions, a composer may continue to receive royalties for many years.

WAYS OF GETTING MORE INFORMATION

Young people interested in becoming composers should study music and learn to play an instrument, such as piano. They may join or form their own musical group and try their hand at writing music for the group to perform.

For more information about music schools that offer training in musical composition, write to:

National Association of Schools of Music
11250 Roger Bacon Drive, Number 21
Reston, VA 22090

A composer practices an arrangement for a musical piece he has written.

COMPUTER AIDED DESIGN TECHNICIANS

SCHOOL SUBJECTS:
COMPUTER SCIENCE, SHOP (TRADE/VO-TECH EDUCATION)

PERSONAL INTERESTS:
COMPUTERS, DRAWING/PAINTING

OUTLOOK:
FASTER THAN THE AVERAGE

OTHER ARTICLES TO LOOK AT:

Computer Aided Manufacturing Technicians

Drafters

Graphic Designers

Industrial Designers

WHAT COMPUTER AIDED DESIGN TECHNICIANS DO

Computer aided design technicians, sometimes known as *CAD technicians* use computers to help design, improve, change, or produce manufactured items and manufacturing systems. Although CAD usually stands for computer aided design, it can also mean computer aided drafting. CAD technicians may be involved in any part of the manufacturing process. CAD technicians work under the direction of CAD engineers and designers, who are experts in applying computer technology to industrial design and manufacturing.

CAD technicians help to design and develop new products. These technicians need both drafting and computer skills. They usually work at specially designed computer work stations. They call up computer data files that contain information about a new product. Then, they use computer programs to change that information into diagrams and drawings of the product. These are displayed on a video-display screen, which acts as an electronic drawing board. Under the direction of a CAD engineer or designer, the CAD technician can make changes in diagrams and drawings. These changes can either be typed into the computer or touched onto the screen with a stylus, or light pen.

Once the changes have been made, technicians use computer programs to display the new diagrams or drawings. After the design of the product has been approved, CAD technicians may have more work to do. They may use the computer to make detailed drawings of the parts to be manufactured, as well as the tools that will be needed.

CAD technicians work in a variety of fields. These include architecture; electronics; the manufacturing of automobiles, aircraft, computers, and missiles; and design organizations. Before this technology was available, designing and drafting was done with pen and paper.

EDUCATION AND TRAINING

CAD technicians must have at least a high school diploma. Most have completed a two-year program at a technical school. Such a program includes courses in basic drafting, machine drawing, architecture, civil drafting (with an emphasis on highways), process piping, electrical, electrical instrumentation, and plumbing. It should also include courses in data processing and in computer programming, systems, and equipment. Some companies have their own training programs.

OUTLOOK AND EARNINGS

The employment outlook for CAD technicians in the next decade is excellent. These workers will help companies become more productive in design and manufacturing.

CAD technicians who are graduates of two-year technical programs often start at about $14,000 to $22,000 a year in the 1990s. Experienced technicians can make from $25,000 to $42,000. Some technicians with special skills, extensive experience, or additional responsibilities can earn even more.

WAYS OF GETTING MORE INFORMATION

It is hard to get a part-time or summer job that deals directly with CAD technology. But part-time jobs in drafting or engineering fields will give you a glimpse of a similar work atmosphere. If you are in high school and interested in a career in CAD technology, join the science club (especially computer and electronics clubs), participate in science fairs, or pursue hobbies that involve computers, drafting, electronics, or mechanical equipment.

For more information, write to the following:

American Design and Drafting Association
PO Box 799
Rockville, MD 20848-0799
Tel: 301-460-6875

Institute of Electrical and Electronics Engineers
1828 L Street NW, Suite 1202
Washington, DC 20036-5104
WWW: http://www.ieee.org/usab

Robotics International of the SME Engineers
PO Box 0930, 1 SME Drive
Dearborn, MI 48121-0930
Tel: 313-271-1500

Adjusting a dimension on the computer screen, a CAD technician develops a design for a new sports stadium.

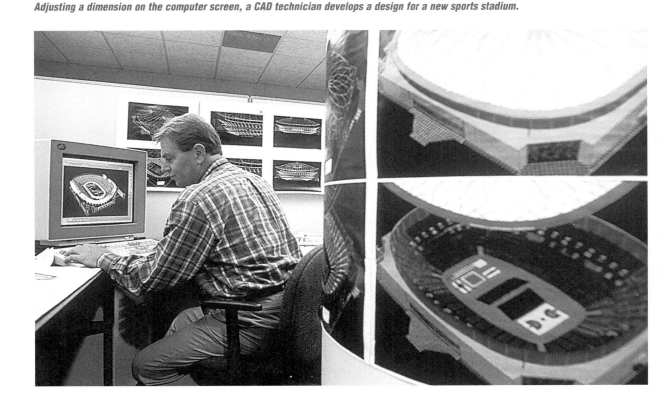

COMPUTER AIDED MANUFACTURING TECHNICIANS

SCHOOL SUBJECTS:
COMPUTER SCIENCE, SHOP (TRADE/VO-TECH EDUCATION)

PERSONAL INTERESTS:
BUILDING THINGS, COMPUTERS

OUTLOOK:
MUCH FASTER THAN THE AVERAGE

OTHER ARTICLES TO LOOK AT:
Computer Aided Design Technicians
Computer Programmers
Electronics Engineering Technicians
Numerical Control Tool Programmers

WHAT COMPUTER AIDED MANUFACTURING TECHNICIANS DO

Computer aided manufacturing (CAM) technicians are usually employed in two different phases of the manufacturing process. Some CAM technicians are involved in the initial design and setup of the process. They organize the materials, parts, and equipment to be used as well as the various steps of the manufacturing process. Other CAM technicians play a bigger role in running, maintaining, and repairing the computer-controlled equipment. In smaller facilities, CAM technicians perform all of these duties.

Like CAD technicians, CAM technicians work under the direction of engineers and designers. CAM technicians work from blueprints that are provided by the engineering and design staff. While the blueprint may come in on paper, it also appears as an electronic file on the company's computer system. Using specially designed software, the CAM technician enters the blueprint's specification into computer programs that control the different machines that will cut, drill, bore, punch, press, and otherwise work on the product as it reaches them. This data is combined with information about materials and conditions on the factory floor. The computer is programmed to determine the best way to produce the needed products. Computers are then used to begin and control automated production processes.

When the production run begins, the CAM technician monitors the program, speeding up, slowing down, or stopping the run when necessary. The CAM technician can also change the program while it is working, adding changes or variations to the product's design. When the run is complete, the CAM technician reports to management, using the data generated during the production run.

CAM technicians work in a variety of fields. These include architecture; electronics; the manufacturing of automobiles, aircraft, computers, and missiles; and design organizations. Before this technology was available, designing and drafting was done with pen and paper.

CAM technicians also work in factories running computer-controlled manufacturing devices, such as robots. They may also help to design, test, install, maintain, and repair such devices. In addition, they may train other workers to install, use, and maintain robots.

EDUCATION AND TRAINING

CAM technicians must have at least a high school diploma. Most have completed a two-year program at a technical school or community college. Such a program should include courses in drafting and basic engineering topics. It should also include courses in data processing and in computer programming, systems, and equipment.

Some companies have their own training programs. Many offer four-year apprenticeship programs, which combine on-the-job training with an associate's degree program.

OUTLOOK AND EARNINGS

CAM technology is one of the fastest growing areas in the manufacturing industries. Computer-automated systems are becoming increasingly prevalent as companies try to compete on an international scale. As a result, skilled CAM workers will be needed to operate and maintain this equipment.

Apprentice CAM technicians generally earn about $14,000 a year until they complete their apprenticeship requirements. Starting salaries for CAM technicians average $18,000 per year. The most experienced technicians earn as much as $40,000 a year.

WAYS OF GETTING MORE INFORMATION

Those who are interested in a career in CAM technology should get involved in extracurricular activities such as electronics and computer clubs. It might be possible to arrange a visit to a local manufacturing facility to speak with CAM technicians about their jobs. Finally, part-time or summer jobs at a manufacturing plant may be available to provide some first-hand experience.

For more information, contact:

Computer Aided Manufacturing International
1250 East Copeland Road, Suite 500
Arlington, TX 76011-8098
Tel: 817-860-1654
WWW: http://www.cam-i.com/cami

Institute of Electrical and Electronics Engineers
1828 L Street NW, Suite 1202
Washington, DC 20036-5104
Tel: 202-785-0017
WWW: http://www.ieee.org/usab

Society of Manufacturing Engineers (SME)
Education Department
One SME Drive
PO Box 930
Dearborn, MI 48121-0930
Tel: 313-271-1500
WWW: http://www.sme.org

This CAM technician demonstrates the importance of extensive computer knowledge: he is using one computer to help in the manufacturing of another.

COMPUTER AND OFFICE MACHINE TECHNICIANS

SCHOOL SUBJECTS:
COMPUTER SCIENCE, SHOP
(TRADE/VO-TECH EDUCATION)

PERSONAL INTERESTS:
COMPUTERS, FIXING THINGS

OUTLOOK:
FASTER THAN THE AVERAGE

OTHER ARTICLES TO LOOK AT:

Computer Operators

Computer Programmers

Electrical and Electronics Engineers

Electromechanical Technicians

Electronics Engineering Technicians

WHAT COMPUTER AND OFFICE MACHINE TECHNICIANS DO

Businesses use computers and office machines to do a variety of daily tasks. Since the 1960s, computers have played an important role in business, research, and government. Today, computers are a part of everyone's lives.

Although computers and office machines have gotten smaller, they are still incredibly complex machines. Highly skilled electronics technicians are needed to keep computers and office machines operating properly and efficiently. *Computer and office machine technicians* service, install, calibrate, operate, maintain, and repair computers, peripherals, and other office machines.

Computer and office machine technicians may work for a computer manufacturer, a large corporation, or a repair shop. Technicians who work for a manufacturer learn how their company's products work and how to repair them when they break.

Sometimes, technicians employed by a computer manufacturer may be headquartered at a customer's workplace where they help to plan and install new computer systems. They also perform regular maintenance to make sure the equipment continues to operate properly. If the equipment breaks down, technicians will work together with the customers to fix it.

Some technicians work in the maintenance or service department of large corporations. They work with many different types of machines, both mechanical and electronic.

Some computer and office machine technicians work for companies or repair shops that specialize in providing maintenance services to computer and office machine users. When equipment breaks down or needs regular maintenance, technicians are sent to the customer's offices to provide the necessary services.

EDUCATION AND TRAINING

Because computers and office machines are such complex electronic devices, the technicians who work on them must have excellent engineering, electrical, and mechanical skills. They should know basic mathematics, including algebra and trigonometry. Knowledge of computer programming is also important. Technicians must be able to follow written and spoken instructions and be able to communicate well. The best way to prepare for this career is to attend a special two-year program after high school. These programs are offered by technical institutes and some community colleges. In high school, students should take two years of mathematics, including algebra. They should also take at least three years of language and communication courses, and at least one year of physics or chemistry. Any computer electronics/automotive/engine repair courses offered at the high school level will also be helpful.

OUTLOOK AND EARNINGS

Opportunities for employment in the computer and office machine field are excellent for those with good computer skills. These opportunities are expected to grow in the coming years.

The average starting salary for graduates of two-year special programs is $18,000. The average salary for full-time technicians with some experience is about $28,800. Technicians with even more experience and a higher level of responsibility earn up to $46,000.

WAYS OF GETTING MORE INFORMATION

A great way to explore a career as a computer and office machine technician is to join one of the many computer user groups that have sprung up throughout the country. Many schools also have computer or shop clubs in which students can participate.

For more information about a career as a computer and office machine technician, write or call:

Institute of Electrical and Electronics Engineers
345 East 47th Street
New York, NY 10017
Tel: 212-705-7900

When installing a new computer system, a technician tests the equipment to make sure it is functioning correctly.

COMPUTER NETWORK SPECIALISTS

SCHOOL SUBJECTS:
COMPUTER SCIENCE, MATHEMATICS

PERSONAL INTERESTS:
HELPING PEOPLE: PERSONAL SERVICE, FIGURING OUT HOW THINGS WORK

OUTLOOK:
FASTER THAN THE AVERAGE

OTHER ARTICLES TO LOOK AT:
Computer Programmers
Database Specialists
Technical Support Specialists

WHAT COMPUTER NETWORK SPECIALISTS DO

A computer network is a system of computer hardware, that is, computers, terminals, printers, modems, and other equipment, that is linked together electronically. Networks allow many users to share computer equipment and software at the same time. Networks also allow busy workers to share files, view each other's schedules, and send email.

Computer network specialists work with computer networks, making sure they are running properly at all times. They install, maintain, update, and repair network equipment and files. They might also help train network users on how to use the network. Sometimes, they help their supervisors decide which computer system to buy and help change existing software to better meet the needs of the business. There are many kinds of network specialists. The responsibilities of a specific position depend on the nature and size of the company.

Computer network administrators manage the network. They work with the files and directories on the network's central computer, called the server. The server holds important files like software applications, databases, and electronic mail services, all of which must be updated regularly. Some networks have separate servers for specific operations, such as communications or printing or databases.

Network security specialists concentrate most of their efforts on ensuring that the computer system is safe from internal and external tampering. Security is very important since most companies store highly confidential information on their computers. Network security specialists can tell when unauthorized changes are made in the files and who makes them. They then report these problems to a supervisor and devise better ways to eliminate such errors in the future. One important school database that must be protected by security specialists involves student grades; only authorized personnel have access to these files.

Data recovery operators are responsible for setting up emergency computer sites in case the main computers experience major problems. Business emergencies can be caused by natural catastrophes, like power outages, floods, and earthquakes. Data recovery operators choose an alternative location, decide which hardware and software should be stored there, and designate how often files should be backed up.

EDUCATION AND TRAINING

All computer network specialists have at least some postsecondary training in computers. Most computer professionals have taken a lot of classes in mathematics, science, and computers during high school. After high school, some study computer networking at technical/vocational schools. Many others prefer to earn official certification from a commercial educational center, sponsored by companies such as Novell and Microsoft. Students can become certified as a CNA, Certified Network Administrator, and later as a CNE, Certified Network Engineer. The certification process is difficult and proves to employers that the individual has reached a high level of understanding in the field.

OUTLOOK AND EARNINGS

Since so many businesses are using computer networks, this field is growing very quickly. Many companies will be looking for well-qualified computer network specialists for a long time to come.

Computer network specialists start at about $17,000 to $19,000 per year. After some experience and more training, average salaries rise to $27,000 per year. The best paid network specialists can earn up to $37,000 per year. Most employers of network specialists offer full benefits, including health insurance, sick leave, and paid vacation.

WAYS OF GETTING MORE INFORMATION

For more information, write:

CNE Professional Association
Novell Inc.
122 East 1700 South
South Provo, UT 84606
Tel: 800-453-1267

IEEE Computer Society
1730 Massachusetts Avenue NW
Washington, DC 20036

A computer network specialist discusses the details of a new computer system with the system analyst.

COMPUTER OPERATORS

SCHOOL SUBJECTS:
BUSINESS, ENGLISH

PERSONAL INTERESTS:
COMPUTERS, FIGURING OUT HOW
THINGS WORK

OUTLOOK:
LITTLE CHANGE OR MORE SLOWLY
THAN THE AVERAGE

OTHER ARTICLES TO LOOK AT:

Computer Programmers

Instrumentation Technicians

Secretaries

Stenographers

WHAT COMPUTER OPERATORS DO

Computers use various types of information to solve complicated problems. For a computer to operate correctly, it needs to be fed information in a form that it can understand. *Computer operators* prepare this information to be entered (inputted) into a computer and then load the information into the machine. They read information from checks, bills, and other forms and type it into the computer using a regular keyboard or numbers only keypad. They check the accuracy of their work regularly.

While computer programmers develop the operating instructions for a particular computer system, computer operators actually follow through with these instructions. They use keyboards to enter commands into the computer so that the computer can operate correctly. Their tasks may include setting controls on the computer, loading tapes, disks, and paper, and watching the screen for any messages or abnormalities. Some computer operators prepare printouts for all the people in a company who will be using the computer, and they keep a log of all malfunctions in the system.

As computers become more and more sophisticated, computer operators have to keep up with new technologies. Some companies now have computers, for instance, that can perform some of an operator's easier tasks automatically, such as scanning information for direct input, which frees up some operators to take on the more challenging responsibilities. These responsibilities include investigating and reporting complicated mistakes or glitches that occur in the system to appropriate supervisors. Most jobs for computer operators are in companies, industries or organizations that process a large amount of information. These include banks, insurance companies, government agencies, accounting firms, utilities, and the transportation and manufacturing industries.

EDUCATION AND TRAINING

Most people working as computer operators in large companies are high school graduates. Some have college or technical school education. A large company seeking a computer operator usually looks for applicants who are fast and accurate at typing. They also prefer applicants who are familiar with their machines. So the wider the range of experience an applicant has, the more likely he or she is to find a good job. In smaller companies, requirements for entry-level jobs as computer operators are the same, but might also include typical secretarial skills. Most companies provide on-the-job training courses lasting several days or weeks.

In addition to these requirements, computer operators need to be able to communicate well, both with programmers and the employees using the computer system, and they need to be able to work well with others, since they generally work under close supervision. Some computer operators may advance to jobs as supervisors or even programmers.

OUTLOOK AND EARNINGS

The use of computers has grown tremendously in the past few years, and this growth should continue throughout 2005. As the ability to input information automatically grows, the need for computer operators will decrease. Many operators will be needed, however, to supervise the running of the system and check for accuracy.

The beginning salary for computer operators is about $13,000 per year, with the top 10 percent earning about $21,000. Computer operators working for the federal government start at about $13,000 a year if they have a high school diploma, and $14,500 if they have one year of college. Those with more experience are paid higher starting salaries. Computer operators earn more in the Midwest and the West than in the Northeast and the South.

WAYS OF GETTING MORE INFORMATION

A good way to find out if you would enjoy being a computer operator is to get a part-time job in a computer department or to work as a typist or secretary for a small business that uses a computer system.

Taking computer courses in high school is another good way to experience the work of a computer operator while learning skills that are valuable after graduation.

For more information on a career as a computer operator, write to the following organizations:

Association for Computing Machinery
11 West 42nd Street, 3rd Floor New York, NY 10036

Computer and Communications Industry Association
666 11th Street NW, Suite 600 Washington, DC 20001

Organizational
Skills

People Skills

A computer operator uses the training she received from her employer to run this program.

COMPUTER PROGRAMMERS

SCHOOL SUBJECTS:
COMPUTERS, MATHEMATICS

PERSONAL INTERESTS:
COMPUTERS, FIGURING OUT HOW THINGS WORK

OUTLOOK:
FASTER THAN THE AVERAGE

OTHER ARTICLES TO LOOK AT:

Computer and Office Machine Technicians

Computer Systems Analysts

Database Specialists

WHAT COMPUTER PROGRAMMERS DO

Computer programmers write and code the instructions that control the work of a computer. Computers can perform work only by following these carefully prepared instructions.

Computer programmers work for companies that create and sell computer hardware and software. They also work for all kinds of businesses, from manufacturers of office machines to distributors of machinery and equipment, as well as banks, hospitals, educational systems, and the federal government.

To do their work, programmers have to break down each step of a desired task into a logical series of instructions that the computer can follow. Then they translate the instructions into a specific computer language, such as COBOL or FORTRAN. Then they test each part of the program to make sure it works, correcting any errors or debugging

the program. Finally, they write the instructions for the operators who will use the program. Some programs can be created in a matter of hours, while others may take more than a year of work. It is not uncommon for programmers to work together on teams for a large project.

There are two basic kinds of computer programmers: *systems programmers* and *applications programmers*. Systems programmers must understand and take care of an entire computer system, including its software, its memory, and all of its related equipment, such as terminals, printers, and disk drives.

Applications programmers write the actual programs that do particular tasks—word processing, accounting, data bases, and games. They tend to specialize in a field such as business, engineering, or science. Systems programmers will often help applications programmers with complicated tasks.

EDUCATION AND TRAINING

Many colleges offer courses and degree programs in computer sciences, and most employers prefer to hire college graduates. A number of two-year programs in data-processing, and junior-level programming are available in junior and community colleges; some companies send employees to a computer school at company expense. Employers whose work is highly technical may want their programmers to be trained in their specific area—for example, a computer programmer for an engineering firm might need an engineering degree. Most employers look for candidates who are patient, persistent, very logical in their thinking, and who can work under pressure without making mistakes.

Because programmers work in so many different industries, there is no standard way to begin as a computer programmer. After learning the basics of computer programming, young people should choose a field that interests them and then seek out programming opportunities within that field. It generally takes up to a year to master all aspects of a programming job, and opportunities for advancement are great.

OUTLOOK AND EARNINGS

As our society continues to rely more and more on computers to store and analyze data, employment opportunities for computer programmers should increase faster than the average through 2005. The best jobs will go to college graduates who know several programming languages and who are trained in a specific field, such as accounting, science, engineering, or management.

The average earnings for full-time programmers are about $35,000 a year, with the top 10 percent earning more than $50,000. Entry positions pay about $20,000 in private business and $18,000 in government. Generally, systems programmers earn more than applications programmers, and those working in the West and the South earn more than those in the Midwest and Northeast.

WAYS OF GETTING MORE INFORMATION

The best way to learn about computers is to use one—either at home surfing the Internet or at school. Join a school computer club and ask a librarian for books on the history, use, and programming of computers.

For more information, write to:

Association for Computing Machinery
11 West 42nd Street, 3rd Floor
New York, NY 10036

Data Processing Management Association
505 Busse Highway
Park Ridge, IL 60068

Using a schematic plan, a computer programmer works out a programming problem.

COMPUTER SYSTEMS ANALYSTS

SCHOOL SUBJECTS:
COMPUTER SCIENCE, MATHEMATICS

PERSONAL INTERESTS:
COMPUTERS, FIGURING OUT HOW
THINGS WORK

OUTLOOK:
FASTER THAN THE AVERAGE

OTHER ARTICLES TO LOOK AT:
Computer Network Specialists
Computer Operators
Computer Programmers
Database Specialists
Software Engineers

WHAT COMPUTER SYSTEMS ANALYSTS DO

Computer systems analysts help banks, government offices, and businesses of all kinds understand their computer systems. As more and more offices change from keeping records by hand to storing data in computers, analysts who can tailor computer systems and programs to the needs of a business, or even to the needs of just one department within a business, will become very important to any organization.

Computer systems analysts work with both the hardware and software parts of computer systems. The hardware includes the large items such as the computer itself, the monitor, and the keyboard; the software includes the computer programs, which are written and stored on diskettes, and the documentation (the manuals or guidebooks) that goes with the programs. Analysts design the best mix of hardware and software for the needs of the organization they are working for.

A computer systems analyst for the personnel department of a large company, for example, would first talk with the manager about what areas the computer could help with. The manager might be interested in knowing about how a new policy of giving employees longer paid vacations at Christmas has affected company profits for the month of December. The analyst can then show the manager what computer program to use, what data to enter, how to read the charts or graphs that the computer produces, and so on. The work of the analyst thus frees the manager to review the raw data—in this case, the numbers that show company profits were the same as in the previous Decembers—and decide how this information should affect company policy.

Once analysts have the computer system set up and running, they advise on possible equipment and programming changes. Often, two or more people in a department each have their own computer, but they must be able to connect with and use information from others' computers. Analysts must then work with all the different computers in a department or an organization so the computers can connect with each other; this system of computers connecting with each other is called networking.

The areas analysts specialize in are as different as the businesses themselves; some deal with basic accounting while others help decide such complex questions as the flight path of a space shuttle.

EDUCATION AND TRAINING

Computer systems analysts need to have at least a bachelor's degree in computer science. Analysts going into specialized areas (aeronautics, for example) usually have graduate degrees as well. Also, proficiency in mathematics, engineering, accounting, or business will be helpful in some instances.

In addition to a college degree, job experience as a computer programmer is very helpful. Many businesses hire systems analyst trainees from the ranks of their computer programmers. Computer systems analysts with several years of experience are often promoted into managerial jobs, especially as businesses find they need top staff members with an understanding of computers.

The Institute for Certification of Computer Professionals offers voluntary certification to computer systems analysts. Analysts take classes and exams to become a Certified Systems Professional (CSP). Certification is an added credential for job hunters.

OUTLOOK AND EARNINGS

This field is one of the fastest growing, and companies are always looking for qualified analysts, especially those with graduate degrees in computer science. As more businesses automate, more analysts will be needed to make the right decisions concerning new software and other technology and to keep current systems running smoothly. Also, computer systems analysts will be increasingly relied upon to work as consultants on a per project basis with a potential client. They will analyze business needs and suggest proper systems to answer them.

Starting salaries for computer systems analysts average about $30,000. With several years of experience analysts can earn from $37,000 to $43,000 per year. Computer systems analysts with many years of experience and additional responsibilities can earn salaries of $50,000 a year and higher. Salaries for analysts in government are somewhat lower than the average for private industry. Earnings also depend on years of experience

and the type of business one works for.

WAYS OF GETTING MORE INFORMATION

For more information, write to :

Association for Systems Management
1433 West Bagley Road
PO Box 38370
Cleveland, OH 44138
Tel: 216-234-2930

For more information on certification, contact:

Institute for Certification of Computing Professionals
2200 East Devon Avenue, Suite 268
Des Plaines, IL 60018-4503
Tel: 847-299-4227

Two computer systems analysts discuss the information path on a flow chart for their computer system.

COMPUTER TRAINERS

SCHOOL SUBJECTS:
COMPUTER SCIENCE, MATHEMATICS

PERSONAL INTERESTS:
COMPUTERS, TEACHING

OUTLOOK:
FASTER THAN THE AVERAGE

OTHER ARTICLES TO LOOK AT:

Adult and Vocational Education Teachers

Computer Network Specialists

Technical Support Specialists

WHAT COMPUTER TRAINERS DO

Today's employees and students need to know how to send email, how to surf the World Wide Web, and how to use word processing programs. However, many people become frustrated when faced with a blank computer screen and a thick instruction manual. Sometimes, too, the computers and programs are too complex to be explained fully and clearly by a manual. *Computer trainers* teach people how to use computers, software, and other new technology. When a business installs new hardware and software, computer trainers work one-on-one with the employees, or they lead seminars. They may also offer instruction over the Internet. With technology changing every day, computer trainers are often called upon for support and instruction.

Computer trainers teach people how to use computer programs. For example a company's accounting department may need a computer trainer to teach its accounting clerks how to use a spreadsheet program, which is used to make graphs and charts, and to calculate sums. Other common business programs include database programs, which keep track of such things as customer names, addresses, and phone numbers, and word processing programs, which are used to create documents, letters, and reports. Some computer trainers may also teach computer programming languages such as C or Visual Basic.

Many magazines, corporations, advertisers, and individuals are setting up home pages on the World Wide Web. A computer trainer can help them use the language needed to design a page, and teach them how to update the page. Desktop publishing programs and laser printers allow individuals and businesses to create interesting graphics and full-color pages for brochures and newsletters. Computer trainers can help users get started in these programs. Some computer trainers may also help offices set up their own office network. With a network, all the computers in an office are linked. Employees then share programs and files, conference with other employees, and send electronic mail.

Computer trainers may be self-employed and work on a freelance basis, or they may work for a computer training school or computer service company.

EDUCATION AND TRAINING

Most community colleges, universities, and vocational schools offer computer courses. Computer service companies and training schools also offer courses in specific software programs. Though college courses and training will make you an attractive candidate for a job with a computer service company, the most important quality is a lot of computer knowledge. Some people gain this knowledge simply by working with computers on a regular basis, either at home, or in the work place. Computer experience can come from working in the sales department of a computer store or software company; teaching experience can be gained by leading courses within the community or in a computer store. Education requirements vary at computer training schools and computer services companies, but to work as a teacher in the computer department of a community college, a bachelor's degree is the minimum requirement.

OUTLOOK AND EARNINGS

The outlook for computer trainers is good because more people are using computers than ever before. Most people do not have the time to teach themselves through trial and error and thick computer books; they need an experienced teacher to get them up to speed quickly.

Computer trainers who are self-employed charge by the hour. Depending on the size of the cities in which they work, and their experience, a computer trainer will charge anywhere from $15 an hour to over $100 an hour.

A computer trainer can find full-time employment with businesses that offer computer service and support, with computer and software manufacturers, and with large corporations. An entry-level position with one of these businesses may pay as low as $18,000 per year (or less in a small town), and as high as $60,000 or more per year.

WAYS OF GETTING MORE INFORMATION

There are a number of computer magazines available at your local newsstand or library. Some of these magazines publish articles written specifically for people unfamiliar with computers. The World Wide Web is also a great resource for information on the latest software and technology. You can even download some software from the Internet for free. Also, people on the Internet are usually eager to answer your questions about computers and software; literally thousands of sites are devoted to computers and computer training.

For more information on a career as a computer trainer, write the following:

Computer Enhancement Systems
4133 East Freedom Center.
Ooltewah, TN 37363
Tel: 423-892-8985
WWW:http://www.pwgroup.com/
ces/focus.shtml

A computer trainer helps a student set up a table in a word processing program.

CONGRESSIONAL AIDES

SCHOOL SUBJECTS:
CIVICS/GOVERNMENT, SPEECH

PERSONAL INTERESTS:
DEBATING, HELPING PEOPLE:
PERSONAL SERVICE

OUTLOOK:
LITTLE CHANGE OR MORE SLOWLY
THAN THE AVERAGE

OTHER ARTICLES TO LOOK AT:

Appointed and Elected Officials

Fund-Raisers

Lobbyists

WHAT CONGRESSIONAL AIDES DO

Congressional aides are the men and women behind the scenes whose work makes it possible for senators and representatives to do their jobs. Congress consists of two branches, the Senate and the House of Representatives. Each state in the country elects two senators for a term of six years. The number of representatives each state can elect is based on the state's population. Representatives serve two-year terms. Both senators and representatives appoint aides to serve on their staffs. These usually include an *administrative assistant*, a *press secretary*, an *office manager*, a *legislative correspondent*, and a *state*, or *district director*. These congressional aides can play an important roll in helping senators and representatives get elected and re-elected. They often organize fund-raising campaigns and stuff envelopes with information about the congressperson's qualifications and opinions. Since the main responsibility of Congress is to make federal laws, members of Congress spend six months of each year in Washington, D.C., where they

meet from January until the end of July. This means that they have two offices: one in the nation's capital and the other in their home state. Their aides help business run smoothly in both offices.

Aides work on either a personal or committee staff. The committee staff focuses primarily on the construction and passage of legislation, while the personal staff deals with matters concerning the home district or state. Aides do a variety of office work in addition to stuffing envelopes. They sort the mail, keep the files in order, type letters, answer the telephone, maintain a computer base of constituents (voters from the home state), conduct opinion polls, do research about pending bills, and receive drop-in visitors. They often serve as a sounding board for their congress member's ideas. Some even write speeches and position papers that describe how a senator or representative feels about a certain issue.

EDUCATION AND TRAINING

Most aides are young and have little experience, but they have a great deal of loyalty to their elected official. A college degree is usually required of a personal congressional aide, while most committee aides have an advanced degree in law or journalism. They attend committees with the Congress member and meet with lobbyists and special interest groups. Many aides are appointed through personal friendship or by contacts made when serving as a volunteer in an election campaign, for instance.

All congressional aides need to have good communications skills—both written and spoken. They must be courteous and efficient. They need to be able to analyze information and to do research. They must also be able to organize the enormous amount of paperwork and information that comes into a Congress member's office. In school, those interested in becoming a congressional aide should learn secretarial skills and take classes in public speaking, math, English, bookkeeping, history, economics, and political science. Whenever possible, interested students should volunteer to help a candidate in an election campaign and learn the ins and outs of fund-raising.

OUTLOOK AND EARNINGS

Wages for most positions are higher in the Senate than they are in the House. Average salaries for the various positions range from $21,000 to $81,000.

WAYS OF GETTING MORE INFORMATION

Language Arts

Organizational Skills

People Skills

For more information, write:

The Congressional Management Foundation
513 Capitol Court NE , Suite 100
Washington, DC 20002
Tel: 202-546-0100

Democratic National Committee
430 South Capitol Street SE
Washington, DC 20003
Tel: 202-863-8000

Republican National Committee
310 First Street SE
Washington, DC 20003
Tel: 202-863-8500

Good communication skills are vital to congressional aides, who must listen carefully to their employers and articulate their own ideas as well.

CONSERVATORS AND CONSERVATION TECHNICIANS

SCHOOL SUBJECTS:
ART, CHEMISTRY

PERSONAL INTERESTS:
DRAWING/PAINTING, FIXING THINGS

OUTLOOK:
ABOUT AS FAST AS THE AVERAGE

OTHER ARTICLES TO LOOK AT:

Anthropologists

Archaeologists

Archivists

Artists

Assessors and Appraisers

WHAT CONSERVATORS AND CONSERVATION TECHNICIANS DO

Conservators and *conservation technicians* are specially-trained professionals who analyze and assess the condition of artifacts and art objects. These objects may include natural objects, such as bones and fossils, or man-made objects such as paintings, sculpture, metal, and paper. Conservation workers need a working knowledge of chemistry and scientific technique in order to plan and carry out conservation treatment and projects. They may work in private practice or in museums, historical societies, or state institutions.

Conservation workers usually specialize in a particular area of work, such as the preservation of books and paper, photographs, paintings, textiles, or wooden objects. Other conservators specialize in archaeological or ethnographical (human culture) materials. The main job of conservators is to conserve or preserve items so that they can be enjoyed and further studied in the future. They undertake these duties in accordance with generally accepted standards of ethics and professional guidelines. They may study an object, such as a Native-American ceremonial headdress, to determine its condition, and stabilize its structure. They attempt to establish the best environment where the artifact can be preserved. Areas that are too hot or too cold, or that are high in humidity, can cause the item to become damaged or further deteriorate. Conservator's responsibilities may also include documenting the condition of the structure using written and visual recording. They design programs for preventative care and oversee conservation treatments. A conservator's tools can include microscopes and cameras, including equipment for specialized processes such as infra-red and ultra-violet photography, and x-ray processes.

Conservation technicians help conservators in preserving and restoring artifacts and art objects. To do this, they study descriptions and other information about the object. They may perform physical and chemical tests. If an object is metal, a technician may be instructed to clean it by gently rubbing it with a cloth or by applying chemical solvents Statues can sometimes be washed with soap solutions, while silver and some types of furniture can be polished. If an object is damaged, conservation technicians may reassemble the broken pieces using solder or glue. They may repaint an object if the original paint is missing or faded, using paint of the same color and chemical make-up as the original. Technicians also build and repair picture frames and remount paintings in frames.

EDUCATION AND TRAINING

In the past, most conservation workers learned their craft through an apprenticeship with an established conservator. Nowadays, graduate training is the most recognized route into the conservation field. Graduate schools are highly selective, so it is important to carefully plan your academic future. Undergraduate course work should include classes in science, including inorganic and organic chemistry, the humanities (art, history, archaeology, and anthropology), and studio art. Some graduate schools consider work experience and internships as comparable to course work. Conservation technicians will need at least some education beyond high school to get a job in this field.

OUTLOOK AND EARNINGS

Increasing interest in cultural material of all forms has brought about a need for qualified conservation workers. This interest is offset by recent decreases in government funding of educational and arts programs. Museums may be forced to limit their conservation staffs, and instead rely on small staffs assisted by private conservation companies. As a result, private industry and for-profit companies will grow, while museum staffs may experience reductions in employment.

Salaries for conservation staff vary greatly by experience, specialty, region, job description, and employer. The average salary for a chief art museum conservator is $54,000. Senior conservators earn $40,000 to $50,000 a year. Associate conservators average $37,000 annually. These positions and their salaries are comparable to other university, museum, and library positions. Conservation technicians may earn starting salaries of $18,000 to $22,000 per year.

WAYS OF GETTING MORE INFORMATION

If you are interested in a career as a conservation worker, contact a local museum or art conservation laboratory to arrange a visit.

For more information, contact:

The American Institute for Conservation of Historic and Artistic Works (AIC)
1717 K Street NW Suite 301
Washington, DC 20006
Tel: 202-452-9545
WWW:vnyaic2aol.com

The work of the conservator is painstakingly slow because the objects on which they work are usually priceless and irreplaceable.

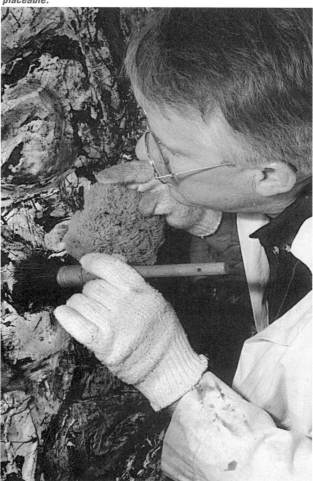

CONSTRUCTION INSPECTORS

SCHOOL SUBJECTS:
MATHEMATICS, SHOP (TRADE/VO-TECH EDUCATION)

PERSONAL INTERESTS:
BUILDING THINGS, FIXING THINGS

OUTLOOK:
FASTER THAN THE AVERAGE

OTHER ARTICLES TO LOOK AT:

Carpenters

Construction Laborers

Electricians

Mechanical Engineers

WHAT CONSTRUCTION INSPECTORS DO

Construction inspectors make sure that all new structures of any kind—hospitals, schools, housing projects, administrative buildings, bridges, highways, dams, sewer and water systems, military installations, and so on—are built legally, properly, safely, and at a reasonable cost. Construction inspectors work for local, federal, and state governments as well as for private industries, such as engineering and architectural firms. They are hired to visit construction sites, test for defects, and take photographs. They use tape measures, survey instruments, metering devices and equipment that measures the strength of concrete. They keep logs of their work and write reports that tell whether or not the structures are built soundly and meet all the necessary codes and contract specifications. Where special natural hazards exists, such as the danger of hurricanes or earthquakes, inspectors have to check to make sure extra regulations are followed.

There are seven categories of construction inspectors: building, electrical, elevator, home, mechanical, plumbing, and public works. *Building inspectors* check for structural quality. They look at plans, visit the work site, and make a final inspection when the building is completed. *Electrical inspectors* check out all the components of a structure's electrical system, including wiring, lighting, sound and security systems, and generators. *Elevator inspectors* examine not only elevators, but escalators, moving sidewalks in airports, amusement park rides, and ski lifts. *Home inspectors* often work for people interested in buying a home; they look at the roof, the pipes, the electrical system, and the plumbing. *Mechanical inspectors* inspect the mechanical parts of gas pipes, gas tanks, and big kitchen appliances. *Plumbing inspectors* check plumbing systems, including how water is supplied to a structure and how waste is removed from it. *Public works inspectors* check all government-built facilities, including water and sewer systems, highways, bridges, dams, and streets to make sure they will function safely.

Whatever their specialty, construction inspectors must pay great attention to detail, be able to spot and correct problems, and communicate well with all kinds of people.

EDUCATION AND TRAINING

Government construction inspectors must be at least high school graduates with a working knowledge of the materials used in construction. Those who have studied engineering or architecture for at least two years in college or those who have attended a community or junior college with courses in construction technology and building inspection will have an advantage on the available jobs.

Construction inspectors receive most of their training on the job and most have proved themselves with several years' experience in private industry, either as a construction contractor or as a trade worker such as carpenter, electrician, plumber, or pipefitter. Some states require that inspectors pass examinations on construction techniques, building materials, and code requirements.

OUTLOOK AND EARNINGS

As the concern for public safety continues to rise, the demand for inspectors should grow about as fast as average even if construction activity does not increase. Applicants who have some college education, are already certified inspectors, or who have experience as carpenters, electricians, or plumbers will have the best opportunities.

Most inspectors earn between $17,500 and $41,000 a year, with building inspectors making the most. The average salary for inspectors working for the federal government is about $27,000 a year, a little higher than the average of $25,700 for all other inspectors. Inspectors in large cities, and in the North and the West, earn the highest salaries.

WAYS OF GETTING MORE INFORMATION

Summer jobs on a construction site or as a carpenter's or plumber's assistant are often available. Also, shop, math and science classes in high school will be valuable.

Manual Skills

Sciences and Mathematics

For more information, contact:

Building Officials and Code Administrators International
*4051 West Flossmoor Road
Country Club Hills, IL 60477
708-799-2300*

International Conference of Building Officials
*5360 South Workman Mill Road
Whittier, CA 90601
310-699-0541*

Southern Building Code Congress International
*900 Montclair Road
Birmingham, AL 35213
205-591-1853*

Holding the blueprints for a building, a construction inspector greets the construction engineer before checking the building site for possible problems.

CONSTRUCTION LABORERS

SCHOOL SUBJECTS:
MATHEMATICS, SHOP (TRADE/
VO-TECH EDUCATION)

PERSONAL INTERESTS:
BUILDING THINGS, FIXING THINGS

OUTLOOK:
AS FAST AS THE AVERAGE

OTHER ARTICLES TO LOOK AT:

Bricklayers and Stonemasons

Carpenters

Plasterers

Roustabouts

WHAT CONSTRUCTION LABORERS DO

Construction laborers are part of the team that builds homes, offices, highways, bridges, apartment buildings, and other structures. They load and unload bricks and other materials, clean up rubble, and pour and spread concrete. They bring tools, materials, and equipment to more skilled workers at a construction site. They may set up scaffolding, dig trenches, and build braces to support the sides of excavations. They work alongside carpenters, electricians, plumbers, and bricklayers and stonemasons, carrying their equipment and assisting in other ways. They also operate heavy machinery, such as jackhammers, cement mixers, front-end loaders, hoists, and laser beam equipment used to align and grade ditches and tunnels.

Construction laborers help out wherever they are needed. They may hold a ladder so a carpenter can work on a ceiling, or they may stack bricks in a corner for later use. They may also sweep up loose stones or help connect plumbing pipes.

Although construction laborers are assistants, they are trained in the methods, materials, and operations used in construction work. This is especially true of those who work with the explosives used to blast rocks away before construction can begin. They must be aware of the effects of different explosives under varying rock conditions. This knowledge is generally gained from on-the-job training from supervisors.

The tasks facing construction laborers are physically demanding and repetitive. Not only do they have to lift and carry heavy objects, they also have to kneel, crouch, crawl, and squeeze into awkward positions. Sometimes they have to work high up off the ground, and they always must be prepared to work in all kinds of weather conditions. Today, construction work usually continues year-round, and working outdoors during the winter can be difficult.

Construction work can also involve travel to remote or isolated areas to build pipelines, shipping terminals, and for other large projects. In addition, construction laborers are sometimes exposed to harmful chemicals, fumes, odors, and dangerous machinery, and they must wear special safety clothing and helmets. On the positive side, construction laborers spend most of their working time outdoors.

EDUCATION AND TRAINING

The best way to become a construction laborer is to apply directly to local contractors who undertake all types of construction work. Contractors normally hire people who are at least 18 years old, in good physical condition, and show a willingness and ability to learn. Laborers are then given on-the-job training.

Apprenticeships are the best way to acquire specialized skills. Apprenticeships usually last 2 years and are sponsored by local unions and contractors.

Although no formal education is needed to become a laborer, only those with at least a high school education are likely to have a chance to become supervisors or advanced workers (such as carpenters and bricklayers and stonemasons).

OUTLOOK AND EARNINGS

As long as the construction industry remains reasonably strong, construction laborers should continue to find good employment possibilities into the next century. An economic slowdown, bad weather in a particular area, and other factors may limit the number of jobs available in construction. However, this is a very big field with a lot of turnover, so there will always be some job openings. Construction laborers may not always work all year round.

Construction laborers ordinarily earn at least $12 per hour, but because they don't work every day, yearly earnings are hard to estimate. Overall in the 1990s, full-time laborers earned between $16,000 and $29,000.

WAYS OF GETTING MORE INFORMATION

A good way to find out if you would enjoy being a construction worker is to look for a summer job as a laborer at a construction site.

In addition, contact the following for more information about being a construction worker:

Associated General Contractors of America
1957 E Street NW
Washington, DC 20006
Tel: 202-393-2040
Email: 73264.15@compuserv

Laborers' International Union of North America
905 16th Street NW
Washington, DC 20006
202-737-8320

Construction workers assemble a support structure for a building under progress.

COOKS, CHEFS, AND BAKERS

SCHOOL SUBJECTS:
FAMILY AND CONSUMER SCIENCE,
MATHEMATICS

PERSONAL INTERESTS:
FOOD, SCULPTING

OUTLOOK:
FASTER THAN THE AVERAGE

OTHER ARTICLES TO LOOK AT:

Caterers

Dietitians

Food Service Workers

Restaurant Managers

Waiters and Waitresses

WHAT COOKS, CHEFS, AND BAKERS DO

Cooks, chefs, and bakers prepare and cook food in restaurants, hotels, cafeterias, and other eating places. They plan menus, order food, measure and mix ingredients, cook and test the food, and arrange it on plates. Some specialize in a certain area, such as cutting meat, boning fish, fixing sauces, or making salads, soups, or desserts. Chefs may do many of these things, but their major job is to oversee all the activities in the kitchen. They also create recipes, train cooks, and keep track of work schedules. Some chefs specialize in one cooking style, such as French or Italian.

Bakers prepare cakes, pastries, cookies, rolls, muffins, biscuits, and breads for bakeries, hotels, restaurants, cafeterias, and large food-chain stores. Though cooks and chefs sometimes also bake, bakers specialize in preparing only baked goods. A baker's responsibilities include coordinating the baked goods that are to appear on restaurant menus, ordering supplies, creating recipes, measuring and mixing ingredients, and testing the results. Some bakers specialize in one particular kind of baked good, such as cakes or cookies.

Cooks and chefs may work a long week of 48 hours or more. This usually includes evening and weekend work because that is when many people are dining out. Bakers who own their own businesses can determine their own hours, but bakers often start work very early in the morning to have freshly baked goods ready for breakfast time.

EDUCATION AND TRAINING

Many cooks, chefs, and bakers enter the profession through on-the-job training in restaurants or hotels. Although a high school education is not always required, it is vital for those who wish to move up to better jobs. The best job opportunities are available to those who graduate from a special cooking school or culinary institute. These schools have classes in menu planning, food costs, purchasing, food storage, sanitation, and health standards, as well as cooking and baking techniques. Graduates may then have to serve an apprenticeship or work in a supporting role before being hired as a head chef or baker in a top restaurant or hotel.

In high school, students can prepare for a career as a cook, chef, or baker by taking classes in family and consumer science. Since many cooking terms are derived from French, foreign languages courses should also be helpful.

OUTLOOK AND EARNINGS

Job opportunities for cooks, chefs, and bakers should be quite good through 2005. People with high and medium-high incomes will be dining out more.

Cooks' and chefs' salaries depend on how skilled they are, what type of food they prepare, and where they work. Salaries are usually higher in restaurants that serve higher-priced meals. Cooks and chefs in famous restaurants and hotels, especially those on the West Coast, earn the highest salaries, generally between $40,000 and $80,000. A few famous chefs can earn much more. The average hourly wage of a chef is $9.80 per hour (about $20,380 per year). Most cooks earn between $6 and $10 an hour, and most chefs earn between $18,000 and $40,000 per year. A baker's salary depends on his or her specialty, experience, skill, and reputation, as well as the establishment in which he or she works. Bakers earn anywhere from $10,000 to $50,000 a year or more.

WAYS OF GETTING MORE INFORMATION

Young people interested in becoming cooks, chefs, or bakers can begin by experimenting at home. Some restaurants hire high school students as kitchen helpers and waiters and waitresses.

For more information, write to:

American Culinary Federation
PO Box 3466
St. Augustine, FL 32085

Council on Hotel, Restaurant, and Institutional Education
1200 17th Street NW
Washington, DC 20036

Educational Foundation of the National Restaurant Association
250 South Wacker Drive, Suite 1400
Chicago, IL 60606

This baker must be especially skilled in breadmaking techniques to prepare so many loaves at once.

COREMAKERS

SCHOOL SUBJECTS:
PHYSICAL EDUCATION, SHOP
(TRADE/VO-TECH EDUCATION)

PERSONAL INTERESTS:
BUILDING THINGS, SCULPTING

OUTLOOK:
DECLINE

OTHER ARTICLES TO LOOK AT:

Forge Shop Workers

Machinists

Molders

Patternmakers

Tool and Die Makers

WHAT COREMAKERS DO

Coremakers prepare the cores, usually made of sand, that are used as molds when making castings of metal articles and machinery parts. These articles and parts include many thousands of the metal objects that are basic to our lives, from automobile engines to water faucets to scissors. In the casting process, molten metal is poured around the core, where it solidifies. When the core is removed, the desired cavity or shape remains in the metal. Cores are made in different sizes and shapes depending upon the size and shape of the metal object to be cast.

Coremakers begin their work by cleaning the core box, which is a block of wood or metal hollowed out to the shape of the desired core. The box is then partially filled with sand, and the sand is compacted in the box by hand, mallet, or other tool. The core box is then put on a machine that packs the sand into the box even more tightly. When the sand has been compacted as much as

possible, it is taken out of the box and baked until it is solid. It is then ready to be used in a metal mold.

There are several specialized jobs that coremakers may have. A *machine coremaker,* for example, makes cores with machines rather than by hand. They generally set up, adjust, and operate machines that make sand cores by forcing sand into specially shaped hollow forms. They are usually employed in large factories where a great many identical parts must be made. A *core-blower operator* runs machines that blow sand into a core box to make a core. A *core checker* uses various tools to make sure that the cores that have been produced are of the correct size and shape. A *core-oven tender* puts cores into the oven and raises the heat to the proper temperature to harden and strengthen the cores. *Coreroom foundry workers* assist coremakers in various ways, such as hauling sand, fastening sections of cores together, and transporting cores to and from the ovens.

EDUCATION AND TRAINING

Most employers today generally prefer to hire people with a high school diploma for helpers' jobs in coremaking operations. New workers usually learn the basics of coremaking by working closely with a skilled coremaker and through on-the-job training. At first, they learn to make simple cores and operate core ovens. They advance to more difficult tasks as they learn new skills.

Sometimes coremakers enter an apprenticeship program to become a coremaker.

This program lasts four years and provides extensive training in all the skills needed to be a fully qualified coremaker. Trainees work as helpers or beginner coremakers and also have classroom instruction in subjects such as mathematics and the study of metals. Opportunities for apprenticeship programs can be very difficult to find, as fewer companies offer them nowadays. Helpful classes to take in high school are English, mathematics, computers, and shop. Learning to read blueprints and use tools is especially useful.

Some coremaking jobs involve heavy work, and physical strength is necessary; however, workers involved with making small cores do not need much strength.

OUTLOOK AND EARNINGS

It is very difficult to find a job as a coremaker as automation has reduced the number of coremakers needed. Most currently employed coremakers are highly skilled workers, and opportunities for new workers to enter this field are extremely limited.

Coremakers make salaries ranging from $30,000 to $32,000 a year.

WAYS OF GETTING MORE INFORMATION

A young person interested in this kind of work may be able to arrange a visit to a foundry through a teacher or school counselor. At a foundry, students can watch the work in progress and see workers involved in different activities.

School and public librarians can also help interested students locate books on minerals and metals and their processing.

Additionally, jewelry-making is a hobby that gives good experience in casting and shaping metals.

For more information, write to:

American Foundrymen's Society
505 State Street
Des Plaines, IL 60016-8399

Glass, Molders, Pottery, Plastics and Allied Workers International Union
608 East Baltimore Pike
Media, PA 19063-0607

A coremaker removes completed ceramic cores from a tray.

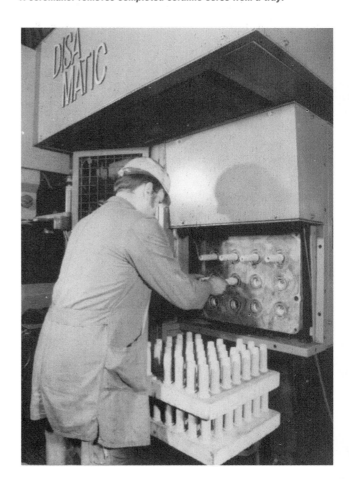

CORRECTIONS OFFICERS

SCHOOL SUBJECTS:
PHYSICAL EDUCATION, PSYCHOLOGY

PERSONAL INTERESTS:
HELPING PEOPLE: EMOTIONALLY,
SPORTS

OUTLOOK:
MUCH FASTER THAN THE AVER-
AGE

OTHER ARTICLES TO LOOK AT:
FBI Agents
Polygraph Examiners
Private Investigators
Security Guards

WHAT CORRECTIONS OFFICERS DO

Corrections officers guard persons who have
been arrested and are awaiting trial. They
also guard those who have been tried, found
guilty, and sentenced to serve time in prison.
They search prisoners and their cells for
weapons and drugs and check locks, bars on
windows and doors, and gates for signs of
tampering. Prisoners must be under guard at
all times—while eating, sleeping, exercising,
and working. Corrections officers count prisoners from time to time to make sure they
are all present. Some officers are stationed at
gates and on towers to prevent escapes.
Corrections officers carefully observe the
attitude and behavior of prison inmates and
remain alert for potential conflicts. Often,
the officers will attempt to settle disputes
before they erupt into violence. When a dis-
turbance or crime occurs at the prison, officers are responsible for stopping it and helping to investigate the cause.

Corrections officers are also responsible
for giving work assignments to prisoners and
supervising them as they carry out their
tasks. Officers check prisoners' cells for
unclean conditions and fire hazards.
Sometimes they may check prisoners' mail
for forbidden items. If a prisoner is injured,
they give first aid. When visitors come to the
prison, officers check their identification
before taking them to the visiting area.

These workers may give help and
advice to prisoners and help them
adjust to prison life. They may
also suggest where to look for a
job after release from prison.
Sometimes officers help prisoners get in touch with their
families. They may try to help
prisoners with their personal
problems.

Corrections officers usually keep
a daily record of their activities. They
make regular reports to their supervisors, the
head corrections officers.

In small towns, corrections officers are
sometimes called *jailers.* These officers may
act as deputy sheriffs or police officers when
they are not performing guard duties.

Many corrections officers work at prisons, prison camps, and reform schools run
by state governments. Others work at city
and county jails. Still others work at prisons
run by the federal government. Many correctional facilities are also run by private companies that employ corrections officers.

EDUCATION AND TRAINING

Corrections officers generally must be at
least 18 to 21 years old and have completed
high school, although many positions require
some post-secondary education or related
work experience. Most states and some local
governments train corrections officers on the
job. These workers spend two to six months
under the supervision of experienced officers.
The federal government and some states have

special schools for training corrections officers in programs that last from four to eight weeks.

In many states, applicants have to pass physical fitness, eyesight, and hearing tests. Some states require one or two years of experience in corrections or related police work.

OUTLOOK AND EARNINGS

The employment outlook for corrections officers is good. Crowded prisons have created a need for more officers. New prisons are being built and others are being enlarged.

The average salary for beginning corrections officers is $18,400, although salaries vary widely from state to state and at the different levels of government. Starting salaries for federal corrections officers range from

A corrections officer patrols the recreation area of a prison.

$21,000 to $28,000 per year, depending on location. At the state level, salaries range from $15,000 to $35,000 per year.

The average salary for all experienced officers is $23,000 per year, with some officers earning $30,000 to $40,000 per year and more.

WAYS OF GETTING MORE INFORMATION

For more information, write to the following:

American Correctional Association
4380 Forbes Boulevard
Lanham, MD 20706

Contact Center, Inc.
PO Box 81826
Lincoln, NE 68501

COSMETOLOGISTS

SCHOOL SUBJECTS:
BUSINESS, HEALTH

PERSONAL INTERESTS:
HELPING PEOPLE: PERSONAL
SERVICE, MANAGEMENT

OUTLOOK:
ABOUT AS FAST AS THE AVERAGE

OTHER ARTICLES TO LOOK AT:

Dog Groomers

Funeral Directors

Manufacturers' Sales Representatives

WHAT COSMETOLOGISTS DO

Cosmetologists help people look their best. They cut hair, apply makeup, give manicures, and do a variety of other jobs. Their services were once considered luxuries and were available only to the very wealthy, but now beauty shops are everywhere, and they cater to everyone. The work of *barbers* and cosmetologists is closely linked, although barbers usually work on men's hair and cosmetologists on women's. Barbers cut, shampoo, color and bleach hair, and trim and shape beards and mustaches. They also give shaves, facials, scalp treatments, and conditioning massages, and they advise customers regarding styling and grooming. They may fit and groom artificial hair pieces such as wigs and toupees. Cosmetologists and barbers who specialize in haircuts and styles are often called *hairstylists*.

Some cosmetologists are experts in makeup and give facials, do makeup analysis, and advise customers on what products to use. Others specialize in manicures, pedicures, and scalp treatments. They may also shape and tint eyelashes and eyebrows and use various techniques such as waxing to remove undesirable hair from a customer's face or body. In small shops (and most beauty shops are quite small) cosmetologists may do all of these things. Some cosmetologists and barbers may be employed in a large city department store, a hospital, or a hotel. Others may style hair or apply makeup in a fashion center, a photographic center, or in a television or movie studio.

Most cosmetologists and barbers work 40 hours a week, and their working hours often include Saturdays and evenings, when it is most convenient for customers to come in. They spend much of their day standing. It is important for both barbers and cosmetologists to make their customers feel at ease and to engage them in polite conversation.

EDUCATION AND TRAINING

The educational requirement for barbers and cosmetologists varies from state to state but usually an applicant must have completed at least the eighth grade, and in some states a high school diploma is required.

Both cosmetologists and barbers must pass a state-administered examination and receive a state license. The requirements for a cosmetologist's license vary from state to state, but usually an applicant must have between 1,000 hours (six months) and 2,500 hours (15 months) of combined on-the-job and classroom training. Barbers also have to train at a state-approved barber school for nine to twelve months and complete an apprenticeship program. Training courses at these schools include classes on personal hygiene, anatomy, skin and scalp disease, applied chemistry, applied electricity, and shop sanitation. Students often begin practical work on mannequins and on each other. As they become more experienced, they begin styling customers who come into the school shop because of its lower prices.

OUTLOOK AND EARNINGS

Barbers' and cosmetologists' salaries depend on experience, speed, the prices charged by the shop, and on the shop's salary arrangement—that is, whether the shop pays only a commission or a commission plus a salary. Cosmetologists and barbers receive a good part of their income from tips. Generally, barbers and cosmetologists earn between $20,000 and $25,000 a year, but those who own their own shops may earn $30,000 or more. A beginning employee might earn about $12,000. Stylists who work in exclusive salons in large cities earn considerably more.

WAYS OF GETTING MORE INFORMATION

For more information about a career as a barber or cosmetologist, write to the following group:

National Accreditation Commission of Cosmetology Arts and Sciences
901 North Stuart Street, Suite 900
Arlington, VA 22203

A cosmetologist applies dye and foil wrap to a customer's hair in a special coloring process.

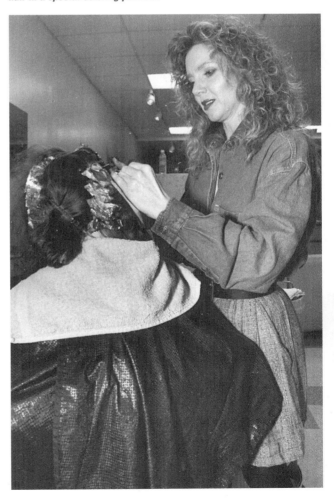

COST ESTIMATORS

SCHOOL SUBJECTS:
BUSINESS, MATHEMATICS

PERSONAL INTERESTS:
BUILDING THINGS, COMPUTERS

OUTLOOK:
ABOUT AS FAST AS THE AVERAGE

OTHER ARTICLES TO LOOK AT:

Accountants

Carpenters

Civil Engineers

Insurance Claims Representatives

WHAT COST ESTIMATORS DO

Cost estimators figure out how much it will cost to build or make something. Builders and manufacturers need cost estimators when they plan a new project or a new product. Cost estimators must have good judgment because their evaluations may involve budgets in the millions of dollars.

Builders first show their plans to a cost estimator who thinks about all the things that go into a large building project. How much will the builder have to pay for labor? What equipment will the builder have to buy or rent? How much will all the materials—stone, wood, plaster, or cement—cost? How much will it cost to bring all the materials to the building site?

Cost estimators must gather the necessary information to answer all these questions. Then they put together an estimate. If a project is very complicated, there may be a need for several cost estimators to handle different parts of the project. For example, one estimator may work only on the cost of elec-

trical work, while another covers the cost of transportation. Then a chief estimator will put all these separate reports together in one complete estimate.

Estimators working for manufacturers have to figure out how much it will cost to train workers to produce a new product. They must determine what parts and materials cost and how much labor will be needed to make it. Because a manufacturer will probably be making a product for years, estimators must also predict how much and how fast these costs will rise. They must also consider what equipment is needed and how quickly the equipment will wear out and have to be replaced.

If a builder or manufacturer needs an estimate in a hurry, the cost estimator has to work long hours to get it done on time. Because estimators may have to make decisions very quickly, and because a great deal of money may be involved, cost estimators must work well under pressure.

EDUCATION AND TRAINING

Builders and manufacturers want cost estimators to know all about their particular business. For this reason, on-the-job training is important for any cost estimator. Many cost estimators begin as trades people—for example, carpenters or plumbers—who gain experience in figuring out how much a given job will cost.

High school students interested in this profession should take courses in mathematics and English. Many technical schools and community colleges offer two-year programs that specialize in manufacturing and construction processes. Accounting courses are also helpful. The federal government and some other employers require cost estimators to have a college degree in either civil engineering or mathematics.

The American Society of Professional Estimators and the Society of Cost Estimations Analysis gives certificates to cost estimators who have three to seven years experience and pass a written and an oral test. This certification is not required; it is a way of proving that estimators know their jobs well.

OUTLOOK AND EARNINGS

Because the work of cost estimators depends entirely on manufacturing and construction, the employment of cost estimators is sensitive to economic fluctuations. This will continue to be true over the next 10 years.

Beginning salaries for cost estimators range from $16,000 to $24,000 per year, depending on the candidate's experience, the size of the employer and the type of work. College graduates with a degree in engineering can earn starting salaries of $30,000 or more. Highly experienced estimators can earn $75,000 or more.

WAYS OF GETTING MORE INFORMATION

One way to practice doing what a cost estimator does is to create budgets for various projects, either at home or at school, and then evaluate the accuracy of the budget after the project is completed.

Watching the construction of a building or taking a factory tour will give those interested in a career as a cost estimator an idea of all the different kinds of workers, materials, and equipment involved.

For more information, contact:

AACE International
PO Box 1557
Morgantown, WV 26507
Tel: 304-296-8444

American Society of Professional Estimators
11141 Georgia Avenue, Suite 412
Wheaton, MD 20902
Tel: 301-929-8848

Society of Cost Estimating Analysis
101 South Whiting Street, Suite 313
Alexandria, VA 22304
Tel: 703-751-8069

Organizational Skills

Sciences and Mathematics

A cost estimator reviews details of a building plan with the client.

COSTUME DESIGNERS

OTHER ARTICLES TO LOOK AT:

Actors and Actresses

Artists

Fashion Designers

Stage Production Workers

Tailors and Dressmakers

SCHOOL SUBJECTS:
FAMILY AND CONSUMER SCIENCE, THEATER/DANCE

PERSONAL INTERESTS:
CLOTHES, DRAWING/PAINTING

OUTLOOK:
ABOUT AS FAST AS THE AVERAGE

WHAT COSTUME DESIGNERS DO

Costume designers create, coordinate, and organize the costumes seen in the theater, on television, and in the movies. They also create costumes for figure skaters, ballroom dancers, circus performers, and others. When a show is to be performed, the costume designer reads the script, then decides what types of costumes are needed for each character. Through the use of a costume's color, style, and texture, the designer can express a character's personality and tell the audience more about his or her lifestyle.

If the story takes place in the past, research is done at the library to make certain that the clothing styles are correct for the time period. For modern settings, a knowledge of styles and trends is necessary Many costume designers also research previous productions of a play to see the kinds of costumes that were used and how well they worked then.

The costume designer consults with the director for design approval; with the stage designer to be certain that the furniture and backdrops do not clash with the costumes; and with the lighting designer to make certain that the lighting will not change the appearance of colors on stage.

The costume designer then compiles all the information, and makes color sketches or renderings of the outfits and accessories needed for each character. The costume designer then decides whether to rent, purchase, or sew the costume. Most often, these choices are determined by the show's budget. A major part of the costume designer's work is in the shopping for clothing and accessories (often from resale shops), fabrics, and sewing supplies, and in supervising the assistants who do the sewing work.

Typically the costume shop is a small workroom which is crowded with people working on the various stages of costume creation: sewing, cutting, draping, and fitting. Costume designers need to be able to work in a busy setting, have patience for changes, and get along with people of all dispositions.

Costume designers usually have irregular hours, and when showtime approaches, they may work long hours seven days a week to coordinate fittings and last-minute changes. When the show is in production, the work does not end —costumes need to be cleaned, ironed, and repaired as needed to appear fresh for each camera shoot or stage performance. Sometimes there is a wardrobe supervisor who handles these tasks.

EDUCATION AND TRAINING

To become a costume designer, it is necessary to have a high school education and a college degree. If a costume design major is unavailable, working in a strong theater department may provide similar experience. Such departments usually hire students to help sew and create the costumes.

High school and college students should take as many English and literature courses as possible, to learn how to interpret drama. Courses in history are helpful in researching historical costumes and time periods. Courses in sewing, art, designing, and draping are also beneficial.

OUTLOOK AND EARNINGS

Payment in the field varies widely. Costume designers usually earn a flat rate per show or per costume. A show in a small theater may pay $400–$500. Larger shows run from $1,000 to $18,000 and more for a Broadway show running about eight weeks. For movies and television, salaries can go much higher.

WAYS OF GETTING MORE INFORMATION

Students interested in experiencing the work of costume designers may be able to participate behind the scenes in school theatrical productions.

For more information, write to:

Costume Designers Guild
13949 Ventura Boulevard
Sherman Oaks, CA 91423

National Costumers Association
3038 Hayes Avenue
Fremont, OH 43420

A costume designer works on a detailed and colorful outfit. Many of these elaborate costumes will reflect the personalities of the characters wearing them.

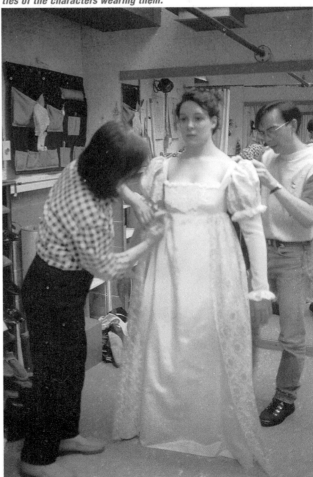

COUNTER AND RETAIL CLERKS

SCHOOL SUBJECTS:
MATHEMATICS, SPEECH

PERSONAL INTERESTS:
HELPING PEOPLE: PERSONAL
SERVICE, PERFORMING
REPETITIVE TASKS

OUTLOOK:
FASTER THAN THE AVERAGE

**OTHER
ARTICLES TO
LOOK AT:**

Bank Services Occupations

Cashiers

Clerks

Postal Clerks

Retail Sales Workers

WHAT COUNTER AND RETAIL CLERKS DO

Counter and retail clerks take orders and receive payments for a wide variety of services. They are the public representatives of businesses that provide goods and services. They work in supermarkets, drugstores, convenience stores, cleaners, computer shops, athletic and footwear boutiques, and photo-finishing stores, among others. Many counter and retail clerks work in the rental industry. They may work as clerks at a car rental agency at an airport, in video stores, or at other establishments that rent goods or services to the consumer.

Counter and retail clerks take orders and receive payments from the public. They keep records of receipts and sales using a cash register, computer terminal, or by hand. They are responsible for keeping track of the money in their register throughout the day and balancing their money when their shift ends. Clerks also bag or wrap the customers' purchases, and sometimes arrange for their delivery. Counter and retail clerks are some-

times responsible for the display and presentation of products in their store. They may clean shelves or sweep floors, if necessary. In supermarkets and grocery stores, clerks stock shelves and bag food purchases for customers.

In smaller shops with no sales personnel or in a situation when a salesperson is unavailable, counter and retail clerks assist customers with purchases or rentals by demonstrating the merchandise or answering the customers' questions.

There are many examples of the wide variety of counter and retail clerks. *Video-rental clerks* greet customers, check out tapes, and accept payment. When the customers return their rentals, the clerks check the condition of the tape and put them back onto the shelves. *Bicycle-rental clerks* prepare rental forms and quote rates to customers. They answer customer questions about the operation of the bikes. They often take a deposit to cover any accidents or possible damage. When the customers return the bikes, clerks check them to make certain they are in good working order. *Shoe repair shop clerks* receive shoes that need to be cleaned or repaired. They examine the shoes and quote a price and gives a receipt to the customer. The clerk marks the shoes with a tag that specifies what work needs to be done and the name of the customer, then sends them to the work department. At the specified date, the clerk returns the repaired or cleaned shoes to the customer and collects payment.

EDUCATION AND TRAINING

There are no formal educational requirements necessary for becoming a counter and retail clerk. Most employers like to hire high school graduates, but there are many jobs available for those who are still in school.

Counter and retail clerks should have a pleasant personality and be able to get along with a wide range of people. They should be courteous, responsible, and willing to make the extra effort to satisfy customers. Clerks should be neat and well groomed. They also should have legible handwriting and the ability to perform simple arithmetic quickly.

OUTLOOK AND EARNINGS

Job opportunities for counter and retail workers are expected to grow faster than the average in the next decade. Salary is usually low and many companies offer few or no benefits. Many people work at these jobs on a part-time basis to earn extra income or until they complete school.

Beginning counter and retail workers usually earn minimum wage. Experienced clerks earn between $6.00 and $9.50 per hour. The most experienced workers with the most responsibility and experience can earn as much as $12.85 an hour. Workers who are members of a union earn considerably more than those are not.

WAYS OF GETTING MORE INFORMATION

For more information, contact:

National Retail Federation
326 7th Street NW, Suite 1000
Washington, DC 20004
Tel: 202-783-7971

A retail clerk must be courteous and efficient when ringing up a customer's merchandise.

COURT REPORTERS

SCHOOL SUBJECTS:
CIVICS/GOVERNMENT, ENGLISH
(WRITING/LITERATURE)

PERSONAL INTERESTS:
COMPUTERS, FOREIGN LANGUAGE

OUTLOOK:
FASTER THAN THE AVERAGE

OTHER ARTICLES TO LOOK AT:

Lawyers

Paralegals

Secretaries

Stenographers

WHAT COURT REPORTERS DO

Court reporters record the testimony given at hearings and trials. They use symbols, or shorthand, to rapidly record what is said. In a courtroom, people may speak between 250 and 300 words per minute. Court reporters must record each word that is spoken. They use a stenotype machine to do this. This machine has a keyboard with 24 keys. Each key has a symbol on it and each symbol or combination of symbols stands for a sound, word, or a phrase. As testimony is given, the court reporter records it by striking the proper keys. The symbols are printed on a strip of paper and recorded on a computer disk.

Because court reporters make the official record of trials, they cannot miss a word or phrase. If they do, they must interrupt the trial and ask to have the words repeated. The judge sometimes asks the reporter to read aloud testimony that has already been recorded.

Court reporters use computers to help them in their work. Computer programs are used to change the symbols and words of a stenotype machine into standard English. The computer can then print out a record of the trial. Thus, the reporter does not have to retype it or read it into a tape recorder.

Most court reporters work in city, county, state, or federal courts. Some work for private companies, recording business meetings and conventions. Others work for freelance reporting companies that provide reporters for trials and business meetings.

Most court reporters work 37 to 40 hours per week. At times, however, they may have to work much longer hours. They must be on hand before a trial starts, and they have to wait while the jury is reaching a verdict. It may sometimes be necessary to work evenings and even weekends. Court reporters who are assigned to a particular judge may have to travel to various trial locations.

EDUCATION AND TRAINING

Court reporters must have a high school diploma. They are also required to take a training program in shorthand reporting. These programs usually take from two to four years to complete. Students learn how to write at least 225 words a minute on a stenotype machine. They also study typing, English, law, and medical and legal terms. Programs in shorthand reporting are offered at community colleges, business and vocational schools, and at some universities.

Some states require court reporters to be licensed. Others require them to be certified by the National Shorthand Reporters Association. Court reporters who work for the federal government may have to pass a civil service exam.

OUTLOOK AND EARNINGS

Employment opportunities for skilled court reporters should continue to grow through the 1990s because courts will have to handle rising numbers of both civil and criminal cases. The largest number of openings will probably be found in and around large cities. Those with computer training should have the best chance to get high-paying jobs.

Beginning court reporters may earn between $21,000 and $30,000 a year. Experienced reporters can earn $30,000 to $70,000 a year or more. Freelance reporters usually earn between $15 and $35 an hour.

Language Arts

Organizational Skills

WAYS OF GETTING MORE INFORMATION

For more information about a career as a court reporter, write to the following:

National Court Reporters Association
*8224 Old Courthouse Road
Vienna, VA 22182*

A court reporter transcribes a discussion of pre-trial proceedings.

CREATIVE ARTS THERAPISTS

SCHOOL SUBJECTS:
ART, EDUCATION

PERSONAL INTERESTS:
HELPING PEOPLE: EMOTIONALLY, TEACHING

OUTLOOK:
FASTER THAN THE AVERAGE

OTHER ARTICLES TO LOOK AT:
Actors and Actresses
Artists
Ceramic Artists
Child Life Specialists
Musicians

WHAT CREATIVE ARTS THERAPISTS DO

Creative arts therapists treat and rehabilitate people with mental, physical, and emotional disabilities. They usually work as part of a health care team with physicians, nurses, psychiatrists, psychologists, and social workers. Therapists often work in hospitals, schools, rehabilitation centers, shelters for battered women, substance abuse programs, hospices, correctional facilities, and other locations. Some therapists have their own private practices.

The main goal of a creative arts therapist is to improve their patients physically, mentally, and emotionally. Before they begin any treatment, they meet with the team of other health care professionals. After determining the strength, limitations, and interests of their patient, they create a program to promote positive change and growth in the patient. The creative arts therapist continues to confer with the other health care workers as the program progresses, and alters the program according to the patient's progress. How these goals are reached depends on the unique specialty of the therapist in question.

Music therapists use musical lessons and activities to improve a patient's self confidence, self-awareness, to relieve states of depression, and to improve physical dexterity. For example, a music therapist treating a patient with Alzheimer's might play songs from the patient's past in order to stimulate their long- and short-term memory, soothe their feelings of agitation, and increase their sense of reality. *Art therapists* use art in much the same manner. The art therapist may encourage and teach patients to express their thoughts, feelings, and anxieties via sketching, drawing, painting, or sculpting. Art therapy is especially helpful in revealing patterns of domestic abuse in families. Children involved in such a situation may depict scenes of family life with violent details or portray a certain family member as especially frightening or threatening. *Dance/movement therapists* develop and conduct dance/movement sessions to help improve physical, mental, and emotional health of their patients. Dance and movement therapy is also used as a way of assessing a patient's progress toward reaching therapeutic goals.

Other types of creative arts therapists include, *drama therapists,* who use role-playing, pantomime (the telling of a story by the use of expressive body or facial movements), puppetry, improvisation, and original scripted dramatization to evaluate and treat patients; and *poetry therapists* and *bibilotherapists,* who use the written and spoken word to treat patients.

EDUCATION AND TRAINING

A master's degree is usually required for work as a creative arts therapist. Degree programs in specific creative art therapy fields are offered at a good number of colleges and universities. At this time, however, there is no degree program offered for poetry therapy. Most creative arts therapists must be certified or registered by the national association that is specific to their specialty. Requirements vary by association. Creative arts therapists who work in public schools must also be licensed by the department of education in the state they work in.

OUTLOOK AND EARNINGS

Creative arts therapy programs are growing rapidly. Many new positions are being created each year for trained workers. Job openings in nursing homes will increase as the elderly population continues to grow. Advances in medical technology and the recent practice of early discharge from hospitals should also create new opportunities in managed care facilities, chronic pain clinics, and cancer care facilities. The outlook for creative arts therapists will continue to brighten as more people become aware of the need to help disabled persons in creative ways.

Starting salaries for creative arts therapists generally range between $20,000 and $30,000. Therapists with experience usually earn from $25,000 to $35,000. Those creative arts therapists who have administrative or managerial duties can earn from $35,000 to $50,000 a year. Salaries for therapists who work for the government range from $27,000 to $50,000 per year.

WAYS OF GETTING MORE INFORMATION

Those interested in this career should try to arrange to see a creative arts therapist at work. A summer job as an aide at a camp for disabled children may help provide insight

into the demands and rewards of a career in this field. General experience can be gained through volunteering at a hospital, nursing home, or other care facility.

For more information, contact:

American Art Therapy Association
1202 Allanson Road
Mundelein, IL 60060
Tel: 708-949-6064

National Association for Music Therapy
8455 Colesville Road, Suite 930
Silver Spring, MD 20910-3392
Tel: 301-589-3300

National Association of Drama Therapy
44 Taylor Place
Branford, CT 06405
Tel: 203-481-1161

Creative arts therapists work with all kinds of people, young and old. Not only must they be creative themselves, they must inspire creativity in others.

CUSTOMS OFFICIALS

SCHOOL SUBJECTS:
CIVICS/GOVERNMENT, ENGLISH

PERSONAL INTERESTS:
HELPING PEOPLE: PERSONAL
SERVICE, FIGURING OUT HOW
THINGS WORK

OUTLOOK:
FASTER THAN THE AVERAGE

OTHER ARTICLES TO LOOK AT:

Border Patrol Officers

Deputy U.S. Marshals

Detectives

FBI Agents

WHAT CUSTOMS OFFICIALS DO

Customs officials work as observant detectives to make sure nothing illegal, such as drugs, is smuggled into the United States. They are employed by the federal government to enforce the laws that regulate goods coming into the country (imports) and goods leaving the country (exports). They work at airports, seaports, and border crossings of every entry and exit point of the United States. Their main responsibility is to make sure that no illegal merchandise, called contraband, is smuggled into the country. Customs officials need to be observant and tricky to search out all the possible hiding places in luggage or clothes that people might use to conceal contraband. It is possible that they might run into criminals in the course of their work. Federal law prevents other items besides drugs from being transported across borders; these include certain plants and foods that could carry insects and disease. The importation of many species of animals, and products made from them, is also prohibited by law. The special customs inspectors whose job it is to prevent smuggling are called *customs patrol officers*; they may board and search suspect ships or aircraft.

Another important part of the job of a customs inspector is to determine taxes, called duties, on imports and exports. Inspectors check the luggage and personal items of airline and shipboard passengers and crew members as well as the ship's or airplane's cargo. They need to make sure that all merchandise is declared honestly, that duties are paid, and that no contraband is present. Travellers sometimes try to hide expensive imports to avoid paying high duties on them. Customs officials need to be as alert to these tax-evaders as to drug dealers. They also examine packages that are mailed into the country. They check the baggage of travelers who come by car or train across the borders of Canada and Mexico. This allows them to also conduct a first screening of immigrants to the country.

The United States imports many products, which are then sold or used for industry. The merchandise includes bales of cotton from India, rugs from Iran, diamonds from Africa, and wool from Ireland. Customs officials examine, count, weigh, gauge, measure, and sample commercial cargoes in order to check these figures against shipping papers and determine how much import duty (tax) should be paid. *Customs warehouse officers* guard the goods on the pier or in the warehouse to prevent theft, damage, and fire.

Merchandise for delivery to commercial importers is examined by *customs import specialists*, who consider import quotas and make sure trademark laws are observed. They may have to consult computerized lists and databases for this information. They need to know about a law passed in 1930 that exempts certain goods from import tax. These items are antiques made before 1830. Other goods that are duty-free include gifts such as perfume and liquor that international travellers can purchase at airport shops.

EDUCATION AND TRAINING

Customs workers must be United States citizens, and they must be at least 21 years old. They must have earned at least a high school diploma, but a college degree is preferred. Applicants who do not have a college degree must have at least three years of related work experience. Customs inspectors, like all employees of the federal government, must pass a physical examination and undergo a security check. They must also pass a standardized test administered by the federal government. The test is called the Professional and Administrative Career Examination (PACE).

OUTLOOK AND EARNINGS

Employment as a customs inspector is steady work that is not affected by changes in the economy. Currently the government employs over five thousand customs inspectors at an average annual salary of about $30,000. Beginning customs officials start at either $19,400 or $24,000 per year depending on their level of education or experience, and customs officials may earn up to $37,000 per year or more. Although they usually work 40 hours a week, they often work overtime or long into the night. United States entry and exit points need to be supervised 24 hours a day, which means that many inspectors work the night shift. While a workday is usually routine, the growing problem of drug smuggling could bring a customs inspector into contact with dangerous criminals.

WAYS OF GETTING MORE INFORMATION

Information on federal government jobs is available from offices of the state employment service, area offices of the U.S. Office of Personnel Management, and Federal Job Information Centers throughout the country.

For more information, contact:

U.S. Customs Service
Office of Human Resources
1301 Constitution Avenue NW
Washington, DC 20229
Tel: 202-927-6724

A customs inspector in San Juan, Puerto Rico, checks a bag for illegal merchandise through airport security.

DANCERS

SCHOOL SUBJECTS:
MUSIC, THEATER/DANCE

PERSONAL INTERESTS:
DANCING, MUSIC

OUTLOOK:
FASTER THAN THE AVERAGE

OTHER ARTICLES TO LOOK AT:

Actors and Actresses

Athletes

Choreographers

Musicians

Recreation Workers

WHAT DANCERS DO

Dancers perform dances, either as members of a group or as solo performers. Through their body movements they tell a story, express an idea or feeling, or simply entertain their audience. There are several basic types of dancers. *Ballet dancers* require the most rigorous training and perform dances that express a story or theme. Most other types of dancers need some ballet training. *Acrobatic dancers* perform in a difficult gymnastic style. *Interpretive* or *modern dancers* express moods or ideas, often using facial expressions as well as body movements. Jazz dance, for instance, is a form of modern dance. *Tap dancers* keep time with the music by tapping out rhythms with their tap shoes.

Dancers may perform in classical ballets, musical stage shows, folk dance shows, television dance numbers, or other popular dance productions. Because dancing jobs are not always available, many dancers work as part-time dance instructors. Dancers who create new ballets or dance routines are called *choreographers*. *Dance directors* are those who train other dancers in performing a new production.

EDUCATION AND TRAINING

Dancers usually begin training around the age of 10 to 12, or even as early as age seven or eight. They may study with private teachers or in ballet schools. Dancers who show promise in their early teens may receive professional training in a regional ballet school or a major ballet company. By the age of 17 or 18, dancers often begin trying out for positions in professional dance companies.

Training never ends, however, even for professional ballet dancers. They may take 10 to 12 dance classes a week for 11 to 12 months of the year. They also spend many hours in rehearsals to make their performances as good as they can be. Because dancers must be in extremely good physical health to perform well, they must always maintain a nutritious diet.

Many colleges and universities offer degrees in dance. Although a college degree is not required for dancers, it can be very useful. Those who teach dance in a college or university often are required to have a degree. Also, the professional life of a dancer can be rather short. With a college degree, a dancer is better able to move into other career fields.

OUTLOOK AND EARNINGS

Job opportunities for dancers throughout the 1990s will be better than average. However, there will still be more dancers seeking jobs than there are openings for them. Local ballet companies are expected to offer the most job opportunities. Because more people have become interested in dance in recent years, there will also be job openings for dance teachers.

Minimum salaries for dancers are usually set by their unions' contracts. The minimum weekly salary for new dancers in ballet and modern performances is about $555. A new ballet dancer being paid for a single show makes about $230 plus extra pay for each rehearsal. Dancers receive extra money for room and board when they go on tour. Dancers on one-hour television shows earn an average of $570 per show. Dancers typically work 30 hours a week, including rehearsals, matinees, and evening performances. Because dance work is not regular, most dancers take other temporary jobs to raise their incomes.

WAYS OF GETTING MORE INFORMATION

The only way to prepare for a dancing career is to dance. Most communities have dance schools where young people can take dance classes.

For more information, write to:

American Dance Guild
33 West 21st Street, 3rd Floor
New York, NY 10010

American Guild of Musical Artists
1727 Broadway
New York, NY 10019

National Dance Association
1900 Association Drive
Reston, VA 22091

To reach the point of performing in front of a live audience, these dancers have spent many tiring weeks in rehearsal.

DATABASE SPECIALISTS

SCHOOL SUBJECTS:
COMPUTER SCIENCE, MATHEMATICS

PERSONAL INTERESTS:
COMPUTERS, FIGURING OUT HOW THINGS WORK

OUTLOOK:
FASTER THAN THE AVERAGE

OTHER ARTICLES TO LOOK AT:

Computer Programmers

Computer Systems Analysts

WHAT DATABASE SPECIALISTS DO

Business, industry, and the government rely on computers to store and organize huge amounts of information. The collection of information stored in a computer is called a database. For example, all of the information needed by a large corporation to issue weekly paychecks to its employees is one type of database. Information about all of the books and other materials available in a library, including their location, is another.

Database specialists work for utilities, stores, investment companies, insurance companies, publishing houses, telecommunications firms, and for all branches of government. They are responsible for setting up and maintaining databases. They purchase computer equipment and create computer programs that will collect, analyze, store, and transmit information.

Database specialists work in three major areas. First, some specialists figure out the type of computer system needed by their company. This means that the database specialist must know all about the latest developments in computer technology. A database manager meets with top-level company officials to discuss the company's needs. Together they decide what type of hardware and software will be required to set up a certain type of database. Then a database design analyst writes a proposal that states the company's needs, the type of equipment that will meet those needs, and how much the equipment will cost.

The second area of responsibility of database specialists is to set up and maintain the computer system that the company buys. Database managers and administrators must decide how to organize and store the information in the database. This involves creating a computer program or a series of programs and training employees to enter information into those programs. Decisions are made on how best to organize data for quick retrieval.

Computer programs sometimes crash, or work improperly. Database specialists must make sure that a copy of the program and the database is available in case of a crash. Specialists are also responsible for protecting the database from people or organizations who are not supposed to see it. A company's database contains important, and sometimes secret, information.

Very large companies may have many databases. Sometimes it is necessary for these databases to share information. Database managers see to it that these different databases can talk, or communicate with each other, even if they are located in different parts of the country.

The third responsibility of database specialists is to train and supervise the employees that will help create and maintain the database and every day users of the database.

EDUCATION AND TRAINING

Those interested in this profession should take as many computer courses as possible in high school. In addition, they should study mathematics, accounting, science, English, and communications. An associate's degree in a computer-related technology is required for entry-level database administrators.

A bachelor's degree in computer science or business administration is necessary however, for advanced positions. Those people with a master's degree will have even greater opportunities.

No license or certificate is needed. However, database specialists can become certified for jobs in the computer field by passing a test given by the Institute for Certification of Computer Professionals.

OUTLOOK AND EARNINGS

Employment in the computer field should increase through 2005. Most jobs will be in big cities.

A person with an associate's degree can earn $17,000 per year to start. Those with bachelor's degrees earn up to $37,000. Database specialists with master's degrees earn even more.

WAYS OF GETTING MORE INFORMATION

For more information, write to the following:

Association for Systems Management
24587 Bagley Road
Cleveland, OH 44138
Tel: 216-243-6900

Data Processing Management Association
505 Busse Highway
Park Ridge, IL 60068

Consulting recent publications, a database manager updates a computer file used by clients for information services.

DEMOGRAPHERS

SCHOOL SUBJECTS:
MATHEMATICS, SOCIOLOGY

PERSONAL INTERESTS:
COMPUTERS, FIGURING OUT HOW THINGS WORK

OUTLOOK:
FASTER THAN THE AVERAGE

OTHER ARTICLES TO LOOK AT:
Actuaries
Marketing Researchers
Mathematicians
Sociologists

WHAT DEMOGRAPHERS DO

Demographers collect and study facts about their society's population—births, marriages, deaths, education and income levels, and so on. They use these facts to develop population studies that tell what the society is really like, and to forecast economic and social trends. For example, a demographer may discover, through studying birth rates of a particular community, that the population of school-age children is growing faster than expected, and that new schools will therefore have to be built. Or the demographer may collect facts about how many of these children have been sick with measles—which in turn could be studied to determine how effective the measles vaccine is.

Demographers work for both government agencies and private companies. Local, state, and federal government agencies use the demographer's forecasts to help them provide enough of the right kinds of transportation, education, police, and health services. Private companies (such as retail chains) need the demographer's collections of facts, or statistics, for help in making marketing decisions, such as the best location to open a new store. Demographers may also teach in colleges and universities or work as consultants for private companies or communities as a whole.

Whoever they work for, demographers rely on computers to help them gather and analyze the millions of pieces of information they need to make their forecasts. Still, it is up to the individual demographer to know how to interpret the statistics and put them together in a meaningful way.

EDUCATION AND TRAINING

A college degree in sociology or public health with special studies in demography is always required to work as a demographer. Most entry-level jobs require a master's degree. Students interested in this field should be good at solving logical problems and have an aptitude with numbers and mathematics, especially algebra and geometry. Recommended college courses include classes in statistics, public policy, social research methods, and computer applications. High school students interested in this career should take classes in social studies, English and mathematics.

No licenses or certificates are necessary, but demographers who work for the federal government may need to pass civil service examinations. As the field gets more competitive, many demographers (especially those wishing to work for the federal government) will get a doctorate in sociology. The most successful demographers keep up with advances in their field by continuing education throughout their careers and by specializing in one area.

After graduation from college, hopeful demographers may apply directly to private research firms or other companies that do population studies. However, because they will most likely need a graduate degree, aspiring demographers should apply to a graduate program. (College placement offices will prove helpful in both cases.) Government jobs are listed with the Civil Service Commission, and demographers who wish to teach will find leads through their graduate schools.

OUTLOOK AND EARNINGS

There is a tremendous amount of fact-gathering and social science research going on in the United States, and the need for trained demographers to analyze this research should increase through the year 2000. Job opportunities will be greatest in and around large cities, because that is where many colleges, universities, and other research facilities are located. In addition, there may be an increasing demand for demographers in international organizations such as the World Bank, the United Nations, and the World Health Organization. These demographers will be needed to help developing countries analyze their own growing populations and plan for services to accommodate the growth.

A demographer with a bachelor's degree can expect to earn between $19,000 and $23,000 per year in the 1990s. Those who have a graduate degree should start at around $26,000 to $30,000 a year. After several years of experience, good demographers earn between $34,000 and $40,000.

For more information, write to:

Population Association of America
1429 Duke Street
Alexandria, VA 22314

Population Reference Bureau
777 14th Street NW, Suite 800
Washington, DC 20005

A demographer reviews data on public health statistics.

DENTAL ASSISTANTS

SCHOOL SUBJECTS:
BUSINESS, HEALTH

PERSONAL INTERESTS:
HELPING PEOPLE: PHYSICAL
HEALTH/MEDICINE, TEACHING

OUTLOOK:
MUCH FASTER THAN THE
AVERAGE

OTHER ARTICLES TO LOOK AT:
Dental Hygienists
Dentists
Medical Technologists
Physician Assistants

WHAT DENTAL ASSISTANTS DO

Dental assistants help dentists examine and treat patients. They also carry out administrative and clerical tasks that make the dentist's office run smoothly.

Dental assistants usually greet patients, take them to the examining room, and prepare them for examining by covering their clothing with paper or cloth to protect it from water and stains. They also adjust the chair and its headrest to the proper height. Many dental assistants take X rays of patients' teeth and develop the film for the dentist. During examinations and dental procedures, dental assistants hand instruments to the dentist as they are needed and use suction devices to keep the patient's mouth dry. When the examination or procedure is over, assistants may give patients instructions for taking care of their teeth and keeping the mouth clean and healthy between office visits.

Dental assistants also help with a variety of other tasks, such as making plaster casts of a patient's teeth, making dentures, or in some states, applying medications to teeth

and gums or removing excess material after cavities have been filled. Dental assistants may help dentists with any emergencies that arise during dental procedures.

In addition to assisting the dentist with dental procedures, many dental assistants work in the front office on clerical and administrative tasks. They keep patient records, answer the telephone, schedule appointments, prepare bills, collect payments, and issue receipts. They may also keep an inventory of dental supplies and order them when necessary.

Dental assistants are not the same as dental hygienists, who are licensed to clean and polish teeth.

EDUCATION AND TRAINING

Many dental assistant positions require little or no experience and no education beyond high school. Assistants in such positions can learn their skills on the job. However, some assistants go on to receive training after high school at one of the many technical institutes and community and junior colleges that offer dental assisting programs. Armed forces schools also train some dental assistants. Students who attend two-year college programs receive associate degrees, while those who attend technical schools finish after one year and earn a certificate or diploma. To enter these programs, candidates must have a high school diploma, and some schools require that applicants have received good grades in science, typing, and English.

Accredited programs—those meeting the standards set by professional organizations in the field—instruct students in dental assisting skills through the combination of both classroom lectures and laboratory experience. Students take courses in English, speech, and psychology, as well as anatomy, microbiology, and nutrition.

High school students who wish to work as dental assistants may prepare by taking courses in general science, biology, health, chemistry, and business management. Typing is also important for dental assistants.

OUTLOOK AND EARNINGS

The employment outlook for dental assistants is excellent. Because the demand for dental care will increase in coming years, the need for assistants should increase as well.

Salaries of dental assistants vary according to their duties, experience, and geographical location. According to the American Dental Association's 1993 Survey of Dental Practice, full-time dental assistants working for general dentists earn an average annual salary of between $17,000 and $23,000.

WAYS OF GETTING MORE INFORMATION

For more information, write to:

American Dental Assistants Association
203 North LaSalle Street, Suite 1320
Chicago, IL 60601
Tel: 312-541-1320

American Dental Association
211 East Chicago Avenue
Chicago, IL 60611
Tel: 312-440-2500
WWW: http://www.ada.org/prac/careers/dc-menu.html

Dental Assisting National Board
216 East Ontario Street
Chicago, IL 60611
Tel: 312-642-3368

Aiding in a routine procedure, the dental assistant takes notes on the condition of the patient's teeth.

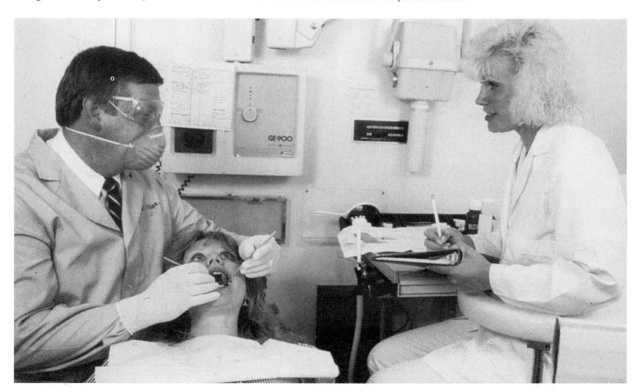

DENTAL HYGIENISTS

SCHOOL SUBJECTS:
BIOLOGY, HEALTH

PERSONAL INTERESTS:
HELPING PEOPLE: PHYSICAL
HEALTH/MEDICINE, TEACHING

OUTLOOK:
MUCH FASTER THAN THE AVERAGE

OTHER ARTICLES TO LOOK AT:

Dental Assistants

Dental Laboratory Technicians

Dentists

WHAT DENTAL HYGIENISTS DO

Dental hygienists are the only assistants working for dentists who are licensed to clean patients' teeth. Their primary job is to remove plaque and other deposits from the teeth, polish teeth, and massage gums. They also promote good oral health to patients, explaining how to select toothbrushes and use floss, what kinds of foods are bad for the teeth, and the effects of various habits, such as smoking, on teeth. The main goal of a dental hygienist is to help the patient prevent tooth decay and maintain a healthy mouth.

Hygienists who work for dentists in private practice may do more than clean teeth. They may take and develop X rays, mix materials to fill cavities, sterilize instruments, assist in surgery, and keep charts of patients' teeth. Some hygienists perform office duties as well, such as answering phone calls and making appointments for patients.

Not all hygienists work for dentists. Some work in schools where they clean and examine students' teeth and show them how to prevent tooth decay. They stress brushing and flossing teeth correctly and eating the right foods. They also keep records of the students' teeth and notify parents of any problems or need for additional treatment.

Some dental hygienists work for local, state, or federal public health agencies. They clean the teeth of adults and children in public health clinics and other public facilities and educate them in the proper care of teeth. A few hygienists work on research projects. Others who are qualified will teach in a dental hygiene school.

EDUCATION AND TRAINING

Dental hygienists must have a high school diploma, complete two or four years of college at an approved (accredited) dental hygiene school, and pass the National Board exams or a licensing exam in a particular state.

There are two types of dental hygiene programs: a four-year college program offering a bachelor's degree and a two-year program leading to a dental hygiene certification. The two-year program is widely offered, but more employers are now requiring a four-year degree.

Courses in such a program will include classes in anatomy, physiology, chemistry, pharmacology, nutrition, and other sciences. In addition, students learn to handle delicate instruments, gain experience in the dental laboratory, and practice working with patients in clinics. Before graduation, students are given a test to determine whether or not they are ready to work in the profession.

After graduation from an accredited school, state licensing examinations are required. Upon passing the exam, students are qualified to practice as registered dental hygienists. It is also important for aspiring dental hygienists to be able to help people relax, as many people are afraid of having work done on their teeth. In addition, hygienists need to be clean, neat, and in good health themselves.

A dental hygienist who wishes to teach, conduct research, or work in a school health program is often required to have a master's degree.

OUTLOOK AND EARNINGS

Employment opportunities for dental hygienists are very promising in the 1990s. As the population increases and more employers offer dental insurance, more jobs for dental hygienists will become available.

The salaries that dental hygienists earn will depend on their education, experience, and employer. Hygienists working in private dentists' offices earn higher incomes than those working in school systems, public health agencies, hospitals, factories, or the armed forces.

Most dental hygienists earn between $15,000 and $25,000 a year. Those who conduct research or teach will earn higher salaries.

WAYS OF GETTING MORE INFORMATION

Talking to a family dentist or dental hygienist is one way to explore this career. Interested high school students should take courses in biology, health, chemistry, psychology, speech, and mathematics.

For more information, write to:

American Association of Dental Examiners
211 East Chicago Avenue, Suite 760
Chicago, IL 60611
Tel: 312-440-7464

American Dental Association
211 East Chicago Avenue
Chicago, IL 60611
Tel: 312-440-2500
WWW: http://www.ada.org/prac/careers/dc-menu.html

American Dental Hygienists' Association
444 North Michigan Avenue, Suite 3400
Chicago, IL 60611

Manual Skills

People Skills

A dental hygienist cleans the teeth of a patient.

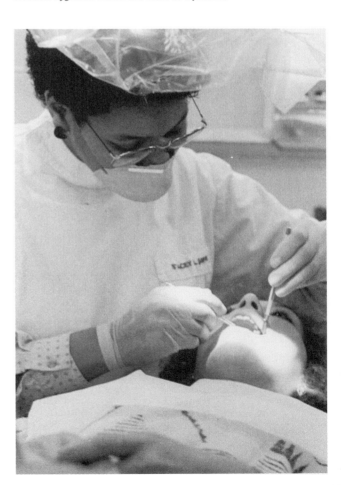

DENTAL LABORATORY TECHNICIANS

SCHOOL SUBJECTS:
ART, CHEMISTRY

PERSONAL INTERESTS:
BUILDING THINGS, SCULPTING

OUTLOOK:
FASTER THAN THE AVERAGE

OTHER ARTICLES TO LOOK AT:

Dental Assistants

Dental Hygienists

Dentists

Orthotists and Prosthetists

WHAT DENTAL LABORATORY TECHNICIANS DO

Even though *dental laboratory technicians* are never seen by the patient, they are very important to the success of many different kinds of dental treatment. When someone loses a tooth, for example, the dentist writes a prescription for a new one and the technician makes it in a laboratory.

There are four main kinds of laboratory work in which a technician can specialize. The first area is *orthodontics*. These technicians make braces for straightening teeth by bending wires into complicated shapes that will fit over the crooked teeth. The braces, retainers, or tooth bands that these technicians make are not meant to be permanent, but will stay in a patient's mouth for a long time and so must fit well and feel comfortable.

Dental ceramicists make real-looking porcelain teeth to replace missing ones or to fit over natural teeth that may have been damaged or that are just not attractive.

Ceramicists apply porcelain paste over a metal frame to make crowns, bridges, and tooth coverings. Their work involves a great deal of knowledge and creativity, and they are usually the best paid technicians.

Some *dental laboratory technicians* specialize in making and repairing full and partial dentures. Full dentures are false teeth worn by people who have had all their teeth removed on the upper or lower jaws or on both jaws. Partial dentures are the missing teeth that are placed in a jaw alongside the natural teeth. Dentures are made by putting ceramic teeth in a wax model and then building up wax over it to hold the set in place.

Crown and bridge specialists restore the missing parts of a natural tooth that has broken. They use plastic and metal appliances that are permanently cemented to the natural tooth. Technicians in this area must be skilled at melting and casting metals.

Most technicians work in privately owned labs that employ only about six or seven people. Many large labs specialize in one type of work, while the smaller ones tend to employ technicians for the whole range of jobs.

EDUCATION AND TRAINING

Dental lab technicians should have a good mix of patience and artistic talent, and they must also be able to follow written instructions precisely. All technicians must have graduated from high school, but the methods of training following high school vary. Three to four years of on-the-job training is the way some start in the profession. Many others take two-year college courses in applied science. Classwork in such a program includes tooth construction, processing and repairing dentures, and making crowns.

Experienced technicians often take a written and practical test that leads to certification by the National Board for Certification in Dental Technology.

OUTLOOK AND EARNINGS

The demand for dental laboratory technicians is relatively high and should continue to grow going into the next century. The fact that the overall population is aging—the number of elderly people is growing in relation to other age groups—means that this type of dental care will be in greater demand.

The salaries for dental laboratory technicians working full time in commercial labs range from $15,000 to $33,000. Those with the most education and experience, and those with specialized skills, such as ceramicists, will earn the most. Technicians who are promoted to supervisor or manager and those who are self-employed earn more than the average.

WAYS OF GETTING MORE INFORMATION

A local dentist may be able to arrange a visit with an area laboratory so that students may visit and get a first hand look at the technician's work.

For additional information, write to:

American Dental Association
211 East Chicago Avenue
Chicago, IL 60611
Tel: 312-440-2500
WWW:
http://www.ada.org/prac/careers/dc-menu.html

National Association of Dental Laboratories
3801 Mount Vernon Avenue
Alexandria, VA 22305
Tel: 703-683-5263

A dental laboratory technician removes the plaster off a cast for teeth.

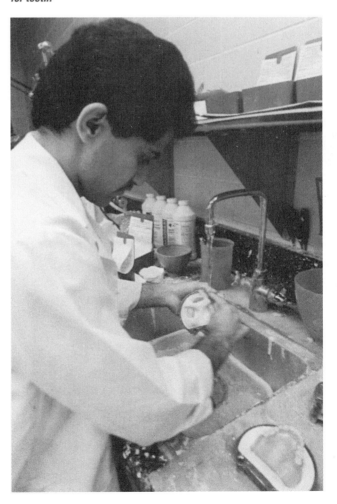

DENTISTS

SCHOOL SUBJECTS:
CHEMISTRY, HEALTH

PERSONAL INTERESTS:
HELPING PEOPLE: PHYSICAL
HEALTH/MEDICINE, SCIENCE

OUTLOOK:
FASTER THAN THE AVERAGE

OTHER ARTICLES TO LOOK AT:
Dental Assistants
Dental Hygienists
Dental Laboratory Technicians
Physicians

WHAT DENTISTS DO

Dentists help people to have healthy teeth and gums. They do this by cleaning, filling, repairing, replacing, and straightening teeth. Dentists who are general practitioners do many kinds of dental work. They take X rays, fill cavities, clean teeth, and pull diseased teeth. Dentists also talk to their patients about how they can prevent tooth and mouth problems and give them instructions on proper brushing, flossing, and diet. They must also be able to recognize unique problems that demand the care of a dental specialist.

Specialists are devoted to just one kind of dental problem. *Orthodontists* use braces and other devices to correct irregular growth of teeth and jaws. *Oral surgeons* perform difficult tooth-pulling jobs, remove tumors, and fix broken jaws. *Periodontists* treat diseased gums. *Prosthodontists* make artificial teeth and dentures. *Pedodontists* specialize in treating children's dental problems. *Oral patholo-gists* examine mouth tumors and lesions and determine their cause. *Endodontists* treat patients who need root canal work.

A few dentists work for the federal government in hospitals or clinics, and others teach, conduct research, or hold positions in dental schools. But the vast majority of dentists, about 90 percent, have their own private practice. Since they work for themselves, they have to know about administrative and managerial matters, such as leasing office space, hiring employees, running an office, keeping books, and stocking equipment. These dentists set their own hours, but most of them work at least forty hours a week, including some time on weekends. For beginning dentists, it takes many hours of work to help pay for the expensive equipment they need.

EDUCATION AND TRAINING

To become a dentist, a person must complete three to four years of college-level predental education; three out of four dentists have a bachelor's or master's degree. Next, to be admitted to a certified dental school, the student must pass the Dental Admissions Test. Training at a dental school then takes at least four years. In dental school, students take basic sciences, including anatomy, biochemistry, microbiology, and physiology, and they learn how to treat patients. Upon graduation, a dentist must take a state examination to receive a license to practice dentistry in that state. Dentists who wish to enter a specialized field spend an additional two to three years studying that specialty.

Besides having basic dental skills, a dentist should be able to get along well with other people. Good vision, good manual skills, and some artistic ability are also important. In high school, science and math courses are a good preparation for a career in dentistry.

OUTLOOK AND EARNINGS

Opportunities for dentists are expected to remain good throughout the 1990s. Because of scientific advances in dentistry, the need for dental specialists will be especially high. Oral pathologists and orthodontists, for instance, will be in great demand.

Dentists just out of school who are beginning a private practice often earn only enough to cover their expenses. Some may start by working for an established dentist until they can earn their own reputation and save enough money to equip an office. After a few years in a private practice, a dentist who is a general practitioner earns an average of $70,000 in annual income. Specialists average $100,000 a year. Dentists working for the federal government start at about $26,400 a year, and those with more experience earn an average annual salary of $54,000.

WAYS OF GETTING MORE INFORMATION

Young people interested in becoming dentists can observe their own dentist at work and ask questions about the profession. Most dentists also can provide brochures that explain the structure of teeth and proper dental care.

Manual Skills

People Skills

Sciences and Mathematics

For more information about a career as a dentist, write to:

American Association of Dental Schools
1625 Massachusetts Avenue NW
Washington, DC 20036
Tel: 202-667-9433
Email: aads@aads.jhu.edu

American Dental Association
211 East Chicago Avenue
Chicago, IL 60611
Tel: 312-440-2500
WWW: http://www.ada.org/prac/careers/dc-menu.html

Dentists must protect their patients from infection during treatment.

DEPUTY U.S. MARSHALS

SCHOOL SUBJECTS:
CIVICS/GOVERNMENT, PHYSICAL EDUCATION

PERSONAL INTERESTS:
HELPING PEOPLE: PERSONAL SERVICE, SPORTS

OUTLOOK:
ABOUT AS FAST AS THE AVERAGE

OTHER ARTICLES TO LOOK AT:

Border Patrol Officers

Detectives

FBI Agents

Police Officers

WHAT DEPUTY U.S. MARSHALS DO

Deputy U.S. marshals are law enforcement officers who protect and enforce the decisions of the U.S. judiciary system. The judiciary system includes judges, the Supreme Court, and the Department of Justice. The Marshal Service is the oldest federal law enforcement agency. Since the time of George Washington, it has been responsible for upholding the law of the land.

Deputy U.S. marshals are assigned to many different kinds of duties. They transport federal criminals to prison, sometimes in government-owned jets. They are on guard in our federal courtrooms and protect judges and jury members who are involved in important legal cases that put their lives in possible danger. They are also responsible for serving subpoenas, summonses, and other legal writs that are essential to the functioning of the court system.

Marshals investigate and track down fugitives (criminals who are running from the law), even those who have escaped to another country. They also track down those fugitives

here who are wanted by foreign nations. In hunting down fugitives, marshals often work with state and local police departments and with other law enforcement agencies.

The Marshal Service operates the nation's witness relocation program. This program is designed to encourage witnesses to testify in federal trials when they feel that their testimony would put them in danger, such as in organized crime cases. The Marshal Service provides personal protection for the witness up until he or she testifies in court. After the trial is over, the Marshal Service helps the witness move to a new city and take on a new name and identity, keeping him or her anonymous and safe from reprisals. This successful program has been recognized as a very valuable tool in the government's efforts against major criminal activity and organized crime.

U.S. marshals also operate the program for confiscating property that has been purchased from the profits of certain illegal activities such as drug dealing. The marshals seize the houses, boats, and other property that criminals have purchased. They then hold it and maintain it until the property is sold or put up for auction. Hundreds of millions of dollars in seized assets are in the custody of the Marshal Service.

The Marshal Service is able to respond to emergency situations such as riots, terrorist incidents, or hostage situations when federal law is violated or federal property is endangered. A highly trained force of deputy U.S. marshals called the Special Operations Group (SOG) is deployed in these situations. Deputies also protect shipments of weapons systems for the U.S. Air Force.

U.S. deputy marshals have some of the most unique and exciting duties in law enforcement. They have been ready to protect our system of justice for more than 200 years.

There are more than 95 districts across the U.S. and Puerto Rico, Guam, the Virgin Islands, and the Northern Marianas to which marshals are assigned. Each district is managed by a U.S. marshal who is appointed by the president. Beneath the marshal is the chief deputy U.S. marshal who directs a staff of supervisors, deputy U.S. marshals, and other support staff. In addition, specialists in witness security, court security, seized property, and enforcement provide professional expertise for each district field office.

EDUCATION AND TRAINING

Like other federal officers, deputy U.S. marshals are trained at the Federal Law Enforcement Training Center in Glynco Naval Air Station in Georgia. They complete a three-month training program that teaches them about laws, proper procedures, firearm use, and physical training.

To enter this program, applicants first take a civil service exam. They are then interviewed to see if they have the makings of a good deputy marshal. Applicants must have a minimum of some college education, work experience, or a combination of both. Any law enforcement experience and the applicants' educational level are also considered. A point system weighs all these qualifications and determines who will be admitted. Competition for these jobs is strong, with an average of 15 applicants for every opening.

OUTLOOK AND EARNINGS

The U.S. Marshal Service is likely to keep growing at an average pace through 2005. Beginning deputies earn $19,000 to $24,000 annually. Those with five years of experience usually earn around $30,000. Chief deputy marshals earn $55,000 or more.

WAYS OF GETTING MORE INFORMATION

A good way to find out about this career is to contact the marshal's office of your local federal district.

For more information, write to:

U.S. Marshal Service
Law Enforcement Recruiting Branch
Arlington, VA 22202

Escorting a prisoner to court, this U.S. marshal must make sure he does not escape.

DERMATOLOGISTS

SCHOOL SUBJECTS:
BIOLOGY, HEALTH

PERSONAL INTERESTS:
HELPING PEOPLE: PHYSICAL
HEALTH/MEDICINE, SCIENCE

OUTLOOK:
FASTER THAN THE AVERAGE

OTHER ARTICLES TO LOOK AT:

Allergists

Nurses

Physicians

Surgeons

WHAT DERMATOLOGISTS DO

Dermatologists study, diagnose, and treat diseases and ailments of the skin, hair, mucous membranes, nails, and related tissues or structures. They may also perform cosmetic services, such as the removal of scars or hair transplants.

The work of a dermatologist begins with a diagnosis to determine the cause of a disease or condition. For example, if a patient exhibits a mysterious red rash on their arms and legs that does not seem to go away, a dermatologist will use a variety of factors to determine what is wrong. He or she will study the patient's past medical history, conduct a visual examination, and sometimes take blood samples, smears of the affected skin, microscopic scrapings, or biopsy specimens of the skin. The dermatologist may order cultures for fungi or bacteria, or perform tests to reveal allergies or immunologic diseases. Skin, blood, or tissue samplesare sent to a laboratory for testing and analysis.

Dermatologists use a variety of medicines and treatments to cure their patients. They treat some skin problems with oral medications, such as antibiotics. Certain types of inflammations of the skin, such as eczema and dermatitis, psoriasis, and acne, can be treated with creams, ointments or other medications. Dermatologists also use ultraviolet light and radiation therapy.

Some dermatological problems require surgery. Dermatologists may use traditional surgery which cuts away the affected skin. Other methods are cryosurgery (freezing the tissue), lasers, and cauterization (electrical current).

Not all surgeries that dermatologists perform are major. Many procedures can be performed on an outpatient basis in the office of the dermatologist, using local anesthesia. Warts, cysts, moles, scars, and boils can all be taken care of in the office. Hair transplants and laser treatments for such problems as cysts, disfiguring birth defects, birthmarks, and spider veins, can also usually be performed in a dermatologist's office.

A good number of serious diseases can first show themselves in a skin condition. Dermatologists are trained to recognize these symptoms and recommend these patient's to other specialists. Dermatologists often consult with such specialists from other fields in order to make a correct diagnosis.

There are many subspecialties in the field of dermatology. *Dermatoimmunologists* focus on diseases of the immune system, such as allergies. *Pediatric dermatologists* treat children with skin disorders. *Occupational dermatologists* treat occupational disorders, such as forms of dermatitis caused by biological or chemical irritants. Other dermatologists combine their private practice with a teaching career at a medical school. Still others work in research, developing treatments and cures for skin ailments.

EDUCATION AND TRAINING

Those interested in becoming dermatologists must first earn a bachelor's degree. Students then take the Medical College Admission Test and apply to a medical school. After acceptance, students must complete four years of study and training, which will earn them a degree of Doctor of Medicine (MD). After medical school, physicians must pass a standard examination given by the National Board of Medical Examiners. Then they begin their residency to learn a specialty. Only about half of those who apply to residency programs are accepted, and the field of dermatology is especially competitive. The American Board of Dermatology, an organization that certifies dermatologists, requires four years of residency training, three of which must be training in dermatology. They administer written and sometimes practical examinations, and certify those who meet their standards.

OUTLOOK AND EARNINGS

The employment of all physicians is expected to increase faster than the average for all occupations in the next decade. The population as a whole is growing older, requiring more health care for those in their later years. Demand for dermatologists has increased as the public has become more aware of the effects of radiation exposure from the sun and air pollution on the skin. The public has also become more aware of the benefits of good dermatological health.

Physicians begin to earn a salary when they start their residencies. First year salaries for residents begin at $25,800 and increase to $33,300 in the last year of residency. Beginning dermatologists can expect to earn $80,000 per year, while experienced dermatologists who have their own practices or are full partners in a group practice, can earn up to $120,000. Average salaries range from $120,000 to $150,000 annually.

WAYS OF GETTING MORE INFORMATION

For more information, contact:

American Academy of Dermatology
PO Box 4014
Schaumburg, IL 60168-4014
Tel: 847-330-0230

American Board of Dermatology
Henry Ford Hospital
1 Ford Place
Detroit, MI 48202-3450
Tel: 313-874-1088

Dermatologists' eyes are trained to spot skin problems.

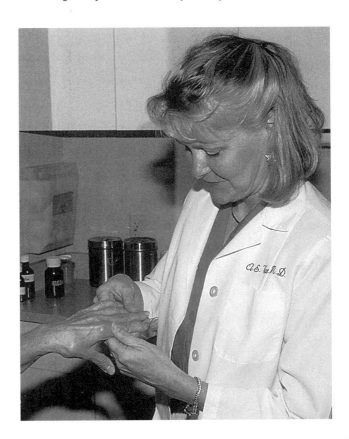

DETECTIVES

OTHER ARTICLES TO LOOK AT:

FBI Agents

Forensic Experts

Police Officers

Private Investigators

Spies

WHAT DETECTIVES DO

Detectives are plain-clothes police officers assigned to either investigate crimes already committed or to try to prevent crimes that are expected to occur. They spend much of their time walking the streets, trying to blend in to a neighborhood or an area that has a specific crime problem they have been assigned to investigate, and collecting information from various sources.

The great majority of detectives spend three to five years as uniformed police officers on the street before being promoted to a detective position. *Police detectives* work on cases involving murder, arson, fraud, and property crimes. Some may specialize in one area, such as fingerprinting or handwriting analysis. Detectives must know how to protect evidence from being destroyed or altered. Good detectives are very observant and can remember faces, names, and anything unusual about a suspected criminal, such as a peculiar way of dressing or speaking. They also have to be aggressive in wanting to remove criminals from the street, and they have to be able to work independently, without constant supervision. After a crime has been committed, detectives must work quickly, as it becomes more difficult to solve a crime after too much time has passed. Police officers who become detectives have usually made more arrests than their peers. Detectives often work in teams, and since criminals are more likely to suspect a man of being a detective, often the most effective teams consist of men and women working together.

Narcotic squad detectives have very dangerous jobs which can also be very rewarding. They are people who get much satisfaction from apprehending someone who is dealing illegal drugs. About 80 percent of all crimes involve narcotics, either drugs or alcohol, and people trafficking in drugs are often particularly experienced and vicious criminals. Outsmarting them and catching them in the act of selling drugs is a serious challenge. Often, narcotics squad detectives will know far in advance that someone is selling drugs but may not have enough real evidence or witnesses willing to testify against that person in order to make an arrest and be assured of obtaining a conviction.

These detectives have to know how to recognize and test narcotics, know the chemical makeup of drugs, keep a trail of evidence, and seal it. They have to know self-defense, how to use a search warrant, and how to seize property. They often have to stay up long hours to observe drug activities, and sometimes they have to infiltrate a suspected drug operation by pretending to be interested buyers themselves. This is called a sting operation, and it can be very dangerous, especially if the detective's true identity is revealed to the dealer.

EDUCATION AND TRAINING

A person interested in joining a police force needs a high school diploma, and preferably at least two years of college. Many police departments encourage candidates to attend special police academies or universities with courses in law enforcement.

Candidates need to be at least 21 years old, and they have to pass rigorous physical exams, including tests of strength and agility as well as vision. They should be individuals of high moral character, and their background will be investigated to assure they themselves haven't committed any crimes. Once a person has joined the police force, basic training is provided. Those who wish to become detectives need to put in their time on the job and demonstrate that they are street smart, knowledgeable in the use of weapons, and physically and mentally fit.

OUTLOOK AND EARNINGS

Salaries of police officers and detectives vary according to where they work and the size of their department, with larger urban police departments paying the most. While police officers have an average starting salary of between $20,000 to $23,000, detectives start at about $25,000 to $28,000, and experienced detectives may earn as much as $40,000 per year or more. The average starting salary for narcotics squad detectives in the U.S. Drug Enforcement Agency is $34,000. Experienced detectives with the DEA make up to $54,000. A chief of detectives in a city such as New York may earn $80,000 or more.

WAYS OF GETTING MORE INFORMATION

Neighborhood police may be willing to talk to interested students about their work.

For further information, write to:

National Association of Chiefs of Police
3801 Biscayne Boulevard
Miami, FL 33137

International Narcotics Enforcement Officers Association
112 State Street
Albany, NY 12207

A detective takes measurements of a damaged car.

DEVELOPMENT DIRECTORS

SCHOOL SUBJECTS:
BUSINESS, ECONOMICS

PERSONAL INTERESTS:
MANAGEMENT, SELLING/
MAKING A DEAL

OUTLOOK:
ABOUT AS FAST AS THE
AVERAGE

OTHER ARTICLES TO LOOK AT:
Advertising Account Executives
Fund-Raisers
Grants Coordinators
Marketing Researchers
Public Relations Specialists

WHAT DEVELOPMENT DIRECTORS DO

Money donations, or philanthropy, is one of the ten largest industries in the United States. Americans donate over $100 billion each year to various organizations, like research centers, hospitals, religious groups, schools, libraries, and other special campaigns. *Development directors* are the people who organize and plan ways to raise funds for charity programs. They are responsible for appeals to large contributors, like corporations, philanthropic foundations, and wealthy persons.

An important part of their job is to find new sources of funds. They must be imaginative and resourceful in thinking of ways to ask people to donate money. For example, a director working for an opera company may ask a wealthy business to provide funds to pay for a well-known opera singer to give a special performance. This is good public

relations for the business because support for the arts enhances its public image.

Successful development directors have many skills, particularly in financial management and accounting, public relations, marketing, and media communications. They also must have strong communications skills because of their contact with volunteers, board members, corporation leaders, and members of the press. It is important that they maintain contacts with corporate industries, so they may give speeches or talks, or attend fund-raising parties.

Most development directors work in social service agencies, research centers, college alumni programs, and cultural institutions like museums and zoos. Others work for consulting firms that specialize in helping to raise and manage funds for nonprofit organizations. In larger organizations and charities, the development director may be in charge of a staff of fund-raisers. In smaller agencies, he or she may be the only person who raises money, and may also have other duties.

EDUCATION AND TRAINING

There are no specific educational requirements for development directors, but most have earned at least a bachelor's degree in liberal arts. Interested high school students should take college-preparatory courses, and they should plan to attend a college or university. A wide range of classes is recommended, including English, speech, foreign languages, public relations, psychology, business administration, social work, and journalism. Most development directors also have a good working knowledge of economics, accounting, and mathematics. Experience on a student council and community volunteer work can help students to develop necessary skills in leadership.

OUTLOOK AND EARNINGS

There is expected to be an increase in jobs for development directors in the next decade, since sources other than government funding will be needed to fund charity efforts. Many well-educated people are interested in becoming directors and there should be stiff competition for these jobs, especially the higher-paying positions in large cities.

Salaries vary widely. Beginning fund-raisers earn about $20,000 per year. The average salary for development directors is $30,000 per year. Very successful directors can earn over $150,000 per year.

WAYS OF GETTING MORE INFORMATION

The best way to get experience in fund-raising is to volunteer at social agencies, your church or school, or other organizations for their revenue drives. You may try to volunteer at your local public radio or television station during their fund-drives. All these methods will help you get an inside look at what it takes to be a successful fund-raiser and development director.

For more information, write to:

American Association of Fund-raising Executives
25 West 43rd Street, Suite 1519
New York, NY 10036
Tel: 212-354-5799

National Society of Fundraising Executives
1101 King Street, Suite 700
Alexandria, VA 22314-2967
Tel: 703-684-0410

While development directors sometimes enjoy socializing at gala fundraising events, much of their time is spent writing letters and making phone calls.

DIAGNOSTIC MEDICAL SONOGRAPHERS

SCHOOL SUBJECTS:
PHYSICS, PHYSIOLOGY

PERSONAL INTERESTS:
HELPING PEOPLE: PHYSICAL
HEALTH/MEDICINE, SCIENCE

OUTLOOK:
FASTER THAN THE AVERAGE

OTHER ARTICLES TO LOOK AT:

Nuclear Medicine Technologists

Physicians

X-Ray Technologists

WHAT DIAGNOSTIC MEDICAL SONOGRAPHERS DO

Diagnostic medical sonographers, or sonographers, use advanced technology, in the form of high frequency sound waves, to produce images of internal organs in the human body. These sound waves are similar to SONAR, which is used to locate objects beneath the water.

Sonographers work on the orders of a physician. They set up the ultrasound equipment for each exam. They describe the imaging process as they move the patient's body into the correct position for the procedure. It is important that sonographers possess "people skills" such as kindness and compassion, while still maintaining a professional attitude. Oftentimes, patients are very old or young, or fearful about the sonogram, and need to be reassured and comforted before the procedure begins. When the patient is properly aligned, the sonographer applies a type of gel to the body which improves the ability to see the image. The sonographer then moves the transducer, a device that directs sound waves, over the specific body area to be imaged, adjusting the equipment according to the proper depth of field and the specific internal organ that needs to be examined. They record diagnostic data on computer disc, magnetic tape, strip printout, film, or videotape. When the procedure is complete, the sonographer is responsible for preparing the recorded images, and also for making notes or observations of what occurred during the exam so as to be able to pass on this information to the attending physician for analysis.

Other duties of sonographers include maintaining patient records, monitoring and adjusting sonographic equipment for accuracy, and, after considerable experience, serving as supervisors, preparing work schedules and evaluating future equipment purchases.

Sonographers need to have a good mind for details, a superior knowledge of the systems and organs of the body, and strong communication skills in order to work successfully with patients and coworkers.

EDUCATION AND TRAINING

Sonographers receive their training from teaching hospitals, colleges and universities, technical programs, or the Armed Forces. Sonography students serve an internship as they complete classroom and laboratory instruction. In grade school, students should take classes in mathematics, science, and speech, and writing. High school students should focus on chemistry, anatomy and physiology, physics, and also mathematics, speech, and technical writing classes.

OUTLOOK AND EARNINGS

As the population ages, and medical technology advances, demand for diagnostic medical sonographers should continue to rise. The average starting salary for a sonographer is $27,000, with experienced technologists earning on average $34,000 per year. Top sonographers can make up to $41,000 a year.

WAYS OF GETTING MORE INFORMATION

Students interested in sonography should speak to a trained sonographer, or visit an ultrasound department. Counselors or teachers may be able to arrange a visit by a technologist, or a field trip to a facility that performs sonographic examinations.

In addition, write to the following organizations for more information:

American Medical Association (AMA)
515 North State Street
Chicago, IL 60610

American Registry of Diagnostic Medical Sonographers (ARDMS)
2368 Victory Parkway, Suite 510
Cincinnati, OH 45206-2810

Society of Diagnostic Medical Sonographers (SDMS)
12770 Coit Road, Suite 508
Dallas, TX 75251

This sonographer performs an ultrasound so that both she and the expectant mother can see the growing baby.

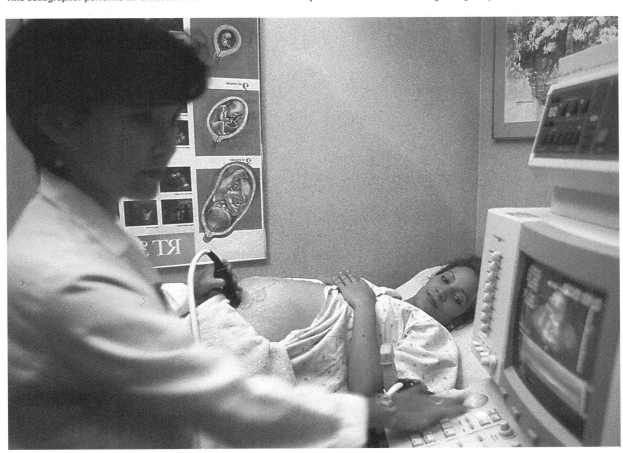

DIALYSIS TECHNICIANS

SCHOOL SUBJECTS:
BIOLOGY, CHEMISTRY

PERSONAL INTERESTS:
HELPING PEOPLE: EMOTIONALLY,
HELPING PEOPLE: PHYSICAL
HEALTH/MEDICINE

OUTLOOK:
ABOUT AS FAST AS AVERAGE

OTHER ARTICLES TO LOOK AT:

Biomedical Equipment Technicians

Cardiovascular Technologists

Diagnostic Medical Sonographers

Nuclear Medicine Technologists

X-Ray Technologists

WHAT DIALYSIS TECHNICIANS DO

Dialysis technicians, also called *nephrology technicians,* or *renal dialysis technicians,* set up and operate *hemodialysis* (artificial kidney) machines for patients with *chronic renal failure (CRF).* Dialysis technicians also maintain and repair this equipment as well as help to educate patients and their families about dialysis. All dialysis technicians work under the supervision of physicians or registered nurses.

Healthy kidneys remove toxic wastes from our blood in the form of urine. CRF is a condition where the kidneys cease to perform this task. Many people, especially diabetics or people who suffer from undetected high blood pressure, develop this condition. These patients require hemodialysis to sustain life. In hemodialysis the patient's blood is circulated through the dialysis machine, which takes over for the kidneys by filtering out impurities, wastes, and excess fluids from the blood. The cleaned blood is then returned to the patient's body.

Dialysis technicians most often work in a hospital or special dialysis center. Some technicians travel to patients' homes and administer dialysis. Technicians are responsible for preparing the patient for dialysis, monitoring the procedure, and responding to any emergencies which occur during the treatment.

Before dialysis, the technician measures the patient's vital signs (including weight, pulse, blood pressure, and temperature) and obtains blood samples and specimens as required. The technician then inserts tubes into a vein or a catheter, which will exchange blood between the patient and the artificial kidney machine throughout the session.

While monitoring the dialysis, technicians must be attentive, precise, and alert. They measure and adjust blood-flow rates as well as check and recheck the patient's vital signs. All of this information is carefully recorded in a log. In addition, technicians must respond to any alarms which occur during the procedure and make appropriate adjustments on the dialysis machine. Should an emergency occur during the session, technicians may have to administer cardiopulmonary resuscitation (CPR).

EDUCATION AND TRAINING

Potential dialysis technicians should have at least a high school diploma or the equivalent. Previous experience caring for the seriously ill, such as volunteering in a hospital, is highly recommended. Presently only a few two-year dialysis preparatory programs exist in technical schools and junior colleges. By far, the majority of technicians learn their skills through on-the-job training.

In most states, dialysis technicians are not required to be registered, certified or licensed. California and New Mexico are the only states that require certification. In some states technicians are required to pass a test before they can work with patients.

OUTLOOK AND EARNINGS

There should continue to be a need for dialysis technicians. The percentage of the population over 60 is increasing, as is the number of people with kidney disease. This means that dialysis technicians will continue to be needed to provide treatment.

Dialysis technicians can earn between $14,000 and $35,000 per year, depending on job performance, responsibilities, locality, and length of service. Some employers pay higher wages to certified technicians than to those who are not certified. Technicians who rise to management positions can earn from $35,000 to $40,000 per year.

WAYS OF GETTING MORE INFORMATION

Volunteering in a hospital, nursing home, or dialysis center can give you a taste of what it is like to care for patients, many of whom are seriously ill. Most hospitals have volunteer programs open to high school students.

For more information about being a dialysis technician, contact:

National Association of Nephrology Technicians/Technologists (NANT)
P.O. Box 2307
Dayton, OH 45401-2307
Tel: 513-223-9765

Dialysis technicians must be skilled at operating their equipment, but they must also be able to put their patients at ease and make them comfortable.

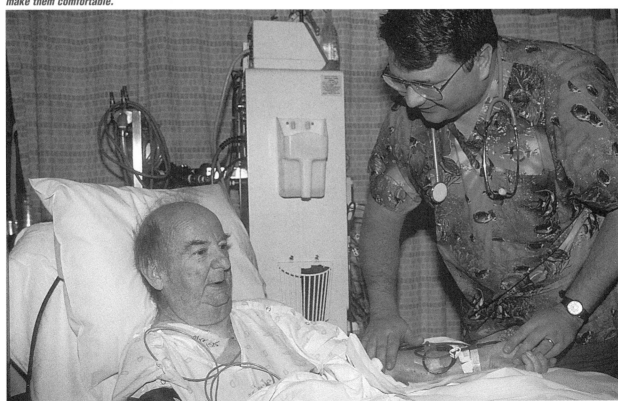

DIESEL MECHANICS

OTHER ARTICLES TO LOOK AT:

Aeronautical and Aerospace Technicians

Automobile Mechanics

Farm Equipment Mechanics

Truck and Delivery Drivers

WHAT DIESEL MECHANICS DO

Diesel mechanics work on the diesel engines that power such machines as buses, ships, automobiles, trucks, locomotives, construction machinery, and farm and highway equipment. Their work can be divided into three basic categories: maintenance, repair, and rebuilding.

Maintenance work involves the day-to-day servicing that keeps the engine running smoothly. This includes checking oil levels, the brake system, steering mechanisms, and wheel bearings; cleaning air and oil filters; removing and checking the various parts of the fuel system; and inspecting the water cooling system.

Despite regular maintenance checks, parts of the diesel engine can wear out or break. When this happens, the diesel mechanic removes, replaces, and adjusts the defective part.

To rebuild an engine a diesel mechanic must take it completely apart. This is usually scheduled at regular intervals such as every 18 months or 100,000 miles. The mechanic uses a variety of instruments to check each part, and then either repairs, adjusts, or replaces it as needed.

The work of diesel mechanics varies according to the kind of machine they are working on. All mechanics must know the principles of diesel engines and must be prepared to do exacting, often strenuous work to keep their engines in good working order. They usually work indoors and are exposed to dirt and grease. Minor cuts and bruises on the hands are the most common injuries that diesel mechanics suffer. They work with heavy tools such as welding and flame-cutting equipment, power wrenches, and lathes and grinding machines.

EDUCATION AND TRAINING

Today's entry-level diesel mechanic has a high school diploma and has completed some formal training. Training can vary from on-the-job or apprenticeship training, to formal classroom work in a technical or vocational school that offers courses in diesel equipment. Because of the time and money it takes to train an apprentice, most employers today prefer to hire only those who have some post-secondary training.

Many diesel mechanics began their training by working on gasoline engines. However, as diesel engines became more complex and sophisticated, it became necessary for diesel mechanics to seek formal training. Some firms, particularly those that manufacture diesel engines, offer their own formal training programs, which can last anywhere from six months to four years. The

National Automotive Technicians Education Foundation offers voluntary certification through many technical schools. NATEF certification is recognized by everyone in the industry. Marine engineers, who are diesel engineers on ships, are trained and licensed by the U.S. Coast Guard.

OUTLOOK AND EARNINGS

This increase has created a demand for skilled mechanics, and their employment outlook is very good. A qualified mechanic may choose from a variety of employers, including dealers of diesel-powered farm and construction equipment, bus and shipping lines, construction and trucking companies, electric power plants, or federal, state, or local governments.

The hourly rate for diesel mechanics varies according to the specific job. Certified mechanics in the transportation industry make the most, an average of $32,000, followed by those in wholesale trade, manufacturing, retail trades, and services industries. The overall average annual salary is about $28,000. Skilled workers can make $39,000 or more. These wages reflect earnings for a 40-hour work week; many mechanics work far longer hours, with time and half paid for overtime. Mechanics own their own hand tools that may cost between $6,000 and $25,000.

WAYS OF GETTING MORE INFORMATION

High school courses in auto shop are excellent for exploring an interest in this career. Part-time and summer jobs in a service station are also often available.

For more information, write to:

International Union, United Automobile, Aerospace and Agricultural Implement Workers of America
*8000 East Jefferson Avenue
Detroit, MI 48214*

National Automotive Technicians Education Foundation (NATEF)
*13505 Dulles Technology Drive
Herndon, VA 22071*

A diesel mechanic repairs the engine block on a large truck.

DIETETIC TECHNICIANS

SCHOOL SUBJECTS:
BIOLOGY, FAMILY AND CONSUMER SCIENCE

PERSONAL INTERESTS:
COOKING, HELPING PEOPLE:
PHYSICAL HEALTH/MEDICINE

OUTLOOK:
ABOUT AS FAST AS THE
AVERAGE

OTHER ARTICLES TO LOOK AT:

Cooks, Chefs, and Bakers

Dietitians

Family and Consumer Scientists

Food Service Workers

Food Technologists

WHAT DIETETIC TECHNICIANS DO

Dietetic technicians work in two basic areas: food-service management and the nutrition care of individuals, also known as clinical nutrition. They normally work as members of a team, under the direction of a dietitian. Most technicians work for hospitals and nursing homes. Some, however, work for health agencies such as public health departments or neighborhood health centers.

Technicians who work in food-service management perform a variety of tasks. They may work in the kitchen, overseeing the actual food preparation. They may supervise dietetic aides, who serve food in the cafeteria and to patients in their rooms. Technicians also may set up the work and time schedules of other food-service employees. In addition, they may train these employees and evaluate their work. Technicians sometimes develop recipes, as well as diet plans for patients. They also may help patients select their menus. Some have the duties of keeping track of food items on hand, ordering supplies, and supervising food storage.

Technicians involved in clinical nutrition work under the supervision of a dietitian. They may interview patients about their eating habits and the foods they prefer. They then give this information to the dietitian, along with reports on each patient's progress. This information may reveal the need for changes to the patients' diets. Technicians also teach patients and their families about good nutrition. They may keep in touch with patients after they leave the hospital to see if they are staying on their diets.

Some dietetic technicians work in community programs. They may teach families how to buy and prepare healthful foods. They may work with those who have special diet problems, such as the elderly. Some technicians work in programs that provide meals for the needy.

Dietetic technicians may also work for schools, colleges, and industrial food-service companies. Some work in research kitchens, under the supervision of a dietitian. These technicians may keep track of supplies, weigh and package food items, inspect equipment, and keep records.

EDUCATION AND TRAINING

Dietetic technicians must have a high school diploma and complete a two-year program that leads to an associate's degree. The program must be approved by the American Dietetic Association. Such programs are offered in many junior and community colleges. They combine classroom work with on-the-job experience. Subjects studied include food science, menu planning, sanitation and safety, and diseases related to poor nutrition. Students also learn how to purchase, store, prepare, and serve food.

OUTLOOK AND EARNINGS

The outlook in the 1990s for dietetic technicians, especially those who are certified, is generally very good. Technicians will be in demand because of society's concern with nutrition and health and also because the elderly, who make up an increasing percentage of the population, often have strict dietary needs. Employers may also prefer to hire technicians in greater numbers since they can perform many of the same duties as dietitians while working for lower salaries.

Earnings vary widely. Beginning technicians are paid about $15,000 a year.

Experienced workers earn between $20,000 and $36,000 a year.

WAYS OF GETTING MORE INFORMATION

School lunch programs may be managed by a dietetic technician. If so, perhaps this technician would be willing to speak to a class or answer questions about the job.

For more information, write to:

American Dietetic Association
216 West Jackson Boulevard
Chicago, IL 60606

Dietetic technicians are employed by cafeterias to make sure the food service provides a balanced diet.

DIETITIANS

SCHOOL SUBJECTS:
FAMILY AND CONSUMER SCIENCE,
HEALTH

PERSONAL INTERESTS:
FOOD, HEALTH

OUTLOOK:
FASTER THAN THE AVERAGE

OTHER ARTICLES TO LOOK AT:

Cooks, Chefs, and Bakers

Food Service Workers

Home Health Aides

Human Services Workers

Physicians

WHAT DIETITIANS DO

Dietitians teach people about healthy nutritional habits. They help people select good foods and show them how to prepare meals so that they can stay healthy. Dietitians, sometimes called *nutritionists*, work in hospitals, community centers, restaurants, businesses, or other locations.

Dietitians are food experts who work directly with people. A dietitian in a hospital will plan the general food menu and also plan diets for patients with special health problems. Some patients may not be allowed to eat meat, salt, or sugar, so dietitians must plan meals with substitutes for these foods. Dietitians may work with pregnant women, people who have high blood pressure, high cholesterol, or any number of health conditions.

As health professionals, dietitians work with physicians and other health care providers. A dietitian will always consult with a patient's medical doctor before planning a special menu. He or she also meets with patients, discusses their concerns and special needs, and then uses this information to plan a menu.

Dietitians not only work with people who are sick, but also help healthy people stay that way. They may work with a community group, for instance, meeting with parents and their children to advise them on how to develop a balanced diet. With the help of a dietitian, families are taught how to plan and prepare meals and how to shop for food wisely and economically.

Dietitians also work with individuals who are overweight, underweight, or have special dietary restrictions or food allergies. They may also work in research, aiding in the discovery of how different types of food will help maintain health and cure people of disease.

EDUCATION AND TRAINING

Dietitians should have good communications skills and be able to work closely with physicians, patients, and other health professionals. Interested high school students should take courses in chemistry, mathematics, biology, family and consumer science, and business. Classes in English, psychology, and sociology are also valuable.

The best way to become a dietitian is to get a bachelor's degree in dietetics, nutrition, food-service management, or a related subject. Many colleges offer programs in these areas, but make sure the program is approved by the American Dietetic Association (ADA). All graduates must complete a training program of about one year in a hospital, school, or other location. During this year, dietitians-in-training are supervised by experienced dietitians.

All dietitians must be licensed. To become licensed, a qualified college graduate must pass an examination. He or she is then fully qualified to practice as an R.D. (Registered Dietitian).

OUTLOOK AND EARNINGS

A career as a dietitian should offer good job opportunities in the 1990s. Health, nutrition, and fitness have become important parts of out lives. As more and more people want to learn about good nutrition, businesses, community social service agencies and research organizations will need trained dietitians.

The average salary is between $25,000 and $35,000 after one to five years of experience. Experienced dietitians may make $35,000 or more. Salaries vary by region.

WAYS OF GETTING MORE INFORMATION

Many helpful books on nutrition are available in stores and libraries. Ask a school or public librarian to help.

For additional information about a career as a dietitian, write to:

American Dietetic Association
216 West Jackson Boulevard
Chicago, IL 60606

A dietitian prepares to test a variety of nutritional supplements to see if they meet her exacting standards.

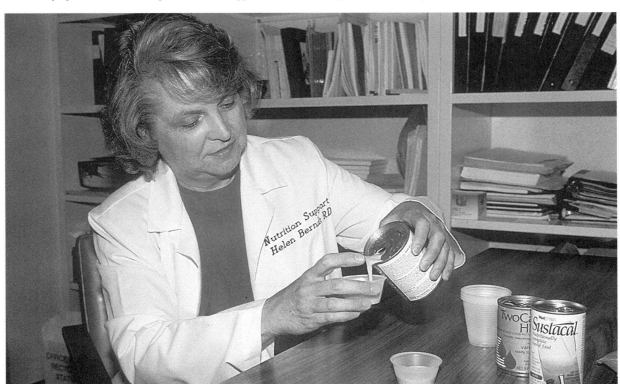

DISC JOKEYS

SCHOOL SUBJECTS:
ENGLISH, SPEECH

PERSONAL INTERESTS:
ENTERTAINING, MUSIC

OUTLOOK:
LITTLE CHANGE OR MORE
SLOWLY THAN THE AVERAGE

OTHER ARTICLES TO LOOK AT:

Electronics Engineering Technicians

Library Media Specialists

Radio and Television Announcers

Radio and Television Newscasters

WHAT DISC JOCKEYS DO

Disc jockeys, or *DJs,* play recorded music on radio or during parties, dances, and special occasions. On the radio they also announce the time, the weather forecast, or important news. Sometimes they interview guests and make public service announcements.

Unlike radio and television newscasters or news reporters, disc jockeys most often do not have to read from a written script. Except for when they do commercials, their comments are usually spontaneous. They also do not have to play any musical selection to the end. Instead, they can fade out any recording to make room for commercials, news, time and traffic checks, or weather reports.

Because most radio shows are live broadcasts and anything may happen on the air, disc jockeys must learn to react calmly under stress and know how to handle unexpected circumstances. The best disc jockeys have

pleasant, soothing voices and a good wit for keeping listeners entertained.

Often, disc jockeys have irregular hours, and most of them work alone. Some have to report for work at a very early hour in the morning or work late into the night. But the work can be exciting. Those who stay with a station for a long time often become famous personalities. As they become known, they are invited to participate in civic activities.

Work in radio stations is usually very pleasant, but it is demanding. It requires that every activity or comment on the air begin and end exactly on time. This can be difficult, especially when the disc jockey has to handle news, commercials, music, weather, and guests within a certain time frame. It takes a lot of skill to work the controls, watch the clock, select music, talk with someone, read reports, and entertain the audience; often several of these tasks must be performed at the same time.

Because disc jockeys play the music their listeners like and about the things their listeners want to talk about, they must always be aware of pleasing their audience. If listeners begin switching stations, ratings will go down, and disc jockeys can lose their jobs.

EDUCATION AND TRAINING

There is no formal education required of a disc jockey. However, many large stations prefer to hire people who have been to college. Some schools train students for broadcasting, but such training will not necessarily improve the chances of an applicant's getting a job at a radio station.

Students interested in becoming disc jockeys and advancing to other broadcasting positions should attend a school that will train them to become an announcer. Or they can apply for any job at a station and work their way up.

OUTLOOK AND EARNINGS

In the broadcasting field there are usually more job applicants than available jobs. As a result, competition is stiff. In general, beginning jobs are easier to get in small radio stations.

Disc jockeys can make anywhere from $12,000 to $80,000 a year or more. Those who work for small stations earn the lowest salaries and may have to work an additional job to make a good income. Top personalities in large market stations earn the most.

WAYS OF GETTING MORE INFORMATION

Summer jobs are sometimes available in radio stations. College students may also have opportunities to work at their university's own radio station or to participate in internship programs.

For more information, write to:

Broadcast Education Association
National Association of Broadcasters
1771 N Street NW
Washington, DC 20036-2891
Tel: 202-429-5355

National Association of Broadcast Employees and Technicians
501 3rd Street NW, 8th Floor
Washington, DC 20001
Tel: 202-434-1254

Radio-Television News Directors Association
1000 Connecticut Avenue NW, Suite 615
Washington, DC 20036
Tel: 202-659-6510

A disc jockey announces the next recording to be played on the radio show.

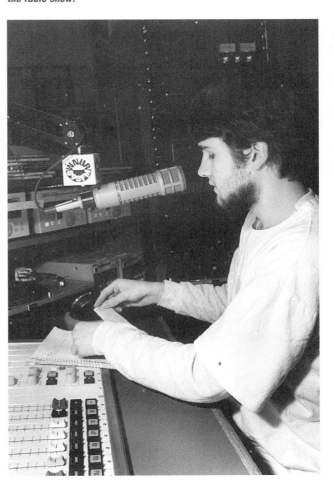

DISPENSING OPTICIANS

SCHOOL SUBJECTS:
BIOLOGY, MATHEMATICS

PERSONAL INTERESTS:
HELPING PEOPLE: PERSONAL
SERVICE, BUILDING THINGS

OUTLOOK:
FASTER THAN THE AVERAGE

OTHER ARTICLES TO LOOK AT:

Instrument Makers

Lens Technicians

Optometric Technicians

Optometrists

WHAT DISPENSING OPTICIANS DO

Dispensing opticians fit people with eyeglasses and contact lenses. Dispensing opticians may work in the optical department of a large department store or in a small store that sells only eyewear. Some dispensing opticians work for ophthalmologists or optometrists who sell glasses to their patients.

When customers come in, dispensing opticians help them select glasses frames. Then the dispensing optician takes the customer's prescription and orders the laboratory to grind the lenses. Sometimes the lenses are ground right on the premises; sometimes the prescription must be sent out to a laboratory to have the lenses made and inserted in the frames.

When the glasses are ready, dispensing opticians make sure the glasses fit the customer properly. They use small hand tools to adjust the frames so the lenses are positioned correctly and the frames are comfortable.

Some dispensing opticians fit contact lenses as well as glasses. They measure the curve of the customer's eye and then give these measurements and the doctor's prescription to an optical mechanic who makes the lenses. Dispensing opticians also teach the customer how to wear and care for the lenses.

EDUCATION AND TRAINING

Dispensing opticians need at least a high school diploma. Many learn on the job, as apprentices. More and more employers prefer to hire those who have graduated from two-year college programs. The job requires good eye-hand coordination and the ability to work well with customers.

In high school, students should study mathematics, and health/mechanical drawing. Community colleges and trade schools offer two-year optician programs giving students the chance to study the science of optics and the techniques of making lenses, as well as business and communications.

Often the companies that sell glasses offer apprenticeship programs. It takes an apprentice two to four years to learn on the job. Larger companies may have formal apprenticeship programs; in small companies, training will be less formal. Dispensing opticians need special training to fit contact lenses. This training is usually offered by contact lens manufacturers.

In some states, dispensing opticians must have a license to fit glasses. To earn the license, they must usually pass an oral and a written exam.

OUTLOOK AND EARNINGS

There will be a growing demand for dispensing opticians in the 1990s because, overall, there will be more older people in the population. Many people start wearing glasses in middle age. Larger cities with more optical stores will have more job openings.

Dispensing opticians who are just starting out earn between $15,000 and $20,000 per year. They average about $25,000, and those with experience earn up to $30,000. Those who advance to become store supervisors or managers or go into business successfully for themselves may earn more.

WAYS OF GETTING MORE INFORMATION

Learning how to use instruments with lenses (telescopes, microscopes, binoculars) is a good way to start learning about the science of optics. Librarians can help you find articles and books about lenses and their uses.

For more information, write to:

American Board of Opticianry
10341 Democracy Lane
Fairfax, VA 22030

National Academy of Opticianry
10111 Martin Luther King Jr.
Highway, Suite 112
Bowie, MD 20715

National Federation of Opticianry Schools
10111 Martin Luther King Jr. Highway,
Suite 112
Bowie, MD 20715

To make sure a pair of glasses fits a customer properly, the dispensing optician makes adjustments in the store.

DIVING TECHNICIANS

SCHOOL SUBJECTS:
PHYSICAL EDUCATION, SHOP
(TRADE/VO-TECH EDUCATION)

PERSONAL INTERESTS:
BOATS, FIXING THINGS

OUTLOOK:
FASTER THAN THE AVERAGE

OTHER ARTICLES TO LOOK AT:

Industrial Safety and Health Technicians

Oceanographers

Welders

WHAT DIVING TECHNICIANS DO

Diving technicians are experts who use scuba gear (an oxygen tank and breathing apparatus) to perform underwater work. Most are commercial divers who inspect, repair, remove, and install underwater equipment and structures. They work on underwater research projects and on building and maintaining oil wells and other submerged structures.

Most diving technicians work for commercial diving contractors. These contractors perform a wide variety of jobs, including building underwater foundations for bridges, placing offshore oil well piping, and fixing damaged ships, barges, or permanent structures located in the water.

Diving technicians must not only be skilled divers but also able to do a variety of tasks both underwater and aboard a sailing vessel. They may repair a hole in a ship while it is in the water or search for missing equipment at sea. Many diving technicians now work on research projects investigating life in the lakes and oceans. They may take underwater photographs or make films or video-

tapes. Some work on salvage projects, such as exploring and retrieving items from wrecked ships at sea. Others help with underwater military projects.

The work is very strenuous and may be dangerous. Divers must be able to use hand tools, such as hammers, wrenches, and metal-cutting equipment, while deep underwater. They must carefully use such diving equipment as air compressors, breathing-gas storage tanks, and communications equipment. Divers stay in contact with workers on the boat to receive instructions and to be alerted to any developing problems.

Divers must swim underwater to a particular area (like the side of an oil well) and then carefully move about to complete their assigned tasks. They sometimes refer to blueprints of a piece of equipment to locate it in the dark waters. They often work as part of a team and must always know what is going on around them and how much oxygen remains.

Other diving technicians are recreation specialists. They may teach scuba diving lessons or coordinate dive programs for resorts or cruise ships.

EDUCATION AND TRAINING

Diving technicians must be excellent swimmers and have the coordination to do complicated tasks underwater.

Working underwater requires close teamwork, so technicians must be able to communicate clearly and get along with others. Mistakes can sometimes result in serious injury or loss of life, so technicians must be able to follow instructions carefully yet also think independently should a situation change.

The best way to become a diving technician is to complete a two-year training program. Some typical requirements for entering a program are a high school diploma with mathematical and science skills, good swimming ability, and good health. The two-year program has classes in diving techniques and the skills needed to work underwater. Programs for recreation specialists offer training in business and communication, as well. Students must complete an approved program to be certified as diving technicians.

OUTLOOK AND EARNINGS

Job opportunities for trained diving technicians are numerous. Petroleum companies need technicians in their search for oil and natural gas, shipping companies need technicians to repair vessels, and research projects need technicians to take underwater photographs and help in other ways.

The average beginning salary is about $17,000 per year for about six to eight months of work, but earnings increase rapidly with experience. Within four years a skilled technician may earn more than $30,000 per year. Technicians rarely work a standard schedule. They may work every day on a project for three months and then have three or four weeks off before they get another assignment. Even working less than most other professionals, technicians earn good salaries.

WAYS OF GETTING MORE INFORMATION

A good way to find out if you would enjoy being a diving technician is to take diving and swimming lessons.

In addition, write or call:

Association of Commercial Diving Educators
c/o Marine Technology Program
Santa Barbara, CA 93109
Tel: 805-965-0581

Association of Diving Contractors
2611 FM 1960 West, Suite F-204
Houston, TX 77068
Tel: 713-893-8388

Rigging nets in the ocean, two diving technicians set up for biological sampling of marine life.

DOG GROOMERS

SCHOOL SUBJECTS:
ART, BIOLOGY

PERSONAL INTERESTS:
ANIMALS, BABY-SITTING/
CHILD CARE

OUTLOOK:
ABOUT AS FAST AS THE
AVERAGE

OTHER ARTICLES TO LOOK AT:

Animal Health Technicians

Biologists

Equestrian Management Workers

Farmers

Veterinary Technicians

WHAT DOG GROOMERS DO

Dog groomers bathe, trim, shape, brush, and comb dogs' coats to make them look good and help them stay healthy. They may be self-employed and work out of their homes or they may work for a pet shop, grooming school, veterinarian's office, animal hospital or shelter, circus, or show kennel.

Though all dogs benefit from regular bathing, brushing, and trimming, some breeds require much more care than others. Poodles make up much of groomers' business, since their coats are among the most highly styled. But the groomer's routine is much the same when working with any dog.

First the dog is thoroughly brushed, and all matted hair is trimmed or combed out. Clipping and shaping come next, followed by nail trimming and ear cleaning. Then comes a bath with gentle, tearless shampoo and, if necessary, a special solution to kill fleas and ticks. After the bath the dog is dried off, either with a towel or, for dogs with long, rough coats, an electric hair dryer. Finally, the dog is given a finishing combing and clipping.

Besides grooming dogs (and sometimes cats), groomers check carefully for any signs of illness or infection in their animals. They examine coats and skin, eyes and ears, muscle tone, and bone structure. They often form a link between owner and veterinarian, advising pet owners when a trip to the vet may be in order.

Groomers must love animals; be physically strong enough to lift heavy animals and work on their feet for long hours; be patient and gentle with nervous pets; have a sense of style for clipping and trimming; and be able to work well with the owners, who are often more nervous than their pets.

EDUCATION AND TRAINING

There are three basic ways to become a dog groomer. Many groomers teach themselves by reading books on the subject and then practicing on their own and friends' pets. Some groomers work in a veterinarian's office or pet shop and learn on the job, beginning with bathing and brushing animals, and working up to rough clipping and expert trimming. Other groomers enroll in an accredited dog grooming course or in one of the many dog grooming schools recognized by the National Dog Groomers Association. Groomers don't need a high school diploma for any of these entry methods, but they may find it helpful for advancement in the job, especially if they want to open a business of their own.

Beginning groomers generally work for other people, either a vet, a pet store owner, or an owner of a dog grooming shop. Experienced groomers often go on to manage or open their own shops, or they may become certified instructors and teach grooming techniques in accredited schools.

OUTLOOK AND EARNINGS

In the 1990s more than 35,000 people work as dog groomers. Pet ownership is expected to continue to grow, and with it a need for experienced, qualified dog groomers. Therefore, the outlook is bright for those who wish to become dog groomers—estimates indicate a need for about 3,000 new groomers each year.

On average, groomers earn about $20,000 a year. Sometimes groomers in a pet store or grooming shop work for a percentage of the income, which means they get 50 to 60 percent of the money paid by their customers. Self-employed groomers with own their own shops may earn anywhere from $25,000 to $55,000 a year.

WAYS OF GETTING MORE INFORMATION

The best way to learn about dog grooming is to get books from the library and then start practicing—on your own or a friend's dog. Visit a local vet or pet shop to see how professional groomers work; part-time work as a groomer's assistant may be available.

For more information about a career as a dog groomer, write to:

New York School of Dog Grooming
248 East 34th Street
New York, NY 10016

National Dog Groomers Association of America
PO Box 101
Clark, PA 16113

Nash Academy of Animal Arts
857 Lane Allen Road
Lexington, KY 40504

A dog groomer carefully trims the fur on a dog's paw.

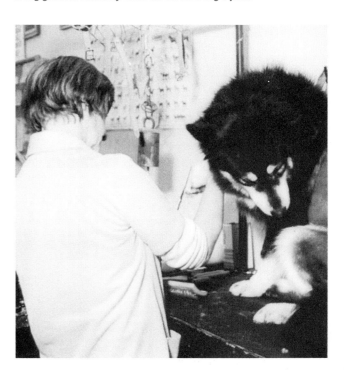

DOOR-TO-DOOR SALES WORKERS

SCHOOL SUBJECTS:
BUSINESS, ECONOMICS

PERSONAL INTERESTS:
SELLING/MAKING A DEAL, TRAVEL

OUTLOOK:
LITTLE CHANGE OR MORE
SLOWLY THAN THE AVERAGE

OTHER ARTICLES TO LOOK AT:

Buyers

Manufacturers' Sales Representatives

Retail Sales Workers

Retail Store Managers

WHAT DOOR-TO-DOOR SALES WORKERS DO

Door-to-door sales workers visit people, usually in their homes, to explain, demonstrate, and sell products. Unlike retail stores, which wait for customers to come to them, they must identify likely customers and arrange to meet with them to show the products and take orders.

Many door-to-door sales workers are *direct company representatives*. Direct company representatives are typically employees of the company whose products they are selling. They might work for a commission (a percentage of the price of an item sold), or they might receive a salary and a commission. Some direct company representatives are self-employed. They are paid only a commission by the company or companies whose products they sell.

Some door-to-door sales workers work as *dealers*. They buy products at wholesale prices from companies and resell them at retail prices.

Door-to-door sales workers use different methods to locate customers. For example, exhibitors set up exhibit booths at places where large numbers of people can be found, such as state fairs. Here the sales worker makes sales presentations to interested people and schedules appointments to visit them later in their homes.

Sales workers involved with group plans invite customers to participate in the selling effort. Under what is called a party plan, for instance, the sales representative asks an interested customer to invite a group of friends to the customer's home for a display and demonstration of the products. The customer receives free products or a discount on products in exchange for using the house and for assembling potential customers.

Whatever the sales plan, door-to-door sales workers must go out and get customers for their product. They must also have strong selling skills in order to win the confidence of the customer, create a desire in the customer to buy the product, and make the sale, all in a brief visit.

EDUCATION AND TRAINING

Most door-to-door sellers have graduated from high school, and many have attended college. No one particular course of study is best for all sales workers, although English, public speaking, and psychology are undoubtedly useful to most.

To be successful, door-to-door sales workers need to bring certain personal qualities to their work. In particular, they must be able to organize their own time. Self-discipline is required to work without supervision and to keep working even after a series of unsuccessful sales calls. Sales workers should also enjoy talking with people and have a friendly personality.

OUTLOOK AND EARNINGS

Job opportunities for door-to-door sales workers are expected to grow in the 1990s.

Door-to-door sales workers often receive a commission instead of a salary. The commission ranges from 10 percent to 40 percent of the retail price of the product they are selling. Earnings are determined almost wholly by the individual sales worker's training, ability, desire to succeed, and the time and effort put into the job. Many earn between $12,000 and $20,000 a year.

WAYS OF GETTING MORE INFORMATION

The best way to learn more about this work is to do some door-to-door selling. Opportunities to do this are often available to members of organizations, such as the Boy Scouts and Girl Scouts, Junior Achievement, and the Junior Sales Club of America.

Interested students can also write for information from the following organization:

Direct Marketing Association
1120 Avenue of the Americas
New York, NY 10036
212/768-7277

A door-to-door sales worker shows her products to a customer in the customer's home.

DRAFTERS

SCHOOL SUBJECTS:
MATHEMATICS, SHOP (TRADE/VO-TECH EDUCATION)

PERSONAL INTERESTS:
BUILDING THINGS, DRAWING/PAINTING

OUTLOOK:
MORE SLOWLY THAN THE AVERAGE

OTHER ARTICLES TO LOOK AT:
Aerospace Engineers
Architects
Civil Engineers
Industrial Designers

WHAT DRAFTERS DO

Drafters are artists who prepare clear, complete, and accurate drawings and plans for engineering and manufacturing purposes. These drawings are based on the rough sketches and calculations of engineers, architects, and industrial designers. To complete their drawings successfully, drafters use their knowledge of machinery, engineering practices, mathematics, building materials, and the physical sciences.

For example, an architect might prepare a rough sketch of an office building. The sketch shows what the building will look like and includes its dimensions—the measurements of its size. However, before the building can be constructed, extremely detailed drawings of every part of the building must be made. These drawings, called blueprints or layouts, are created by drafters.

Drafters work at large, tilted drawing tables. Some also use computer-aided drafting (CAD) systems, sitting at a computer and drawing on a video screen. Regardless of the computer's help, a drafter needs to know how to use a variety of drawing instruments, including protractors, compasses, triangles, squares, drawing pens, and pencils. Some drawings made by a drafter are very small. Others are quite large, occasionally reaching lengths of 25 to 30 feet. Small or large, each drawing must be detailed enough so that the subject of the drawing can be constructed from it.

Drafters have different responsibilities. *Senior drafters,* sometimes called *chief drafters,* use the ideas of architects and engineers to make design layouts. *Detailers* make complete drawings from these design layouts. Complete drawings usually include the dimensions of the object shown and the type of material to be used in constructing it. *Checkers* carefully examine drawings to look for mistakes. *Tracers* correct any mistakes found by the checkers and then trace the finished drawings onto transparent cloth, paper, or plastic film. This makes the drawings easy to reproduce.

Drafters often specialize in a certain type of drawings. *Commercial drafters* do all-around drafting, such as plans for building sites or layouts of offices and factories. *Computer-assisted drafters* use computers to make drawings and layouts of many types of objects, including buildings, electronic parts, or airplanes.

EDUCATION AND TRAINING

In high school, students interested in a career as a drafter should take as many science and mathematics courses as possible. Mechanical drawing classes and wood, metal, or electric shop are also very important. Since good communication skills are necessary, students should take four years of English.

Most beginning drafters must take classes after high school to get a job. Students can enroll in drafting programs offered by community colleges and technical institutes. These two-year programs will include courses in science, mathematics, drawing, sketching, and drafting techniques.

Another alternative after high school is an apprenticeship program. These programs usually run for three to four years, during which the apprentice works on the job and takes classes. At the end of the program, the apprentice becomes a full-fledged drafter.

OUTLOOK AND EARNINGS

Employment for drafters is expected to grow more slowly than the average through the year 2000. During times of slow economic growth, fewer buildings and manufactured products are designed, and therefore, fewer drafters are needed.

The average salary of a full-time drafter is about $30,000. Experienced drafters who work in manufacturing, transportation, and for utility companies earn between $20,000 and $40,000 a year. Senior drafters can make up to $45,000 a year.

WAYS OF GETTING MORE INFORMATION

Mechanical drawing classes are a good introduction to the type of work drafters do. Hobbies that require the use of drawings or blueprints are also informative. These include woodworking, building models, and remodeling projects.

For more information, contact:

American Design Drafting Association
PO Box 799
Rockville, MD 20848-0799
Tel: 301-460-6875

International Federation of Professional and Technical Engineers
8701 Georgia Avenue, Suite 701
Silver Springs, MD 20910
Tel: 301-565-9016

National Association of Trade and Technical Schools
2251 Wisconsin Avenue NW
Washington, DC 20007

Language Arts

Manual Skills

Sciences and Mathematics

Registering the exact design information, a drafter draws an architect's illustration on to a final blueprint.

DRY CLEANING AND LAUNDRY WORKERS

SCHOOL SUBJECTS:
CHEMISTRY, SHOP (TRADE/VO-TECH EDUCATION)

PERSONAL INTERESTS:
CLOTHES, HELPING PEOPLE; PERSONAL SERVICE

OUTLOOK:
MUCH FASTER THAN THE AVERAGE

OTHER ARTICLES TO LOOK AT:

Clerks

Textile Technicians

Textile Workers

Truck and Delivery Drivers

WHAT DRY CLEANING AND LAUNDRY WORKERS DO

Laundry and dry cleaning facilities clean clothes and other articles made from natural and synthetic fibers. *Dry cleaning and laundry workers* dry clean, wash, dry, and press clothing, linens, curtains, rugs, and other articles for families, industries, hospitals, schools, and other institutions. In smaller laundries and dry cleaning plants, one worker may perform several different tasks. In larger plants, however, a worker usually performs only one job in the cleaning process.

Some laundry is picked up from homes and businesses by *sales route drivers*. These drivers also return the laundry after it has been cleaned. Some people bring their laundry to dry cleaning stores. Here, sales clerks take the items from customers, add up the cleaning costs, and fill out cleaning tickets or receipts for the customers to bring back when they pick up their clothes. Then the clerks inspect the items for rips and stains, mark the items to identify the customer to whom they belong, and bundle them for cleaning.

In the cleaning plant, *markers* put tags on articles so they will not be lost. Then they send the items to rooms where they will either be dry cleaned or laundered. If the items are to be dry cleaned, *classifiers* will sort them according to the treatment they need. If the items are to be laundered, sorters may weigh the items and put individual customer's articles into net bags to keep them together.

Laundry spotters brush stains with chemicals or other cleaners until the stains disappear. In dry cleaning plants, *spotters* do the same work. Plants that clean rugs may employ *rug measurers* to record the sizes of the rugs so they can be stretched back to their original sizes after cleaning.

When articles are ready to be cleaned, *laundry laborers* and loaders take the laundry to the washing machines. *Washing machine operators* then wash the articles. When the washing cycle is complete, these operators load the laundry into extractors. Extractors are machines that remove about 50 percent of the water from washed laundry. The damp laundry is then put on a conveyor belt that takes it to driers, conditioners, and other machines.

Dry cleaners operate the machines that clean items using chemicals. *Hand dry cleaners* clean delicate items that need individual attention by hand.

When items are dry or semi-dry, *pressers* or *finishers* operate machines that use heat or steam to press articles. *Silk finishers* work on delicate items. *Flatwork finishers* feed linens into automatic pressing machines. *Puff ironers* press portions of garments that can not be ironed with a flat press by pulling them over heated, metal forms.

EDUCATION AND TRAINING

Most dry cleaning and laundry workers learn their skills on the job. Usually, the only educational requirement is a high school diploma or its equivalent. Courses in sewing and clothing construction are useful. Some large dry cleaning and laundry plants offer formal training programs for new employees.

Another way to learn dry cleaning and laundry skills is through trade associations. These associations publish newsletters and conduct seminars to help workers learn new skills and techniques.

OUTLOOK AND EARNINGS

The job outlook in the 1990s for dry cleaning and laundry workers is favorable. However, continued automation of plants will lessen the need for unskilled or semiskilled workers. Job prospects look best for workers who can do a variety of jobs and have a good knowledge of textiles.

Beginning full-time laundry workers earn between $8,850 and $10,000 a year. Skilled workers may earn $15,000 to $18,000. Some dry cleaning workers earn higher wages. Pressers can often earn more than $15,000 a year, and skilled spotters and dry cleaners can make $20,000 or more. Still, the average wage for all dry cleaning and laundry workers is about $11,000 a year.

WAYS OF GETTING MORE INFORMATION

To find out more about dry cleaning and laundry work, students can arrange to visit a plant, local dry cleaner, or laundromat and talk with the workers.

Students can also write to the following for more information:

International Fabricare Institute
12251 Tech Road
Silver Spring, MD 20904

Neighborhood Cleaners Association
252 West 29th Street
New York, NY 10001

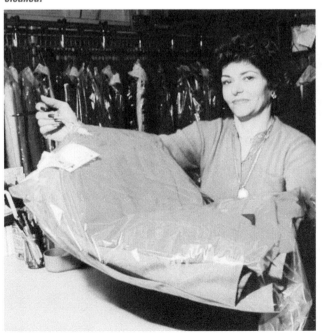

A dry cleaner packages and tags clothes that have been cleaned.

DRYWALL INSTALLERS AND FINISHERS

SCHOOL SUBJECTS:
MATHEMATICS, SHOP (TRADE/VO-TECH EDUCATION)

PERSONAL INTERESTS:
BUILDING THINGS, DRAWING/PAINTING

OUTLOOK:
ABOUT AS FAST AS THE AVERAGE

OTHER ARTICLES TO LOOK AT:
Bricklayers and Stonemasons
Carpenters
Painters and Paperhangers
Plasterers

WHAT DRYWALL INSTALLERS AND FINISHERS DO

Drywall panels consist of a thin layer of plaster between two sheets of heavy paper. They are used in place of wet plaster to make the inside walls and ceilings of houses and other buildings. *Drywall installers* measure the areas to be covered. Then they mark the panels and cut them. They use a keyhole saw to cut openings for electrical outlets, vents, and plumbing fixtures. Next, they fit the pieces of drywall into place and use glue to attach them to the wooden framework. Then they nail or screw them down. Installers usually need a helper to assist with the larger, more awkward pieces.

Large ceiling panels may have to be raised with a special lift. After the drywall is in place, installers usually attach the metal frames, also called beading, on the edges of the walls and the trim for windows, doorways, and vents.

Drywall finishers, also called *tapers*, seal and hide the joints where drywall panels come together and prepare the walls for painting or wallpapering. They mix a quick-drying sealing compound and spread the paste into and over the joints with a special trowel or spatula. While the paste is still wet, the finishers press paper tape over the joint and press it down. When the sealer is dry, they spread a cementing material over the tape. They blend this material into the wall to hide the joint.

Sometimes finishers have to apply second or third coats of sealer to smooth out all the rough areas on the walls. Any cracks or holes and nail and screw heads in the walls or ceiling are also filled with sealer.

With a final sanding of the patched areas, the walls and ceiling are ready to be painted or papered. Some finishers apply textured surfaces to walls and ceilings. To do so, they use trowels, brushes, rollers, or spray guns.

Most drywall installers and finishers work for painting, decorating, drywall contractors. Some installers and finishers operate their own contracting businesses. Others work for general contractors.

Drywall installing and finishing is strenuous work because it requires a lot of standing, bending, and kneeling. Lifting large panels of drywall requires a fair amount of strength and agility.

EDUCATION AND TRAINING

Most employers prefer applicants with a high school diploma. Drywall installers and finishers are trained on the job. Installers begin as helpers to experienced workers. At first, they carry materials, hold panels, and clean up. After a few weeks, they are taught to measure, cut, and install panels. Finisher helpers start out by taping joints and sealing nail holes and scratches. Then they learn to install corner guards and to hide openings around pipes. Both installers and finishers also learn to estimate job costs.

Another way of learning this trade is through apprenticeship programs. Such programs combine classroom study with on-the-job training.

OUTLOOK AND EARNINGS

Drywall continues to replace plaster as a building material because it is cheaper and faster to install. Thus, the need for drywall installers and finishers will continue at an average pace. Jobs will be more plentiful in and around cities, where contractors have enough business to hire full-time drywall workers. In small towns, carpenters often do drywall installation and painters do the finishing.

Salaries of drywall workers range from about $20,000 to $40,000 a year. Trainees receive about half the rate earned by experienced workers. Some contractors pay their workers based on the amount of work completed; others pay an hourly rate.

WAYS OF GETTING MORE INFORMATION

One way to learn more about this trade is to watch drywall installers and finishers at work. Interested high school students can call a drywall contractor and ask to arrange a visit to a construction site. Summer or part-time work as a helper to workers is sometimes available.

For more information, contact:

Canadian Paint and Coatings Association
*#103, 9900 Cavendish Boulevard
Ville St. Laurent, Canada,
PQ H4M 2V2
Tel: 514-745-2611*

International Joint Painting, Decorating, and Drywall Apprenticeship and Manpower Training Fund
*1750 New York Avenue NW
Washington, DC 20006
Tel: 202-783-7770*

A drywall installer assembles the walls and the ceiling in a room under construction.

ECOLOGISTS

SCHOOL SUBJECTS:
BIOLOGY, GEOLOGY

PERSONAL INTERESTS:
THE ENVIRONMENT, SCIENCE

OUTLOOK:
FASTER THAN THE AVERAGE

OTHER ARTICLES TO LOOK AT:
Biologists
Environmental Engineers
Geologists
Paleontologists

WHAT ECOLOGISTS DO

Ecologists study relationships between organisms (plants and animals) and their environment. They care about how such things as pollutants, rainfall, temperature, and altitude affect living organisms. For example, an ecologist may compare the differences and similarities between the beds of clean and polluted rivers, or study how a forest recovers after a fire.

There are a number of subspecialties within the field of ecology. For example, *forest ecologists* research how changes in the environment affect forests. They may study the conditions which cause a certain type of tree to grow abundantly, including its light and soil requirements, and its resistance to insects and disease. Another type of ecologist is the *hydrogeologist,* who studies the relation of waters on or below the surface of the earth. *Geochemists* study the chemistry of the earth, including the effects of pollution on that chemistry.

The ecologist conducts studies on plants and animals in their natural setting and in the laboratory; they use electron microscopes, electronic instruments, computers, and other equipment in their research. Field work may include living in remote areas under primitive conditions and may involve strenuous physical activity. The results from the trips are then written up in technical reports.

The study of ecology helps in efforts to protect, clean up, improve, and preserve our environment. Ecologists are needed to investigate the impact of industry and government actions and to correct past environmental problems. Some work is even done with dangerous organisms or toxic substances in the laboratory.

EDUCATION AND TRAINING

A bachelor of science degree is the minimum degree needed and is adequate for nonresearch jobs such as testing or inspection. Ecologists must be able to work independently or as part of a team. Good written skills are important for writing reports, and physical endurance will aid in field work that may be necessary. For jobs in applied research or management, a master's degree is usually necessary. And, for advancement to administrative positions, positions in college teaching, or independent research, a Ph.D. is generally required.

OUTLOOK AND EARNINGS

The job outlook for environmental workers in general should remain strong going into the next century. Land and water conservation, an area in which many ecologists work, will be somewhat weaker, however. The lack of openings will be caused by strong competition for these popular jobs and the tight budgets on which many environmental organizations operate.

Those entering the field with a bachelor's degree earn between $12,000 and $18,000 per year. Average salaries are $27,000 to $34,000. With experience and a Ph.D., salaries can go as high as $60,000 and more. Among jobs in the public sector, those with the federal government pay the most. Nevertheless, the majority of private sector jobs offer higher salaries than those with the federal government.

WAYS OF GETTING MORE INFORMATION

Students interested in ecology should take related classes while in school to gain a better understanding of the field. Joining a scouting organization or environmental protection group is a great way to gain first-hand experience in the work of an ecologist.

For more information about a career as an ecologist, write or call:

American Geological Institute
4220 King Street
Alexandria, VA 22302
Tel: 703-379-2480

Ecological Society of America
2010 Massachusetts Avenue NW, Suite 420
Washington, DC 20036-1023

Environmental Careers Organization
286 Congress Street
Boston, MA 02210
Tel: 617-426-4375

Cleaning up after an oil spill makes for dirty work for this ecologist. He will also investigate the effect it has on the environment.

ECONOMISTS

OTHER ARTICLES TO LOOK AT:

Accountants

Management Analysts and Consultants

Marketing Researchers

Mathematicians

WHAT ECONOMISTS DO

Everyone makes decisions on how to spend money, but *economists* do it on a grand scale, working with companies and the government to help plan various programs and projects. Economists investigate what people spend their money on and what goods and services are being produced.

Many economists work for businesses to help them plan what to make and how much to charge. An economist may study such factors as how many potential customers there are in a certain area, how much they pay for a product, and which other companies are making the product. The economist would also look at statistics showing how much the product costs to make and where the manufacturer should invest its profits. The economist analyzes these factors and then reports his or her findings to management officials who use this information in future plans.

No matter what the area of study, economists collect and analyze the appropriate statistics. Economists look at numbers and how those numbers are related. For example, an economist may find that salaries are going up

and use that information to explain, in part, why prices are also increasing.

Preparing reports is another important part of the economist's job. He or she may be called on to review important information and then prepare tables and charts and write up the results in clear, direct language.

Economists usually specialize in a specific branch of their field.

Government economists tend to look at larger issues than those who work for private companies. There conclusions may affect governmental policy. A *labor economist* for the government may investigate salaries paid to workers across the country and how many people are employed nationwide. They use this information to determine and report various economic trends. *International economists* study how many local goods are sold to foreign countries and how many foreign goods are bought here. They study statistics to make sure that their government is benefitting from its exchange of goods with other nations. *Financial economists* study credit, money, and other statistics and trends to help develop public policy. *Industrial economists* study the way businesses are organized and suggest ways to use profits or other assets.

EDUCATION AND TRAINING

The best way to become an economist is to get at least a bachelor's degree in economics or business administration. Most economists, though, especially those who want to teach or do research, get a master's degree or doctorate in those fields.

High school students should take courses in mathematics, English, writing, and any available classes in economics or other social sciences. Because of the increasing importance of computers in all types of statistical work, students should learn as much about computers as possible.

OUTLOOK AND EARNINGS

The job market for economists should be very good in the next decade. This is because the rapidly changing economy will cause many businesses to hire economists to analyze business trends, forecast sales, plan purchases, and organize production schedules. Economists who work as teachers will face strong competition for the best jobs.

Salaries vary somewhat according to the work being done. Those who work for private companies earn more than those who work for the government or a college or university. The average beginning salary in private business is about $42,000 a year for those with a bachelor's degree. The average salary of a full-time economist is about $62,000. Economists with advanced degrees earn the most, with the top 10 percent earning about $80,000.

WAYS OF GETTING MORE INFORMATION

For more information, contact:

American Economic Association
2014 Broadway, Suite 305
Nashville, TN 37203
Tel: 615-322-2595
WWW: http:gopher://vuinfo.vanderbilt.edu/ 11/employment/joe

Two economists discuss trends in the stock market before consulting clients who are investing money.

EDUCATION DIRECTORS

SCHOOL SUBJECTS:
EDUCATION, ENGLISH (WRITING/
LITERATURE)

PERSONAL INTERESTS:
MANAGEMENT, TEACHING

OUTLOOK:
LITTLE CHANGE OR MORE
SLOWLY THAN THE AVERAGE

OTHER ARTICLES TO LOOK AT:

College and University Faculty

Museum Attendants and Teachers

Museum Curators

Naturalists

Zoo and Aquarium Directors

WHAT EDUCATION DIRECTORS DO

Museums and zoos are places where people go to observe exhibits with animals or historic objects. *Education directors* are responsible for helping these visitors to learn more about what they have come to see.

Education directors carry out the educational goals of the zoo or museum. For example, goals at many museums and zoos focus on helping children understand more about the exhibits. In museums children often are allowed to handle artifacts or play with objects. In zoos children may be able to pet animals. Education directors develop special projects to help visitors learn more from this type of hands-on experience.

Education directors plan, develop, and administer educational programs. These include tours, lectures, and classes that focus on the history or environment of a particular artifact or animal.

Education directors advise teachers in leading workshops and classes. They help

resource directors find ways to teach, using materials like egg shells or skeletons, and instruments, like microscopes, in resource centers. They work with exhibit designers to create displays, perhaps showing the development of a moth into a butterfly, or adding plants that animals would find in their natural environment. They also work with graphic illustrators to produce signs and illustrations that reveal more about an exhibit. Signs in a gorilla exhibit, for instance, may include a map of Africa to show where gorillas live.

Most education directors at museums work in art, history, or science, but other museums have a special interest such as woodcarvings or circuses. These directors must have some training or experience in such special fields, just as those at zoos must know about animals. Wherever they work, education directors must have a good working knowledge of all the specimens in their collection.

EDUCATION AND TRAINING

Education directors usually begin in another position at a zoo or museum, like a teacher or resource coordinator, and they are promoted into the position, or transfer from one organization to another to reach the desired level. Education directors must have at least a bachelor's degree. Most positions require at least a master's degree, and many, including those at larger zoos and museums, require a doctorate.

Interested high school students should take college-preparatory courses, and they should plan to attend a college or university that offers a liberal arts degree. Some people who plan to become education directors prefer to obtain their bachelor's degree in one of the sciences and a master's degree in a specialized area of education. Students should also make a point of becoming familiar with the practices of museums or zoos. Many museums offer volunteer opportunities. Zoos often provide entry level work in other areas - such as customer service, which can allow a student to observe zoo employees first hand.

OUTLOOK AND EARNINGS

Salaries vary widely, depending on the level of experience and education of the director, and the size and type of employer. In general, education directors can earn from $20,000 to $53,000 a year.

WAYS OF GETTING MORE INFORMATION

A good way to find out if you would enjoy the work of an education director is to get a part-time job as a helper at a museum or zoo, or do some volunteer work.

In addition, contact:

American Association of Botanical Gardens
786 Church Road
Wayne, PA 19087

American Association of Museums
1225 I Street NW, Suite 200
Washington, DC 20005
Tel: 703-860-8000

An education director for a zoo demonstrates the techniques for handling an owl to zoo volunteers.

ELECTRIC POWER WORKERS

SCHOOL SUBJECTS:
MATHEMATICS, SHOP (TRADE/VO-TECH EDUCATION)

PERSONAL INTERESTS:
COMPUTERS, FIGURING OUT HOW THINGS WORK

OUTLOOK:
LITTLE CHANGE OR MORE SLOWLY THAN THE AVERAGE

OTHER ARTICLES TO LOOK AT:

Electricians

Line Installers and Cable Splicers

Power Plant Workers

Telephone Installers and Repairers

WHAT ELECTRIC POWER WORKERS DO

Electric power workers make sure electricity is available whenever it is needed. Without electric power workers to guide and manage the flow of electricity, power would never reach our homes, businesses, factories, and hospitals. Electric power workers are employed in plants fueled by coal, oil, natural gas, and nuclear power.

There are several kinds of electric power workers. The first is *load dispatcher*. Load dispatchers give orders, usually over the phone, about how much electricity should be produced and where it should be released. The amount is decided based on such things as air temperature—for example, more electricity is needed on a hot day when air-conditioners and fans are being used—and the power available for production at any one time. By reading meters and recorders, load dispatchers know at any time how much power is flowing and where. If lines are down or need repair, load dispatchers will arrange for their removal and service. Load dispatchers keep careful records of all normal and emergency situations that occur on their shifts and they are responsible for telling the proper authorities when lines or equipment need attention.

A *substation operator* controls the flow of electricity by flipping switches at the control board at one of the power company's substations. Substation operators monitor and record the board's readings and then give the data on the amount of electricity distributed and used to operators at the main generating plant. These operators then connect or break the flow by pulling levers that control circuit breakers.

Line installers put up the power lines, which consist of poles, cables, and other equipment, that conduct electricity from the power plant to where it will be used. *Ground helpers* aid the line installers in digging the holes and then raising the poles. They may also help in stringing cables from pole to pole or from pole to building. *Trouble shooters* are line workers who service transmission lines that are not working properly. Because they deal with energized lines—that is, lines that have electricity in them—they must take extra precautions to avoid burns or electric shock. And finally, *cable splicers* do work similar to that of line installers, although with cables. Underground cables are used rather than lines in, for example, a large city, where raising a pole on a street corner is too difficult. Cable splicers work in tunnels or on cables buried in yards, under streets, or through buildings, and spend most of their time in maintenance and repair work.

EDUCATION AND TRAINING

Most electric power workers are at least high school graduates who learn the trade either by on-the-job training or through an apprenticeship program. To be prepared for either type of training, high school classwork should include mathematics, physics, and shop. Three to seven years of work as an assistant or junior operator is needed before one can operate a large substation, and seven to ten years experience as a substation operator are needed before becoming a load dispatcher. An apprenticeship program includes classes in such things as blueprint reading, how electricity is made, and rules and codes. Many experts in the field find that those trained in an apprenticeship program are better prepared.

OUTLOOK AND EARNINGS

The job outlook for electric power workers should be about average for the next decade. Electric power will always be needed, but competition will be strong for most jobs. Most jobs will occur as a result of older workers in the field retiring from service.

The earnings for workers in the electric power industry vary by region, but are relatively high. Line installers and cable splicers earn salaries of between $17,500 and $56,600, with an average salary of $37,000 per year. Powerplant worker earn salaries between $27,000 and $52,000 per year. The main union is the International Brotherhood of Electrical Workers.

WAYS OF GETTING MORE INFORMATION

Visit a utility or transmission building site to get a glimpse of all the different types of electric power jobs that are available.

For more information, contact the following:

Edison Electrical Institute
701 Pennsylvania Avenue NW
Washington, DC 20004-2696
Tel: 202-508-5000

International Brotherhood of Electrical Workers
1125 15th Street NW
Washington, DC 20005
Tel: 202-833-7000

Wiring the power lines, an electric power worker wears safety gloves, helmet, and glasses to avoid injury.

ELECTRICAL AND ELECTRONICS ENGINEERS

SCHOOL SUBJECTS:
MATHEMATICS, PHYSICS

PERSONAL INTERESTS:
BUILDING THINGS, FIGURING
OUT HOW THINGS WORK

OUTLOOK:
FASTER THAN THE AVERAGE

OTHER ARTICLES TO LOOK AT:
Aerospace Engineers
Electronics Engineering Technicians
Industrial Engineers
Quality Control Technicians
Robotic Technicians

Because there are so many types of electrical equipment, engineers usually specialize in one area of work. Engineers may work with the broadcasting equipment at radio and television stations, or concentrate on designing stereos, computers, or medical equipment. Electrical and electronics engineers also research new ways to design electrical equipment.

Electrical and electronics engineers not only design new products, they also have supervisory responsibilities. They decide how a piece of equipment should be built and then direct technicians and production workers in their tasks.

WHAT ELECTRICAL AND ELECTRONICS ENGINEERS DO

For electrical equipment to operate properly, it needs to be designed and built by experts who understand wiring and other construction requirements. *Electrical and electronics engineers* design new products, test equipment, and solve any operating problems. They also estimate the time and money it will take to build a new product and then make sure these figures turn out as expected.

Electrical and electronics engineers work on all types of projects. They may design the equipment used by electric companies to generate power or build electric motors used in airplanes. They develop blueprints that show how a piece of equipment should operate and then complete sketches that show how wiring should be connected. Engineers supervise the production of the equipment and test it to make sure it is working properly. An engineer who designs a computer, for example, will review the related diagrams and then test the computer once it is built to correct any problems.

EDUCATION AND TRAINING

Electrical and electronics engineers should have a solid background in mathematics and science and an understanding of how mathematical and scientific concepts can be used to solve technical problems. They must be skillful in making clear sketches of unfinished equipment and have the ability to explain in understandable language how complex equipment operates.

In order to become an electrical and electronics engineer, a bachelor's degree in electrical engineering, electronics engineering, or computer engineering is needed. A degree in mathematics or science is sometimes acceptable, if the person also has a lot of coursework in engineering.

Many electrical and electronics engineers have advanced degrees. A master's degree takes two years of school beyond a bachelor's degree. A Ph.D. takes four extra years of study. Engineers who plan to teach in colleges or do research are usually required to have a Ph.D.

OUTLOOK AND EARNINGS

Job opportunities for electrical and electronics engineers are very good and should remain good throughout the rest of this century. As new products are needed, especially in the communications, automobile, and computer industries, skilled engineers will be needed to design them and oversee the production process.

The average beginning salary for electrical and electronics engineers with a bachelor's degree is about $35,500 per year. Those with a master's degree have average starting salaries between $35,000 and $40,000. After ten years of experience, engineers can earn $51,000 a year or more.

WAYS OF GETTING MORE INFORMATION

For further information, write to:

Institute of Electrical and Electronics Engineers
U.S. Activities
1828 L Street, NW, Suite 1202
Washington, DC 20036-5104

Junior Engineering Technical Society (JETS)
1420 King Street, Suite 405
Alexandria, VA 22314

An electrical engineer explains to others the methods of testing electrical equipment.

ELECTRICIANS

SCHOOL SUBJECTS:
MATHEMATICS, PHYSICS

PERSONAL INTERESTS:
COMPUTERS, FIXING THINGS

OUTLOOK:
ABOUT AS FAST AS THE AVERAGE

OTHER ARTICLES TO LOOK AT:

Communications Equipment Mechanics

Electric Power Workers

Electrical and Electronics Engineers

Telephone Installers and Repairers

WHAT ELECTRICIANS DO

Electricians install and repair the wiring and electrical equipment that supplies light, heat, refrigeration, air conditioning, and other electrically powered services, as well as equipment involved in telecommunications. Electricians work on constructing new buildings, on remodeling old ones, and on making electrical repairs in homes, offices, factories, and other businesses.

Electricians usually specialize in either construction or maintenance. Most construction electricians are employed by contractors or builders. Others have their own small companies. Some work for large employers that need construction electricians fairly constantly, such as large industrial plants or state highway departments.

Many maintenance electricians are employed by manufacturing industries such as those producing automobiles, ships, steel, chemicals, or machinery. Others work for employers such as city governments, shopping centers, or housing complexes. Some

maintenance electricians have their own shops.

Electricians install many types of switches, controls, circuit breakers, wires, lights, signal devices, and other electrical parts. They may work from drawings or blueprints, or they may be told what to do by a supervisor.

In installing wiring, electricians bend conduit (metal pipe or tubing that holds wiring) so that it will fit snugly on the walls, floors, or beams to which it will be attached. They then pull insulated wires or cables through the conduit and connect the wires or cables to circuit breakers, fuse boxes, transformers, or other components. Electricians test the entire circuit to be sure that it is grounded, the connections are properly made, and the circuits are not overloaded.

Maintenance electricians carry out periodic inspections to find and fix problems before they actually occur. They check on the reliability of all sorts of electrical equipment, such as motors, electronic controls, and telephone wiring. They make whatever repairs are necessary and change defective fuses, switches, circuit breakers, and wiring.

EDUCATION AND TRAINING

Most electricians agree that the best way to learn the trade is through an apprenticeship program. Apprenticeship applicants generally are required to be between the ages of 18 and 24 years old. A high school education or its equivalent is desirable. Applicants must take tests to determine their aptitude for the trade.

Most apprenticeship programs involve four years of on-the-job training in which trainees work for several electrical contractors engaged in different types of work. Apprentices learn to operate, care for, and safely handle the tools, equipment, and materials commonly used in the trade, and how to do residential, commercial, and industrial electrical installations and repairs. They also receive a minimum of 144 hours each year of related classroom instruction in such subjects as drafting and electrical layout, blueprint reading, mathematics, and electrical theory, including electronics.

Most cities require electricians to be licensed. To obtain a license, the electrician must pass an examination that requires a thorough knowledge of the craft and of national, state, county, and municipal building codes.

OUTLOOK AND EARNINGS

The employment outlook for electricians is expected to be good through the 1990s.

Most electricians earn between $21,000 and $37,000 a year. Some make as little as $13,350 or less, and some make as much as $45,000 a year or more. But the average salary for full-time electricians who are not self-employed is about $34,000. In general, electricians working in cities tend to be better paid than those in other areas.

WAYS OF GETTING MORE INFORMATION

Anyone interested in becoming an electrician can learn more about this trade by reading some of the many guidebooks available on electronics and then repairing and building radios, working with model electric trains, or fixing electrical appliances.

For additional information on a career as an electrician, write to:

International Brotherhood of Electrical Workers
1125 15th Street NW
Washington, DC 20005

National Electrical Contractors Association
3 Bethesda Metro Center,
Suite 1100
Bethesda, MD 20814

National Joint Apprenticeship and Training Committee for the Electrical Industry
16201 Trade Zone Avenue, Suite 105
Upper Marlboro, MD 20772

Electricians must always be cautious when working with electricity.

ELECTRO-MECHANICAL TECHNICIANS

SCHOOL SUBJECTS:
MATHEMATICS, PHYSICS

PERSONAL INTERESTS:
BUILDING THINGS, FIXING THINGS

OUTLOOK:
FASTER THAN THE AVERAGE

OTHER ARTICLES TO LOOK AT:

Electrical and Electronics Engineers

Electricians

Electronics Engineering Technicians

WHAT ELECTROMECHANICAL TECHNICIANS DO

Electromechanical technicians build, test, adjust, and repair such electromechanical devices as plant automation equipment, environmental control systems, elevator controls, missile controls, and computer tape drivers. An electromechanical device is one in which electronic sensors activate a mechanical operation. Electromechanical technicians work on many different types of electromechanical devices. Technicians who work on product development and manufacturing must be able to think of new ways of using existing electromechanical equipment. They must also be able to imagine new types of electromechanical devices. Technicians may make laboratory studies and do research on problems in assembly and manufacturing techniques.

Operating, testing, and adjusting electromechanical equipment is also an important responsibility of electromechanical technicians. For example, robot welders in automobile manufacturing plants are electromechanical devices. Technicians must constantly check and adjust these devices so that they perform their work flawlessly. Otherwise, the cars coming off the assembly line will not be structurally sound.

Electromechanical technicians also maintain and repair electromechanical devices. These technicians may work at the manufacturing plant where electromechanical devices are returned when repairs are needed. Technicians may also maintain and repair devices in the field—that is, at the locations where the devices are used.

The types of electromechanical devices technicians work on will depend on their skills, level of education, and experience. Some technicians may work on environmental control systems, such as the systems that maintain the proper temperatures and humidity levels in an art museum. These same technicians may not have the skills or experience to work on missile guidance systems.

EDUCATION AND TRAINING

High school students who are interested in a career as an electromechanical technician should take as many mathematics and science courses as possible. Geometry, algebra, physics, and other lab sciences are all good choices. English classes that stress speech and composition skill are also important.

Many colleges and technical institutes have training programs in electromechanical technology. These programs usually take two years to complete. They often include such courses as electricity and electronics, physics, technical graphics, digital computer fundamentals, English composition, and psychology and human relations.

In addition, some companies require new employees to attend special training programs. These programs may take up to a year to complete. During this time, the trainee usually receives both a weekly salary and living expenses.

OUTLOOK AND EARNINGS

Electromechanical technicians are in high demand today, and this trend is expected to continue at least through the next decade.

Salaries for electromechanical technicians depend on the technician's education and experience as well as the size of the firm and where it is located. In general, starting salaries range from $17,000 to $21,000 a year. After several years on the job, technicians earn between $25,000 and $30,000. Some earn $40,000 or more.

WAYS OF GETTING MORE INFORMATION

For information about a career as an electromechanical technician, write to the following:

Institute of Electrical and Electronic Engineers (IEEE)
1828 L Street, NW, Suite 1202
Washington, DC 20036-5104
Tel: 202-785-0017
WWW: http://www.ieee.org/usab

Junior Engineering Technical Society (JETS)
1420 King Street, Suite 405
Alexandria, VA 22314
Tel: 703-548-5387
Email: jets@nas.edu

An electromechanical technician manipulates one of the many circuit boards that operate a facility.

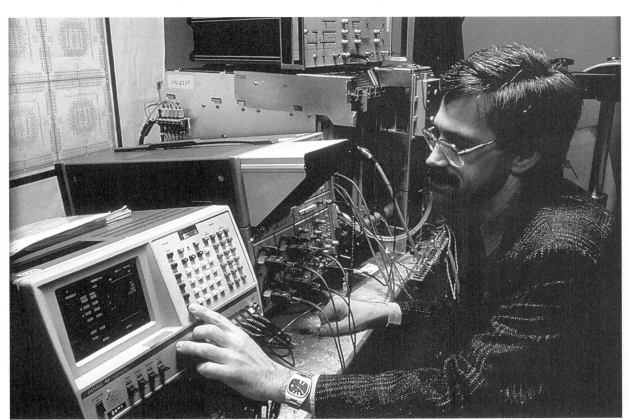

ELECTRONEURO-DIAGNOSTIC TECHNOLOGISTS

SCHOOL SUBJECTS:
BIOLOGY, PHYSIOLOGY

PERSONAL INTERESTS:
COMPUTERS, PERSONAL SERVICE: HEALTH/MEDICINE

OUTLOOK:
MUCH FASTER THAN AVERAGE

OTHER ARTICLES TO LOOK AT:

Biomedical Equipment Technicians

Cardiovascular Technicians

Diagnostic Medical Sonographers

Nurses

X-Ray Technologists

WHAT ELECTRONEURODIAGNOSTIC TECHNOLOGISTS DO

Electroneurodiagnostic technologists, sometimes called *END technologists* or *EEG technologists,* usually work in hospitals and run tests that measure brain damage and heart activity. An EEG, which stands for electroencephalogram, is a test that measures brain waves. When brain waves stop, the patient is considered clinically dead. By recording tracings of brain waves and electrical activity in various parts of the body, EEG technologists are able to provide information that helps doctors diagnose and treat patients.

First, the technologist asks questions about the patient's medical history to record any important information and help the patient feel comfortable with the testing process. They prepare the patients for testing, applying electrodes to certain areas on the head. Placement of electrodes is chosen so the technologist can easily view the brain waves or electrical activity in the results. Sometimes, technologists are given pre-arranged plans for placing the electrodes.

Once prepared, the patient is tested and the impulses of their brain or electrical activity are received and amplified by a machine. Tracings of electric activity are recorded on a moving sheet of paper or optical disks. The technologist notes any irregularities that might occur due to pre-existing injuries or diseases in the patients. They do not interpret the test results, but they ensure that the results are accurate and the data complete. Finally, they determine which sections should be brought to the patient's doctor. Results are given to doctors and used in diagnosis of diseases and injuries such as brain tumors, cerebral vascular strokes, or epilepsy. With the information obtained from electroneurodiagnostic testing, doctors are able to determine the effects of many diseases and injuries on the brain. Then, they are able to prescribe treatment for the patient.

The role of the electroneurodiagnostic technologist can vary. They may be required to handle any emergencies that occur during testing. They may handle other specialized procedures including sleep studies, evoked potential testing, where the brain is tested with specific stimuli, or ambulatory testing, where the patient is tested over a twenty-four-hour period by a small recording device on the patient's side. In addition, EEG technologists may have supervisory or administrative functions. They are responsible for the maintenance of the equipment, and occasionally may need to call on the assistance of a supervisor or equipment technician.

EDUCATION AND TRAINING

EEG technologists must have a high school diploma. In addition, it is usually a requirement to complete a training program. There are two types of post-high school training: on the job training and formal classroom training. After a year of training has been completed, students can take a test for registration as an acknowledgment of the technologist's training. Although registration is not required by employers, it is encouraged and may make job advancement easier. As technologists gain more responsibilities, they will need more training.

OUTLOOK AND EARNINGS

The outlook for EEG technicians is extremely good. It is possible many new positions will open up by the year 2005 due to the growing use of EEGs in surgery, diagnosis and research. Salaries vary according to location, training and other factors, but the average starting salary for an EEG technician is about $19,000 a year. More experienced technicians can make up to $46,000 a year. EEG technologists usually have a full benefits package.

WAYS OF GETTING MORE INFORMATION

It's hard to get experience as an EEG technician without first receiving on-the-job training or classroom education. If you think you might be interested in this type of career, try to get a job as a volunteer at a hospital. At least you will be able to get a general overview of the health care profession. You might ask a teacher to organize a field trip to a hospital, clinic, or doctor's office where you might be able to meet and talk to an EEG technician firsthand.

For a career brochure and list of schools, send $1 to:

American Board of Registration of Electroencephalographic and Evoked Potential Technologists
PO Box 916633
Longwood, FL 32791-6633
Tel: 407-788-6308

For further information write to:

American Society of Electroneurodiagnostic Technologists, Inc.
204 West 7th Street
Carroll, IA 51401
Tel: 712-792-2978

An EEG technologist operates a machine that records the electrical activity in a patient's brain.

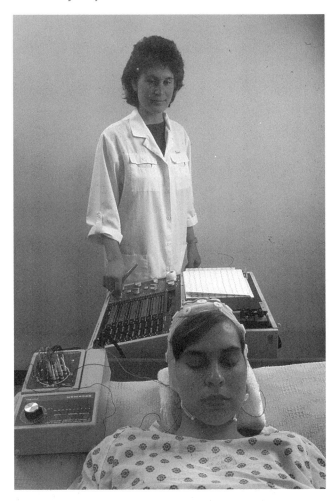

ELECTRONICS ENGINEERING TECHNICIANS

SCHOOL SUBJECTS:
MATHEMATICS, PHYSICS

PERSONAL INTERESTS:
FIGURING OUT HOW THINGS WORK, FIXING THINGS

OUTLOOK:
FASTER THAN THE AVERAGE

OTHER ARTICLES TO LOOK AT:

Electrical and Electronics Engineers

Industrial Engineering Technicians

Instrumentation Technicians

WHAT ELECTRONICS TECHNICIANS DO

Electronics technicians create, assemble, install, operate, maintain, and repair electronic devices such as radios, televisions, computers, stereos, VCRs, and pocket calculators. Some technicians work in product development. These technicians work directly with scientists and engineers. They build, test, and modify experimental electronics products. As part of their work, they use hand tools and small machine tools. They make complex electronic parts and components and use advanced instruments to check the results of their work. Sometimes, they make suggestions to improve the performance or design of an electronic device.

An important part of a technician's job is testing a new product before it is ready to be sold. Before testing new parts and systems, technicians first must study and understand the wiring diagrams and technical manuals that accompany the products they're testing. They learn various tests from the manuals or through special instructions they receive from engineers or other supervisors.

When they do the testing, they usually begin by connecting the part or unit to a special testing device. The device is usually a piece of electronic equipment such as a signal generator, frequency meter, or spectrum analyzer. The technician reads dials on the testing device that indicate electronic characteristics such as the amount of voltage that is going through the unit. The technician then compares the results with the correct level specified in manuals. In this way, the technician can locate a problem such as a short circuit or a defective component. Then he or she replaces the wiring or component or sends instructions to a repair or production department to fix it.

Technicians who work on product development may also become involved in cost estimating. They estimate how much it will cost to manufacture an electronic device. This allows the sales department to figure out how much to charge the consumer.

Electronics technicians may also help manufacture electronics products. They solve production problems, make up production schedules, and supervise and train production employees. Sometimes work in the field may be needed to test a client's equipment.

Other electronics technicians serve as technical writers and editors. They write instruction manuals, books, and test programs. To do this, they talk with engineers, designers, production workers, salespeople, and drafters to gain a thorough knowledge of the product they will write about. Some technical writers also prepare articles for engineering societies and electronics magazines.

EDUCATION AND TRAINING

In high school, students interested in electronics should take two years of mathematics, including geometry and algebra. They should also take physics, chemistry, computer science, and English. An introductory electronics course, shop courses, and courses in mechanical drawing are also useful.

After high school, students should enroll in a two-year training program offered by a community college or technical school. These programs will include courses in physics, technical mathematics, applied electronics, and circuit analysis.

Training programs for electronics technicians are also offered to active-duty members of the armed forces and the reserves. Some companies, such as utility companies, offer on-the-job training programs to high school graduates with good science backgrounds.

Some electronics jobs require certification. Technicians working on radio transmission equipment require a license from the Federal Communications Commission (FCC). Other technicians get voluntary certification to show they have achieved a certain level of competency. This certification is issued by professional associations.

OUTLOOK AND EARNINGS

The electronics industry is one of the fastest growing industries in the United States, and the job outlook for electronics technicians is favorable.

Starting salaries for technicians who have graduated from a two-year training program average about $8,000 to $19,000 a year. The average yearly earnings for full-time electronics technicians are $27,000. Accomplished technicians can earn $40,000 or more.

WAYS OF GETTING MORE INFORMATION

For more information, write to:

International Society of Certified Electronics Technicians
2708 West Berry, Suite #3
Fort Worth, TX 76109-2356

Electronics Technicians Association, International
602 North Jackson
Greencastle, IN 46135

Waiting for the production of one circuit board, an electronics technician examines another board.

ELECTROPLATING WORKERS

SCHOOL SUBJECTS:
CHEMISTRY, SHOP (TRADE/VO-TECH EDU-CATION)

PERSONAL INTERESTS:
BUILDING THINGS

OUTLOOK:
LITTLE CHANGE OR MORE SLOWLY THAN THE AVERAGE

OTHER ARTICLES TO LOOK AT:

Chemical Technicians

Forge Shop Occupations

Iron and Steel Industry Workers

Metallurgical Technicians

Among the special titles some electroplating workers have are *barrel platers,* who operate a mesh barrel that is filled with articles to be plated, *production platers,* who operate automatic plating equipment, and *electroformers,* who prepare objects for plating such as baby shoes or books that don't conduct electricity.

The exact nature of an electroplating worker's job depends on the size of the shop he or she works in. In a large shop, chemists or chemical engineers may make the major decisions. In a small one, however, the electroplating worker is often responsible for the whole process, including ordering chemicals, preparing solutions, plating the products, and inspecting them upon completion.

WHAT ELECTROPLATING WORKERS DO

When an object—a piece of jewelry, for example—is electroplated, it is covered by a layer of gold, silver, brass, or another metal. Electroplating gives objects like car bumpers or electronics parts a hard, protective surface. *Electroplating workers* are the skilled workers who perform this process.

The first thing an electroplating worker does is study a product's specifications and decide which parts need plating, what type of plating to use, and how thickly the metal should be applied. Workers then mix the solution and clean the object that needs to be plated. They place it in tanks for the amount of time necessary for the plating to reach the thickness needed. The metal adheres to the object through an electrical process that is controlled by the plater. When the article is rinsed and dried, the plater looks for any problems and checks the thickness of the metal.

EDUCATION AND TRAINING

Electroplating is a skill that is best learned through a technical program, in a community college or vocational school. Students take classes in chemistry, electricity, physics, and blueprint reading. Some branches of the American Electroplaters and Surface Finishers Society offer courses in the basics of electroplating.

Newly hired workers usually start out as helpers and learn by working under the supervision of a more experienced worker.

OUTLOOK AND EARNINGS

The mechanization of some of the processes used in electroplating is reducing the number of workers needed for this type of work. Skilled workers, who know two or more metals and finishing processes, and who stay up-to-date in technical developments, should be able to find work easily.

Most electroplaters work in the Midwest and the Northeast; that is, near large manufacturing plants that make cars, plumbing fixtures, electronic appliances, hardware, and radio and television products. Other platers work in small shops throughout the United States.

Helpers and entry-level workers without any technical training usually begin at minimum wage and receive regular raises during training. Salaries for regularly employed electroplating workers range from $21,000 to $32,000. Some platers are members of the Metal Polishers, Buffers, Platers and Allied Workers International Union; the International Union, United Automobile, Aerospace and Agricultural Implement Workers of America; or the International Association of Machinists and Aerospace Workers.

WAYS OF GETTING MORE INFORMATION

Those interested in becoming an electroplating worker can look for part-time or summer work in a plating shop where they might be able to assist a plater or work at a related task.

For more information, write to:

American Electroplaters and Surface Finishers Society
12644 Research Parkway
Orlando, FL 32826

National Association of Metal Finishers
401 North Michigan Avenue
Chicago, IL 60611

Two electroplating workers finish the surface of a chrome machine part.

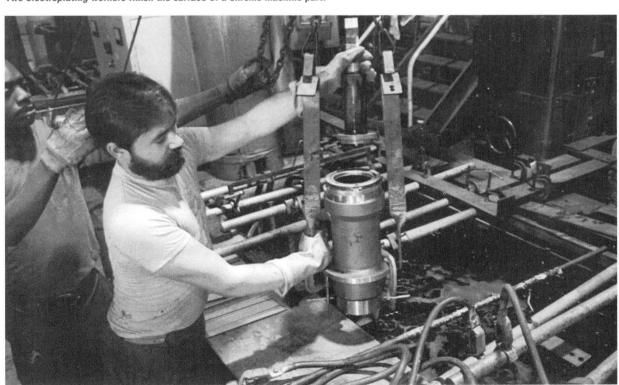

ELEMENTARY SCHOOL TEACHERS

SCHOOL SUBJECTS:
EDUCATION, PSYCHOLOGY

PERSONAL INTERESTS:
BABY-SITTING/CHILD CARE,
TEACHING

OUTLOOK:
FASTER THAN THE AVERAGE

OTHER ARTICLES TO LOOK AT:

Guidance Counselors

Preschool Teachers

Recreation Workers

School Administrators

Secondary School Teachers

WHAT ELEMENTARY SCHOOL TEACHERS DO

Elementary school teachers plan lessons, teach a variety of subjects, and keep class attendance records. Elementary school is usually defined as grades kindergarten through sixth.

Elementary teachers instruct approximately 20 to 30 students in the same grade. They teach a variety of subjects, including reading, spelling, arithmetic, history, civics, English, and geography. They must plan projects, facilitate discussion, and oversee learning activities in all of these areas. Sometimes they link the subjects together under a special theme or event. In some elementary schools, there are special teachers for art and music.

Elementary school teachers use a variety of teaching aids to instruct their pupils. These aids include textbooks, workbooks, magazines, newspapers, maps, charts, and posters.

Elementary school teachers must have a love of learning and be enthusiastic about working with children. They must enjoy being with the age group of students with whom they work and get along well with them. Some elementary school teachers work in multi-age classrooms, where students in a small age range are taught together. Others teach in bilingual classrooms where students are instructed in two languages throughout the day.

After school, elementary school teachers spend time planning the next day's classes and writing up the students' school records. They also grade homework assignments.

Elementary school teachers work with the school principal to solve problems, set up field trips, or plan school assemblies. They also meet with parents to keep them informed about their children's progress, and with school psychologists and social workers to better help students with learning difficulties or other problems.

EDUCATION AND TRAINING

All school teachers must be college graduates and must be certified by the state in which they want to teach. Therefore, high school students should enroll in programs that prepare them to enter college. In college, students studying to be elementary school teachers will take a broad range of courses while majoring in education. Psychology can be an especially useful course to study while in high school or college.

Before graduates can be certified, most states require that students spend time in a real elementary school classroom teaching. Student teachers initially work with a regular teacher at the school, and then are allowed to teach a class alone.

OUTLOOK AND EARNINGS

Job opportunities for elementary school teachers should be good throughout the next decade. Opportunities look best in the West and South, as the population in the United States is growing faster in those areas.

A mid-range salary for elementary school teachers in the United States is about $29,000 per school year. Teachers with master's or doctorate degrees may earn higher salaries.

WAYS OF GETTING MORE INFORMATION

For more information, write to (enclose SASE):

Association for Childhood Education International
11501 Georgia Avenue, Suite 315 Wheaton, MD 20402-1924

National Council for Accreditation of Teacher Education
2010 Massachusetts Avenue, Suite 500 Washington, DC 20036

Elementary school teachers must genuinely enjoy working with children.

ELEVATOR INSTALLERS AND REPAIRERS

SCHOOL SUBJECTS:
MATHEMATICS, SHOP (TRADE/VO-TECH EDUCATION)

PERSONAL INTERESTS:
BUILDING THINGS, FIXING THINGS

OUTLOOK:
ABOUT AS FAST AS THE AVERAGE

OTHER ARTICLES TO LOOK AT:
Construction Inspectors
Construction Laborers
Electricians
Electronics Technicians
Line Installers and Cable Splicers

WHAT ELEVATOR INSTALLERS AND REPAIRERS DO

Elevator installers and repairers, also called *elevator constructors* or *mechanics*, assemble and install elevators, escalators, and dumbwaiters. Today's elevators are usually electronically controlled. They typically have computerized controls called microprocessors, which are programmed to study how many people are using an elevator at any given time and to send elevators up and down when and where they are needed most. Because of these sophisticated devices, elevator installers need to have a strong mechanical ability and a thorough understanding of electronics and hydraulics.

An installer first studies the blueprints of the elevator's planned location in the building to determine where everything is going to fit. Then, he or she directs a crew in installing the guide rails of the car to the walls of the elevator shaft. To set up the elevator's electrical system, the installer runs electrical conduit along the shaft's walls from one floor to the next and then threads plas-

tic-covered electrical wire through it. After installing all the electrical components on each floor and in the main control panel, installers assemble the steel frame of the elevator car at the bottom of the shaft, and connect the platform, walls and door.

In elevators operated by cable, mechanics install a huge electrically powered spool that winds and unwinds a heavy steel cable that connects the car to a counterweight. When the car moves up, the counterweight moves down, and vice versa.

Other elevators function on a hydraulic pumping system, which has a cylinder that pushes the car up from underneath instead of a cable that pulls it up. Regardless of the type of elevator being installed, the entire system has to be checked, adjusted, and tested before it can be used by the public.

Elevator mechanics also install escalators. To do this, they have to put in the steel framework, the electrically powered stairs, and the large track on which the stairs rotate. Then they attach the motors and electrical wiring. Some installers also work on dumbwaiters and similar equipment, such as lifts.

Elevator repairers inspect and adjust elevators that are already installed. Their work involves fixing doors that may come off their tracks and replacing electrical motors, hydraulic pumps, and control panels. They check all cables for wear.

Elevator installers and repairers use a variety of tools and machinery. These include hand tools, power tools, welding machines, cutting torches, rigging equipment, and testing meters and gauges.

The work of elevator installers and repairers is physically demanding because of carrying heavy equipment. It can also be dangerous because of exposure to electricity.

Most elevator installers and repairers work for special contractors who maintain elevators. Others work for elevator manufacturers or for government agencies and businesses that have their own elevator crews.

EDUCATION AND TRAINING

Elevator installers and repairers complete a six-month, on-the-job training program at an elevator factory. After completing this program, trainees work for 60 days on probation, and after six more months they become helpers. Helpers become fully qualified installers within four years and after passing a validated mechanic examination.

Trainees must also take classes in electricity and electronics, if they have not already studied these subjects. Even experienced installers continue to receive training from their employers to keep up with new technological developments. In some areas, installers have to pass a licensing exam.

OUTLOOK AND EARNINGS

Employment of elevator installers and repairers will increase at about the same rate as the average for other occupations through the year 2000. As new buildings are constructed, new jobs will be created for elevator workers. Also, older elevators will need to be replaced by more modern ones. However, because the amount of construction is largely dependent on the general state of the economy, the outlook for elevator installers and repairers is difficult to predict.

Annual earnings for elevator installers and repairers range from $20,000 to $56,000, with the average around $37,000. Supervisors earn between $40,000 and $56,000. Trainees usually begin receiving 50 percent of the salary paid to experienced workers, and helpers start at 70 percent.

WAYS OF GETTING MORE INFORMATION

For additional information contact:

International Union of Elevator Constructors
5565 Sterrett Place, Suite 310
Columbia, MD 21044
Tel: 410-997-9000

National Elevator Industry
11 Larsen Way
Attleboro Falls, MA 02763
Tel: 508-699-2200

An elevator installer checks the operation of a lift at a construction site.

EMERGENCY MEDICAL TECHNICIANS

SCHOOL SUBJECTS:
BIOLOGY, HEALTH

PERSONAL INTERESTS:
HELPING PEOPLE: PERSONAL
SERVICE, HELPING PEOPLE:
PHYSICAL HEALTH/MEDICINE

OUTLOOK:
FASTER THAN THE AVERAGE

OTHER ARTICLES TO LOOK AT:

Fire Fighters

Medical Assistants

Nurses

Physician Assistants

Surgical Technologists

WHAT EMERGENCY MEDICAL TECHNICIANS DO

Emergency medical technicians drive in ambulances or fly in helicopters to the scene of accidents or emergencies and take care of any ill or injured people on the spot. Emergency medical technicians are called EMTs. The ambulances and helicopters they use have two-way radios; a radio message tells the EMTs where they are needed.

EMTs must decide what kind of medical help the victims need and start treating them as quickly as they can. They may have to set broken bones or try to get someone's heart beating or keep someone breathing until they can get the victim to a hospital. EMTs may need to radio hospitals and ask a physician's advice about treatment. Very often the victims of an emergency and the bystanders will be upset. EMTs must go about their work efficiently; they must be able to calm others and stay calm themselves in a crisis.

As soon as they can, EMTs take victims to a hospital. They use stretchers to move victims into the ambulance or helicopter. On the way to the hospital, EMTs radio ahead so the hospital emergency room is ready. They help bring the victims in, and give the hospital staff as much information as they can. EMTs must keep their ambulances and helicopters in good order and make sure that they always have the equipment they need.

EMTs work for hospitals, fire departments, police departments, private ambulance services, or other local first-aid organizations. Some of them, in fire departments, work 56-hour weeks. Most others work 40-hour weeks. But since people need emergency help at all hours, EMTs work nights, weekends, and holidays.

EDUCATION AND TRAINING

Students interested in EMT training must finish high school, be at least 18 years old, and have a driver's license. High school courses in health, science, and English will be helpful. A course in driver education will also be useful because EMTs must drive well. They have to know the roads and travel conditions in their area and be able to drive to an emergency both quickly and safely.

Many hospitals, colleges, and police and fire departments offer the basic EMT training course. The federal government requires this basic training, which teaches students how to deal with common medical emergencies for all EMTS.

The National Registry of Emergency Medical Technicians (NREMT) is an organization that sets standards for EMTs across the country. All EMTs that meet these standards are listed, or registered, with the NREMT. To get on the registry, EMTs must finish the basic training program, have six months work experience, and pass a written and a practical test proving they can handle medical emergencies.

As EMTs get more training and more experience, they can take harder tests from the NREMT to earn registration at a higher level. The middle level is EMT-Intermediate. They are allowed to perform some procedures that basic EMTs are not allowed to perform. The highest level is EMT-Paramedic. EMT-Paramedics are trained in advanced life support skills and are allowed to administer medication and perform certain medical procedures.

All states require EMTs to earn state certification by passing a state exam or passing the basic NREMT registration requirements.

OUTLOOK AND EARNINGS

EMT-Basics can earn anywhere from $18,000 to $31,000. EMT-Intermediates can earn $20,000 to $31,000, and EMT-Paramedics earn between $25,000 and $35,000 per year.

WAYS OF GETTING MORE INFORMATION

For more information write to:

American Ambulance Association
3800 Auburn Boulevard, Suite C
Sacramento, CA 95821

National Association of Emergency Medical Technicians
102 West Leake St.
Clinton, MS 39059

National Registry of Emergency Medical Technicians
Box 29233, 6610 Busch Boulevard
Columbus, OH 43229

A team of emergency medical technicians removes from a helicopter a patient who required airlifting from an accident site.

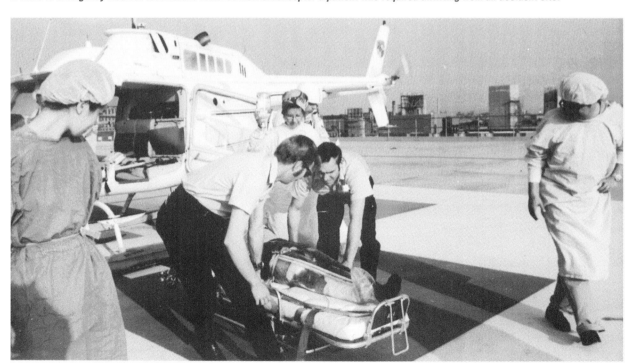

ENERGY CONSERVATION AND USE TECHNICIANS

SCHOOL SUBJECTS:
MATHEMATICS, PHYSICS

PERSONAL INTERESTS:
FIGURING OUT HOW THINGS
WORK, FIXING THINGS

OUTLOOK:
ABOUT AS FAST AS THE AVER-
AGE

OTHER ARTICLES TO LOOK AT:
Architects
Electric Power Workers
Electrical and Electronics Engineers
Operations Research Analysts

WHAT ENERGY CONSERVATION AND USE TECHNICIANS DO

Energy conservation and use technicians study the use of machines in factories, stores, and offices and help determine more effective ways for these machines to use energy. Working under the supervision of engineers or other professionals, they conduct research, perform tests, and repair or replace machines as necessary. Technicians work in a wide variety of locations, including nuclear power plants, research laboratories, and construction companies.

There are four areas in which energy conservation technicians work: energy research and development, energy production, energy use, and energy conservation. Those in research and development often work for the military or another part of government, designing, building, and operating a new laboratory experiment for a physicist, chemist, or engineer. Technicians in energy production often work for power plants, developing and operating systems for converting fuel as efficiently as possible into electricity.

In the field of energy use, a technician might be hired to make heavy industrial equipment work more efficiently. And a technician involved in energy conservation might study how a building such as a hotel could use energy more efficiently.

In all of these categories, the work requires the ability to perform tests and measurements on equipment. For example, an assembly line might not be running efficiently because of a bad motor. A technician would run a series of tests to determine where the problem is and what steps should be taken to correct it. To do this, technicians must know how machines are made and how the parts fit together. Technicians must also be able to read blueprints and other sketches to decide if a better design might increase energy efficiency. A thorough knowledge of complex machinery is necessary to do this job well.

After running tests and measurements, the technician will usually prepare a report of his or her findings and discuss these results with management officials. Technicians may make recommendations, but managers make any final decisions. A manager or supervising engineer might ask the technician to run further tests and present additional findings. After a final decision is made, technicians team up with other workers to see that any necessary corrections are made.

EDUCATION AND TRAINING

Energy conservation and use technicians should have a solid background in how machines operate, be able to read blueprints and sketches, and be able to follow instructions from supervisors. They also need to be good at mathematics and the physical sciences. The ability to describe problems in technical language for engineers and in plain English for people not trained in their field is also a necessity.

The best way to become a technician is to complete a two-year training program at a community college or technical school. The program might be called energy conservation and use technology, or it may be called electric power maintenance, general engineering technology, or something similar. To be accepted into such a program, students should be high school graduates with coursework in mathematics, physics, and chemistry. Other helpful courses are ecology, computers, and mechanical or architectural drafting. Many people receive their training in the military.

OUTLOOK AND EARNINGS

Energy-saving methods are becoming increasingly important to large and small companies and to individual homeowners. For this reason, energy conservation and use technicians should continue to find good job opportunities in the next decade.

The average beginning salary is about $17,000 per year, with experienced technicians earning up to $35,000 annually. Those technicians with five to ten years experience in research, engineering design, or in the maintenance and engineering of machinery may earn $39,000 or more.

WAYS OF GETTING MORE INFORMATION

A science experiment on an energy source, such as a solar heater, is a good way to investigate this career.

For more information about a career in energy conservation and usage, contact the following:

American Institute of Plant Engineers
3975 Erie Avenue
Cincinnati, OH 45208

Institute of Industrial Engineers
25 Technology Park/Atlanta
Norcross, GA 30092

An energy conservation technician studies the air flow from a doorway.

ENVIRONMENTAL ENGINEERS

SCHOOL SUBJECTS:
MATHEMATICS, PHYSICS

PERSONAL INTERESTS:
THE ENVIRONMENT, FIGURING OUT
HOW THINGS WORK

OUTLOOK:
FASTER THAN THE AVERAGE

OTHER ARTICLES TO LOOK AT:
Air Quality Engineers
Civil Engineers
Industrial Engineers

WHAT ENVIRONMENTAL ENGINEERS DO

If a private company or a municipality doesn't handle its waste streams properly, it can face thousands or even millions of dollars in fines for breaking the law. What's a waste stream? It can be anything from wastewater, to solid waste (garbage), to hazardous waste (like radioactive waste), to air pollution. Whatever the waste stream, the environmental engineer plays an important role in controlling it. He or she designs the physical system needed to handle the waste stream.

Depending on his or her specific employer, the environmental engineer may plan a sewage system, design a manufacturing plant's emissions system, or develop a plan for a landfill site needed to bury garbage. Scientists may help decide how to break down the waste, such as by introducing a bacteria that will kill the contaminants in the waste. But engineers figure out how the system will work: where the pipes will go, how the waste will flow through the system, what equipment will be needed.

An environmental engineer may work in the environmental department of a private industrial company, for the Environmental Protection Agency (EPA), or for an engineering consulting firm.

Working for a private industrial company, the environmental engineer usually is part of the company's environmental staff. He or she helps make sure the company is in compliance with environmental laws. That may mean designing new waste systems for the company, or making sure the old ones are up to par. An engineer might, for example, plan the system needed to move wastewater from the manufacturing process area to a treatment area, and then to a discharge site (a place where the treated wastewater can be pumped out). The engineer might write reports explaining the design. He or she also might file certain forms with the government to make sure it knows the company is complying with the laws.

Environmental engineers working for the Environmental Protection Agency (EPA) might not actually design the waste treatment systems themselves. However, they have to know how such systems are designed and built. If there is a pollution problem in their area, they need to figure out if a waste control system is causing the problem, and what might have gone wrong. They have the authority to enforce government regulations on these matters.

Environmental engineers working for an engineering consulting firm may work on many different types of problems. Consulting firms are independent companies that help others get into compliance with environmental laws. Applying engineering expertise, they design and build waste control systems for their clients. They also may deal with the EPA on behalf of their clients, filling out the necessary forms and checking to see what requirements must be met.

Environmental engineers may work in offices part of the time, but also may spend considerable time out in the field inspecting problems and looking for ways to solve them.

EDUCATION AND TRAINING

High school students interested in becoming environmental engineers should take as many science and mathematics courses as possible to prepare for their bachelor's degree. About twenty colleges offer a bachelor's degree in environmental engineering. Another option is to get another type of engineering degree such as civil, industrial or mechanical engineering, with additional courses in environmental engineering. It is a good idea to take advantage of any worksite experience or internships offered through your college.

Registration with the state is required for engineers whose work affects public health, safety or property. It involves obtaining your degree from an accredited engineering college, and passing an engineer-in-training (EIT) at or shortly after your graduation. It also involves passing an examination after you have worked for several years under the supervision of a licensed environmental engineer.

Most employers provide on-the-job training or special training programs for new employees.

OUTLOOK AND EARNINGS

The outlook for jobs as environmental engineers is excellent. There is great demand for people who can design systems to control waste. Engineers are needed in waste water treatment, solid waste management, air qual-

ity control and hazardous waste management.

Those entering the field earn about $23,000 to $35,000 per year. With some experience, $46,000 is about average, and supervisors and those at the top of the field can earn $75,000 or more.

WAYS OF GETTING MORE INFORMATION

Those in high school can gain related experience by volunteering for a local nonprofit environmental organization.

For more information, write to the following:

American Academy of Environmental Engineers
*130 Holiday Court, Suite 100
Annapolis, MD 21401*

Junior Engineering Technical Society (JETS)
*1420 King Street
Alexandria, VA 22314*

Many environmental engineers specialize in one area. Here, an hydrologist is testing the water.

EQUESTRIAN MANAGEMENT WORKERS

SCHOOL SUBJECTS:
AGRICULTURE, BIOLOGY

PERSONAL INTERESTS:
ANIMALS, SPORTS

OUTLOOK:
DECLINE

OTHER ARTICLES TO LOOK AT:

Animal Breeders and Technicians

Farmers

Range Managers

Veterinarians

Zookeepers

WHAT EQUESTRIAN MANAGEMENT WORKERS DO

People who love horses often pursue careers in *equestrian management*. These careers vary widely, but all of them provide the workers with the opportunity to be with horses on a daily basis. *Farriers* are blacksmiths who make horseshoes, fit them, and nail them to horses' hooves. It used to be that all farriers heated the horseshoe's raw metal in a furnace, and hammered it into shape after exactly the right amount of time in the fire. Now most horseshoes are made in factories, and farriers simply shape the horseshoes to the horse's hooves by hammering them. Farriers visit a horse every 6 to 8 weeks to trim hooves, install pads, or put on new shoes. Farriers must choose the correct horseshoe for each horse, depending on what the horse does. A racehorse, a jumping horse, and a horse that pulls carriages, for instance, all require different types of horseshoes.

Horse breeders work with different horses, select mates for them based on desired physical qualities, and raise the offspring. Many horse breeders try to time the breeding so that foals are born in springtime and can be outdoors. Gestation for mares is 11 to 12 months.

Horse trainers specialize in training horses to work in harness or to be ridden. Trainers begin working with young foals soon after birth, as well as old, troubled, or well-trained horses. They teach them to wear halters, saddles, and to respond to the reins. They make sure the horses are accustomed to people, and that they understand certain commands. Trainers also exercise and groom their animals and prepare their food and feed them. Specialized racehorse trainers develop a unique plan for each horse. They exercise the horse a certain number of hours daily, giving the horse time to rest and recover after each session. They clock the horse's speed and work with owners and jockeys on how to elicit the best response from each horse.

Jockeys ride racehorses. They usually work as independent contractors and must find horse owners who will hire them to ride their horses. Owners sometimes hire different jockeys for different races, depending on the type of racetrack being used. Some jockeys have better records on dirt racecourses, for instance, while others excel at racing on the slower-paced artificial turf. Owners may find that a jockey works well with a particular horse and will consistently use that jockey. regardless of the racing surface.

EDUCATION AND TRAINING

A high school diploma will be very helpful for those looking for a job requiring daily contact with horses. Some employers require only a diploma, while others who hire horse trainers, breeders, and jockeys, prefer to hire people who have one or two years of education beyond high school.

There are training programs for farriers that usually last from 10 to 16 weeks. In these programs, people learn how to make, repair, and apply horseshoes, as well as how to handle horses. Some of these programs are offered at local community colleges and require a high school diploma.

OUTLOOK AND EARNINGS

Many farriers are self-employed and can earn between $19,000 and $27,000 annually. There should be some job opportunities for farriers and other equestrian workers, as racetracks, stables, and horse-breeding farms all need trainers, breeders, and farriers.

Average entry-level positions range from $18,000 to $24,000 for graduates of equestrian programs. They work for breed associations, race associations, farriers, sale companies, race tracks, and bloodstock agencies.

There may also be a very limited number of jobs available as carriage drivers, and with police departments, which are reintroducing horse-mounted patrols.

WAYS OF GETTING MORE INFORMATION

Through pony clubs and 4-H organizations many get involved with horses. One can volunteer at a local event or keep up on information through magazines and books.

For more information write to:

National Congress of Animal Trainers and Breeders
Route 1, Box 32 H
Grayslake, IL 60030

American Farrier Association
4089 Iron Works Pike
Lexington, KY 40511

American Horse Council
1700 K Street, NW
Washington, DC 20006

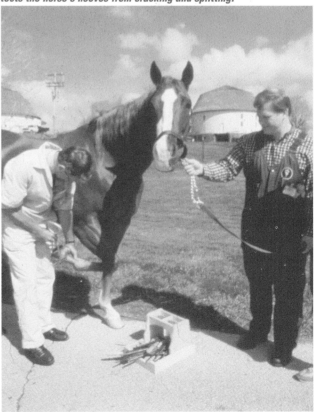

Shoeing a horse may look as though it is uncomfortable for the animal, but it is actually a painless procedure that protects the horse's hooves from cracking and splitting.

ERGONOMISTS AND HUMAN FACTORS SPECIALISTS

SCHOOL SUBJECTS:
MATHEMATICS, PHYSIOLOGY

PERSONAL INTERESTS:
COMPUTERS, HELPING PEOPLE:
PHYSICAL HEALTH/MEDICINE

OUTLOOK:
FASTER THAN THE AVERAGE

OTHER ARTICLES TO LOOK AT:

Industrial Designers

Industrial Engineers

Industrial Safety and Health Technicians

Personnel Specialists

Psychologists

WHAT ERGONOMISTS AND HUMAN FACTORS SPECIALISTS DO

Ergonomists study the workplace to find out how the work environment affects the activities of employees. They do research on how noise, temperature, and lighting affect workers. They study machines to make sure they are safe, efficient, and comfortable to the user. They may also design machines and other equipment. Ergonomists give advice to factory owners, managers, and other top business officials. They help them take the needs of workers into account when changing the workplace. They may also help to design new workplaces.

Ergonomists usually work as part of a team. Each team member deals with one part of the work environment. For example, one ergonomist may deal with machine safety while another ergonomist may deal with noise levels, and a third with the layout of the workplace.

Ergonomists collect information about the workplace and watch employees at work. They study their findings and think of ways that the workplace can be improved. Then, they give a written report of their findings and suggestions to company officials. For example, they may suggest a design for a new machine. Or, they may have an idea for improving the design of an existing machine. In other cases, they may suggest that noise levels be lowered. To make a worker's environment more pleasant, they may suggest painting the walls a different color.

The work of ergonomists is varied. They may, for example, be asked to redesign a computer keyboard or an office chair. Or they may design something as large as a factory. Some ergonomists work with engineers to design systems in which people and machines must work together. Others train workers to use those systems. Still others develop aids for training workers.

Not only are ergonomists concerned with physical comfort in the workplace, but also with the social environment. In the city room of a newspaper, for instance, it might be preferable to have large, wide open spaces in which many people work together so that they can talk and trade information back and forth easily. In a medical practice, on the other hand, small, private offices are better for having quiet conversations and maintaining confidentiality.

Most ergonomists work for large manufacturing companies. Smaller firms may also employ ergonomists, however. Computer companies use them to help in developing effective work environments. Some ergonomists work for the government, designing safe and productive workplaces. Others do research for colleges and universities. Some ergonomists work as freelancers.

EDUCATION AND TRAINING

Most ergonomists have a college degree in either psychology or industrial engineering. Their coursework should include classes in statistics, computer applications, and health sciences, as well as research techniques. The majority of ergonomists also have a master's degree, which is required for most jobs in this field. A doctorate is very helpful for those who want to teach or work at high levels of management.

Certain high school courses are important; these include mathematics, physical sciences, English, psychology, and statistics.

OUTLOOK AND EARNINGS

The outlook for ergonomists is good going into the next century. Because the workplace is becoming increasingly complex, job opportunities should continue to grow, regardless of what happens to the economy.

Beginning ergonomists may earn from $30,000 to $55,000 per year, depending on their level of education. Experienced ergonomists often earn more than $80,000 per year. Freelance ergonomists usually are paid an hourly rate. This rate varies from $60 to $200 an hour, depending upon the ergonomist's education and experience, and the circumstances in which he or she is to work.

WAYS OF GETTING MORE INFORMATION

For more information write to:

Board of Certification in Professional Ergonomics
PO Box 2811
Bellingham, WA 98227
Tel: 360-671-7601

Human Factors and Ergonomics Society
PO Box 1369
Santa Monica, CA 90406
Tel: 310-394-1811

Institute of Industrial Engineers
25 Technology Park
Norcross, GA 30092
Tel: 770-449-0461

An ergonomist conducts a test to measure human static strength.

EXPORT-IMPORT SPECIALISTS

SCHOOL SUBJECTS:
BUSINESS, FOREIGN LANGUAGE

PERSONAL INTERESTS:
COMPUTERS, TRAVEL

OUTLOOK:
ABOUT AS FAST AS THE AVER-
AGE

OTHER ARTICLES TO LOOK AT:

Buyers

Manufacturers' Sales Representatives

Purchasing Agents

Retail Sales Workers

Wholesale Sales Workers

WHAT EXPORT-IMPORT SPECIALISTS DO

Export-import specialists handle the business arrangements for exporting and importing goods to and from foreign countries. They may work out trade agreements with foreign traders and supervise the delivery of the goods. Some export-import specialists work for the government. Others work for companies or for individual people. Many specialists work with both exports and imports, while some handle only one or the other. All specialists, however, must be familiar with international law and trade regulations.

There are many kinds of export-import specialists. *Export managers* handle sales contracts, payments, and shipping of goods to foreign countries. *Customs brokers* handle customs requirements for importers. They inform the importers about customs regulations and prepare the necessary documents. *Wholesalers* buy imported goods and sell them to buyers in this country. They may also buy goods in this country and sell them abroad. Many wholesalers deal in just one type of product, such as clothing or furniture. *Import-export agents* work for import-export firms. They manage shipping, handle permission papers, deal with customs , and solve any problems that arise in the shipping process. *Freight forwarders* are agents for exporters in moving cargo to overseas destinations. They make arrangements for packaging, shipping, and storage, and know the import rules of foreign countries.

EDUCATION AND TRAINING

Although people without a college degree can enter the export-import business, most jobs go to college graduates. The most useful degrees are those in business management, political science, and economics. College courses in international trade, marketing, and business are a good preparation for people entering the field. A master's degree in business administration with a specialty in international trade can lead to better job opportunities. Knowing one or more foreign languages is also an advantage.

Export-import specialists find entry-level jobs with the U.S. Customs Service, seaports and airports, and private companies.

High school students who are interested in export-import careers should take English, geography, social studies, and foreign language courses.

OUTLOOK AND EARNINGS

Job opportunities in the export-import field are expected to be better than average through the next decade. The best opportunities are to be found in large trade centers such as New York, Chicago, Los Angeles, and New Orleans. Highly active industries such as the computer and electronics fields will offer more job openings than others.

Earnings of export-import specialists vary widely, depending on their responsibilities and the size of their firm. Beginning export managers earn $20,000 to $25,000 a year, while those with more experience make more than $37,000. The earnings of customs brokers and freight forwarders may depend on the amount of business they do. Their beginning salary may be $19,000 to $24,000 a year, and with experience they may earn more than $35,000. For wholesalers, earnings depend on how much they buy and sell. They may earn from $23,000 to $90,000 a year, and some may make as much as $150,000 or more. The beginning salary for an import-export agent ranges from $16,000 to $20,000 a year. Those with experience earn $23,000 to $35,000 a year. Agents may also receive a bonus for buying and selling goods.

WAYS OF GETTING MORE INFORMATION

For more information write to:

American Association of Exporters and Importers
11 West 42nd Street
New York, NY 10036
Tel: 212-944-2230

National Customs Brokers & Forwarders Association of America
One World Trade Center, Suite 1153
New York, NY 10048
Tel: 212-432-0500

National Foreign Trade Council
1270 Avenue of the Americas
New York, NY 10020
Tel: 212-399-7128

An importer watches the carving of a statue by a supplier.

FAMILY AND CONSUMER SCIENTISTS

SCHOOL SUBJECTS:
BUSINESS, FAMILY AND CONSUMER
SCIENCE

PERSONAL INTERESTS:
TEACHING, WRITING

OUTLOOK:
MUCH FASTER THAN THE AVER-
AGE

OTHER ARTICLES TO LOOK AT:

Cooks, Chefs, and Bakers

Dietetic Technicians

Dietitians

Food Technologists

Secondary School Teachers

WHAT FAMILY AND CONSUMER SCIENTISTS DO

Family and consumer scientists are concerned with the well-being of the home and family. They improve and help others to improve products, services, and practices which affect that well-being.

Family and consumer scientists do a variety of tasks for a wide range of employers. Some work as teachers in junior and senior high schools. They teach courses such as nutrition, clothing, child development, family relations, and home management. Teachers at the college level prepare students for careers in home economics. They also do research and write articles and textbooks.

The business world offers many opportunities to family and consumer scientists. Some work for manufacturers where they test and improve products and recipes, and prepare booklets on uses of products. They may also plan educational programs and materials. Family and consumer scientists also work

for newspapers, magazines, radio and television stations, publishing companies and advertising agencies. They write about food, fashion, home decoration, budgets, and home management. Some family and consumer scientists work for retail stores. They help customers choose furniture and other household items. They work in advertising, buying, and setting up displays.

Some family and consumer scientists specialize in dietetics. They may work in hospitals, hotels, restaurants, or schools. They plan meals; order food and supervise its preparation; handle budgets; and plan special diets. *Dietitians* may also teach classes in nutrition. *Community* dietitians give advice about nutrition to individuals and groups.

Family and consumer scientists may work as researchers. They create products and develop procedures that make life better for families. Researchers work for colleges and universities, government and private agencies, and private companies.

Health and welfare agencies hire family and consumer scientists. These workers develop community programs in health and nutrition, child care, and money management. They work with families that are having problems with home management.

EDUCATION AND TRAINING

Family and consumer scientists must have at least a bachelor's degree in family and consumer science. Those who do research, teach college, or work as dietitians usually need a master's degree or a doctorate. Many colleges and universities offer degrees in family and consumer scientists. Those family and consumer scientists who plan to teach must complete state requirements for teacher certification, which may vary from state to state.

OUTLOOK AND EARNINGS

The employment outlook for family and consumer scientists is very good for the next decade. Demand will be highest for those in certain specialties. These specialties include research, business, food service management, food science and human nutrition, environment and shelter, and textiles and clothing. Employment for college family and consumer science teachers is expected to decline as a result of declining enrollments.

Earnings for family and consumer scientists depend on a number of factors, including education, experience, specialty, and geographical location. Starting yearly salaries range from $13,000 to $35,000. Family and consumer science teachers in public schools usually earn the same salaries as other teachers. These salaries vary among different school systems. In the late-1990s, the average annual salary for high school teachers was about $37,000. Salary for college and university teachers range from $29,680 for instructors to $63,450 for full professors. Experienced family and consumer scientists in government averaged starting salaries of $25,600 per year.

WAYS OF GETTING MORE INFORMATION

One way to learn more about this field is to talk with a teacher of family and consumer science. This teacher may be able to direct you to other family and consumer scientists who work in your community.

Language Arts

People Skills

Social Sciences

For more information write to:

American Dietetic Association
216 West Jackson Boulevard
Chicago, IL 60606

American Association of Family and Consumer Sciences
1555 King Street
Alexandria, VA 22314

Canadian Home Economist Association
#901, 151 Slates Street
Ottawa, Ontario Canada
K1P 5H3

In a test kitchen, a family and consumer scientist prepares a variety of recipes.

FARM CROP PRODUCTION TECHNICIANS

SCHOOL SUBJECTS:
AGRICULTURE, BUSINESS

PERSONAL INTERESTS:
PLANTS, SCIENCE

OUTLOOK:
ABOUT AS FAST AS THE AVER-
AGE

OTHER ARTICLES TO LOOK AT:

Agribusiness Technicians

Agricultural Scientists

Farmers

Range Managers

Soil Conservation Technicians

WHAT FARM CROP PRODUCTION TECHNICIANS DO

Farm crop production technicians help farmers and others involved in food production get the best results. They help plan what types of grain, wheat, fruit, or other crops to grow and where to plant them, supervise the planting and the ongoing care of the crops, work with farmers as they harvest them, and then provide help in finding buyers for them. Some farm technicians conduct tests and experiments to improve the quantity and quality of crops and to increase the plants' ability to resist disease and insects.

Technicians who specialize in the growth of fruits, nuts, and berries are called *orchard and vineyard technicians*. Those who work with grains, cotton, and other field crops are called *plant technicians*. Other farm technicians work in very specialized areas such as mustard or mushroom farming.

Many technicians work with farmers on a day-to-day or week-to-week basis as they

help them with their crops. They might analyze the soil and water supplies of a farm and study the wind conditions to determine the best place to plant seeds. They may then give instructions on how to apply fertilizers and care for the plants. They also work with the farmer to plan the dates and methods of harvesting and how to store and ship the crops once they are ready to be sold.

Technicians not only work with farmers but with the companies that supply farmers with needed items. For instance, companies that provide seed, fertilizer, machinery, and other products to farmers often hire technicians to go out to farms and sell their products.

Technicians also work with scientists to test new seed crops, new farming methods, and new types of machinery. Some technicians work for the federal government, researching new ways to improve crop production. Others work for companies that process and package the food from farms. By contributing to farm research, technicians ensure that new products and new methods will be available to meet the changing needs of farmers.

EDUCATION AND TRAINING

The best way to become a farm crop production technician is to complete a two-year training program at a community college or technical school. To be accepted into such a program, students should be high school graduates with coursework in mathematics and science. Coursework in English is also important, because much of the work involves interacting with people and preparing reports outlining changes.

The two-year training program will feature courses in soil management, agricultural economics, and farm crop production. Students may choose to specialize in a particular area of interest such as fruit or vegetable production. The training program will include the opportunity to go to farms and receive hands-on experience.

OUTLOOK AND EARNINGS

Although the number of farms in the United States is decreasing, the need for skilled technicians to help in production and research is growing. Individual farmers are looking for assistance in keeping crop productivity up, and the whole industry is in need of researchers to help find solutions to acid rain and other environmental problems. This should lead to a good number of job opportunities in the next decade for skilled technicians.

The average salary of farm crop production technicians is somewhere between $15,000 and $20,000 per year, depending on their education, experience, and the nature of their job. Technicians with advanced degrees who are employed in research or other off-farm jobs earn more.

WAYS OF GETTING MORE INFORMATION

For those who do not live on or near a farm, joining a 4-H club or Future Farmers of America organization is a good way to explore this career. It may also be possible to get a summer job at a farm.

In addition, write to the following organizations for more information about becoming a farm crop production technician:

American Society of Agronomy
Crop Science Society of America
677 South Segue Road
Madison, WI 53711

Future Farmers of America
National FFA Center
Alexandria, VA 22309

A farm crop production technician inspects a shipment of corn that is being unloaded.

FARM EQUIPMENT MECHANICS

SCHOOL SUBJECTS:
AGRICULTURE, SHOP (TRADE/VO-TECH EDUCATION)

PERSONAL INTERESTS:
FIGURING OUT HOW THINGS WORK, FIXING THINGS

OUTLOOK:
ABOUT AS FAST AS THE AVERAGE

OTHER ARTICLES TO LOOK AT:
Automobile Mechanics
Electromechanical Technicians
Mechanical Engineers

WHAT FARM EQUIPMENT MECHANICS DO

In the earliest days of farming, farmers made and maintained their own plows and sickles. If their tools needed repair, they took them into the blacksmith's shop—or even repaired the simple machines themselves. Now, however, the diesel and gasoline tractors, harvesting combines, hay balers, tilling equipment, silo fillers, trucks, and pumps are far too large and complicated for farmers to service themselves.

Farm equipment mechanics keep farm machinery in working order, and repair or overhaul it when it breaks down. They work on farms, in farm equipment repair shops, or for farm equipment dealers. They must know how to provide preventative maintenance, how to locate the cause of trouble when a machine breaks down, and how to repair anything from a failed air-conditioning unit in a tractor cab to a faulty irrigation system. They need both muscle power to lift heavy machine parts, and fine manual dexterity to

work with small components and delicate wiring. Whether they own their own shop or are employed by a farmer or dealer, they must enjoy working independently and in all types of weather.

EDUCATION AND TRAINING

Most employers prefer to hire high school graduates, but they also look for mechanical aptitude and some farm background. High school and vocational school courses in welding, maintenance, electronics, and repair of engines and hydraulic systems would also prove helpful.

Most mechanics learn their trade on the job. They are usually hired by farm equipment dealers or repair shops, and then work for at least two years under an experienced mechanic. There are also a few apprenticeship programs, which combine on-the-job training with classroom study. Some mechanics come from related fields—having served as farm laborers, heavy equipment operators, or automobile mechanics.

During the growing season, when the demand is highest, all farm equipment mechanics work long hours—sometimes 10 to 12 hours a day, seven days a week. During the winter, however, mechanics may work short hours or even be laid off. To avoid unemployment, it is important for farm equipment mechanics to have other skills or to be able to transfer their mechanical skills to other areas.

OUTLOOK AND EARNINGS

Employment for farm equipment mechanics is expected to remain steady going into the next century. New mechanics will be needed to replace those who retire or move into other occupations.

Currently, mechanics who work for farm equipment dealers are paid an average annual wage of about $19,900. Workers with the most experience and those who do the most complicated repairs can earn over $40,000. And mechanics who earn two-year associate degrees in agricultural mechanics and advance to service representative for farm-equipment manufacturers can earn even more.

WAYS OF GETTING MORE INFORMATION

For more information, write to:

National Farm and Power Equipment Dealers Association
10877 Watson Road
St. Louis, MO 63126

Motor and Equipment Manufacturers Association Technical Training Council
300 Sylvan Avenue
Englewood Cliffs, NJ 07632

A farm equipment mechanic works on a combine to ensure that it will perform well during the coming harvest season.

FARMERS

OTHER ARTICLES TO LOOK AT:

Agricultural Scientists

Animal Breeders and Technicians

Farm Crop Production Technicians

Soil Conservation Technicians

WHAT FARMERS DO

Farmers grow crops such as peanuts, corn, wheat, cotton, fruits, or vegetables. They may also raise livestock, chickens and turkeys for food, and keep herds of dairy cattle for milk.

Throughout the history of the United States, farming was mostly a family affair. Today, however, family farms are disappearing. Large farms run by agricultural corporations are taking their place. As farming becomes less a family occupation and more a business, the need for farm operators and managers has increased. *Farm operators and managers* direct all of the activities on farms. Farm operators may own or rent the land.

There are many different types of farmers. Some raise livestock as well as crops. They are called *general farmers*. Many specialize in growing plants. They are the grain farmers, vegetable farmers, tree-fruit-and-nut crop farmers, and tree farmers. Others specialize in animal farming. They are the ani-

mal breeders, fur farmers, livestock ranchers, poultry farmers, worm growers, reptile farmers, beekeepers, and fish farmers.

Farmers need good soil and a lot of water for their crops and animals. Therefore, they need to know how to bring water to their plants (irrigation) and add rich nutrients to the soil (fertilizer). They also need to know how to keep their animals and crops healthy. This involves controlling insects and diseases that will damage or destroy crops or livestock. It also involves providing proper care such as clean, warm shelters, proper food, and special breeding programs.

Crop farmers use large, expensive farm equipment to turn the soil, plant seeds, gather crops, and store them. As a result, they need to know how to run and repair the machines. Often, this becomes a major task. Tractors pull the plows that turn the soil and prepare it for planting. Seed drills plant the seeds in rows, and cultivators till the soil between the rows to control the weeds. Huge harvesting machines cut and sort the crops for storage or for sale.

Farm managers have slightly different responsibilities. Farm managers usually work on large, corporate farms. They are often hired by the owners to oversee different farms' operation. The owner of a large crop farm may hire a manager to oversee general planning, another manager to handle planting and harvesting, and a third manager to handle marketing or storing the crops.

Besides working with the soil, crops, animals, and farm machinery, farmers also have to keep extensive records of their income, expenses, and production schedules.

EDUCATION AND TRAINING

Future farmers can begin their education by joining such organizations as the Future Farmers of America and the 4-H Clubs. There are 4-H clubs for both rural and urban youth. In high school, students should take courses in mathematics and science, especially chemistry, earth science, and botany, the study of plants. Accounting, bookkeeping, and computer courses are also very helpful.

After high school, students should enroll in either a two-year or a four-year course of study in a college of agriculture. For a person with no farm experience, a bachelor's degree in agriculture is essential.

College graduates can be certified as farm managers by the American Society of Farm Managers and Rural Appraisers. To be certified, applicants must pass examinations about the business, financial, and legal aspects of farm management.

OUTLOOK AND EARNINGS

Because farming is such a risky business, those entering the career cannot make it without family support or financial aid. Reports show that the number of farmers or farm laborers is decreasing. Rising costs and the trend toward larger farms are forcing out the small farmers.

Farmers' incomes change from year to year. The amount they earn depends on various things: weather conditions, the condition of their farm machinery, the demand for their crops and livestock, and the costs of feed, land, and equipment. In the late-1990s, salaries for farm operatives and managers range between $15,000 and $30,000.

WAYS OF GETTING MORE INFORMATION

Manual Skills

People Skills

Sciences and Mathematics

For more information, write:

National Farmers Union
250 C 2nd Avenue.
Saskatoon, SK, Canada
27K 2MI

U.S. Department of Agriculture
Washington, DC 20250

A farmer examines one of the ripe vegetables that his farm has produced.

FASHION DESIGNERS

SCHOOL SUBJECTS:
ART, FAMILY AND CONSUMER SCIENCE

PERSONAL INTERESTS:
CLOTHES, DRAWING/PAINTING

OUTLOOK:
ABOUT AS FAST AS THE AVERAGE

OTHER ARTICLES TO LOOK AT:

Costume Designers

Models

Photographers

Textile Technicians

WHAT FASHION DESIGNERS DO

Fashion designers design the coats, dresses, suits, and other clothing that we all wear. Designers in Paris, New York, and other cities make fashion news by developing the new colors and styles that will be worn each year. Most designers, however, work for large department stores and clothes manufacturers and design clothes to meet the constant needs of customers.

In developing a new design or altering an existing one, designers first determine the needs of potential customers. They shop through stores to see which types of clothes are being bought and which are not. Designers may also go to theaters, sporting events, and other locations and regularly examine the latest fashion magazines and catalogs to observe what people are wearing. Keeping up with trends in fashion is very tricky, but important. If a designer's styles are too far ahead of what people want, for example, they will find that purchasers will reject the designs. If, however, designers repeat styles that have been successful in the past, they may find buyers wanting something different.

After a first rough sketch has been prepared, the designer begins to shape the pattern pieces that make the garment. The pieces are drawn to actual size on paper and then cut on a fabric. This fabric is sewn together and fitted on a model. This sample garment is shown to buyers and media representatives, and alterations are made as needed.

In some companies, designers are involved with all aspects of the production of the line, from the original idea to the completed garment. Many designers supervise workrooms while others may work right along with workroom supervisors to solve problems that come up.

Designers may be expected to create between 50 and 150 designs for each season's showings. They work on spring and summer designs during the fall and winter months and on fall and winter clothing during the summer months.

Fashion designers should have an eye for detail and be creative with all of their designs. They must also be able to communicate their ideas visually and work well with their hands. Designers should have the discipline to start projects on their own and meet production deadlines. They should be independent thinkers yet be open to new ideas (because fashions often change) and have a sense of fashion history, too. Because many designers are self-employed, business skills and sales ability are also important.

EDUCATION AND TRAINING

The best way to become a fashion designer is to complete a two-or three-year program in design from a fashion school. Some colleges offer a four-year degree in fine arts with a major in fashion design.

High school students interested in fashion design should take courses in art, clothesmaking, and computer-aided design (CAD).

OUTLOOK AND EARNINGS

There will be a good number of job opportunities for fashion designers in the next decade. Despite strong employment potential, the field is very competitive. Therefore, not all aspiring designers will find work. As always, those with the most skill, training, and experience will have the best chances of success.

Full-time designers who work for large stores or manufacturing companies should earn between $26,400 and $44,000 per year. Those who are self-employed may earn higher salaries, but this is dependent on their design and sales skills.

WAYS OF GETTING MORE INFORMATION

Those interested in fashion design should take every opportunity to attend style shows, visit art galleries, observe clothing worn by fashion leaders, read the latest fashion magazines, and shop through all kinds of clothing stores. Working in a fabric store is a very good way of becoming familiar with the many different kinds of fabrics and sewing notions that are available to designers.

In addition, write to the following organizations for more information:

The Fashion Group
9 Rockefeller Plaza
New York, NY 10020

International Association of Clothing Designers and Executives
475 Park Avenue, 17th Floor
New York, NY 10016
Tel: 212-685-6602

National Association of Schools of Art and Design
1125 Roger Baron Drive, Suite 21
Reston, VA 22090

A fashion designer drapes fabric over a dummy to see exactly how it will look as a blouse.

FAST FOOD WORKERS

SCHOOL SUBJECTS:
BUSINESS, FAMILY AND CONSUMER SCIENCE

PERSONAL INTERESTS:
COOKING, HELPING PEOPLE: PERSONAL SERVICE

OUTLOOK:
MUCH FASTER THAN THE AVERAGE

OTHER ARTICLES TO LOOK AT:

Food Production Workers

Food Service Workers

Waiters and Waitresses

WHAT FAST FOOD WORKERS DO

Fast food workers are employed by hamburger joints, coffee shops, hot dog stands, and other places that promise a quick bite to eat. These workers grill meats, prepare frozen French fries, keep condiment containers filled, and provide hot and cold beverages. They take the customer's order, run the cash register, and keep the restaurant clean. Most fast food restaurants are open seven days a week; some are even open 24 hours a day. To service a fast-moving community, fast food workers are required to keep a restaurant efficient, tidy, and comfortable.

Although a fast food restaurant may employ someone specifically as a cashier, and someone else as short-order cook, and someone else to clean the tables and floors, most restaurants employ people who can do a variety of work. They use many different machines and appliances, including a fryer, a grill, a soft-serve ice cream machine, and a soda fountain. These workers may be required to take orders from the drive-thru using an intercom system. They will have to make change. Perhaps most importantly, although they must work quickly and may have a long line of customers, they always need to remain friendly and courteous.

Though most workers work only part-time, or temporarily, some fast food chains offer workers the chance to advance into management positions. As workers gain more experience they may be given more responsibilities, such as making work schedules, opening and closing the restaurant, and interviewing potential employees.

Some franchise owners work with social service departments to offer work to the elderly, or to people with mental or physical disabilities.

EDUCATION AND TRAINING

From the earliest malt shops and sandwich counters of the 1940s and 1950s, the fast food industry has been a devoted employer of teenagers. High school and college students find most other job opportunities limited, so many fast food restaurants are staffed almost entirely by students. Because fast food work is not usually a career, there is a high turnover in employment. Most people take jobs in fast food restaurants only temporarily to supplement their incomes, pay tuition, or to allow for extra spending money.

OUTLOOK AND EARNINGS

Employment opportunities will continue to be good for fast food workers. Fast food work will continue to be a good source of income for teenagers and others new to the workplace.

Most fast food workers start out at minimum wage, or less if working fewer than 20 hours a week. With more experience, you may be given more responsibilities and a higher wage. Some managers can make around $9.00 an hour.

Other than managers, most fast food workers do not receive benefits. However, some fast food restaurant owners may provide a group insurance plan at a low monthly rate. Tuition payment plans, and other savings programs, may be available with fast food restaurants that employ mostly college students. In some fast food restaurants, workers may serve the customers at their tables, giving them the opportunity to earn tips. However, a waiter or waitress earning tips may be paid a lower wage.

WAYS OF GETTING MORE INFORMATION

Working a few hours a week at a local fast food restaurant is your best opportunity to learn more about the jobs that fast food workers do.

For more information, write:

National Soft Serve and Fast Food Association
9614 Tomstown Road
Waynesboro, PA 17268
Tel: 800-535-7748

Fast food workers must not only help keep their restaurant clean, but must also make sure that their own appearance is tidy.

GLOSSARY

accredited Approved as meeting established standards for providing good training and education. This approval is usually given by an independent organization of professionals to a school or a program in a school. Compare **certified** and **licensed.**

apprentice A person who is learning a trade by working under the supervision of a skilled worker. Apprentices often receive classroom instruction in addition to their supervised practical experience.

apprenticeship 1. A program for training apprentices (see **apprentice**). 2. The period of time when a person is an apprentice. In highly skilled trades, apprenticeships may last three or four years.

associate degree An academic rank or title granted by a community or junior college or similar institution to graduates of a two-year program of education beyond high school.

bachelor's degree An academic rank or title given to a person who has completed a four-year program of study at a college or university. Also called an undergraduate degree.

certified Approved as meeting established requirements for skill, knowledge, and experience in a particular field. People are certified by the organization of professionals in their field. Compare **accredited** and **licensed.**

commission A percentage of the money taken in by a company in sales that is given to the salesperson as pay, either in addition to or instead of a salary.

community college A public two year college, attended by students who do not live at the college. Graduates of a community college receive an associate degree and may transfer to a four-year college or university to complete a bachelor's degree. Compare **junior college** and **technical community college.**

curriculum All the courses available in a school or college; or, the courses offered in a particular subject.

degree An academic distinction given by a college or university to a student who has completed a program of study.

diploma A certificate or document given by a school to show that a person has completed a course or has graduated from the school.

doctorate An academic rank or title (the highest) granted by a graduate school to a person who has completed a two- to three-year program after having received a master's degree.

engineering The profession that is concerned with ways of making practical use of scientific knowledge. Typical engineering activities include planning and managing the building of bridges, dams, roads, chemical plants, machinery, and new industrial products.

freelancer A self-employed person who contracts to do specific jobs.

fringe benefit A payment or benefit to an employee in addition to regular wages or salary. Examples of fringe benefits include a pension, a paid vacation, and health or life insurance.

graduate school A school that people may attend after they have received their bachelor's degree. People who complete an educational program at a graduate school earn a master's degree or a doctorate.

humanities The branches of learning that are concerned with language, the arts, literature, philosophy, and history. Compare **social sciences** and **natural sciences.**

intern An advanced student (usually one with at least some college training) in a professional field who is employed in a job that is intended to provide supervised practical experience for the student.

internship 1. The position or job of an intern (see **intern**). 2. The period of time when a person is an intern.

journeyman A person who has completed an apprenticeship or other training period and is qualified to work in a trade.

junior college A two-year college that offers courses like those in the first half of a four-year college program. Graduates of a junior college usually receive an associate degree and may transfer to a four-year college or university to complete a bachelor's degree. Compare **community college.**

liberal arts The subjects covered by college courses that develop broad general knowledge rather than specific occupational skills. The liberal arts are often considered to include philosophy, literature and the arts, history, language, and some courses in the social sciences and natural sciences.

licensed Having formal permission from the proper authority to carry out an activity that would be illegal without that permission. For example, a person may be licensed to practice medicine or to drive a car. Compare **certified.**

life sciences The natural sciences that are concerned with living organisms and the processes that take place within them (see **natural sciences**).

major (in college) The academic field in which a student specializes and receives a degree.

master's degree An academic rank or title granted by a graduate school to a person who has completed a one- or two-year program after having received a bachelor's degree.

natural sciences All the sciences that are concerned with the objects and processes in nature that can be measured. The natural sciences include biology, chemistry, physics, astronomy, and geology. Compare **humanities** and **social sciences.**

pension An amount of money paid regularly by an employer to a former employee after he or she retires from working.

physical sciences The natural sciences that are concerned mainly with nonliving matter, including physics, chemistry, and astronomy.

private 1. Not owned or controlled by the government (such as private industry or a private employment agency). 2. Intended only for a particular person or group; not open to all (such as a private road or a private club).

public 1.Provided or operated by the government (such as a public library). 2. Open and available to everyone (such as public meeting).

regulatory Having to do with the rules and laws for carrying out an activity. A regulatory agency, for example, is a government organization that sets up required procedures for how certain things should be done.

scholarship A gift of money to a student to help the student pay for further education.

social sciences The branches of learning (such as economics and political science) that are concerned with the behavior of groups of human beings. Compare **humanities** and **natural sciences.**

social studies Courses of study (such as civics, geography, and history) that deal with how human societies work.

starting salary Salary paid to a newly hired employee. The starting salary is usually a smaller amount than is paid to a more experienced worker.

technical college A private or public college offering two- or four-year programs in technical subjects. Technical colleges offer courses in both general

and technical subjects and award associate degrees and bachelor's degrees. Compare **technical community college.**

technical community college A community college that provides training for technicians (see **community college**). Technical community colleges offer courses in both general and technical subjects and award associate degrees. Compare **technical college.**

technical institute A public or private school that offers training in technical subjects. Technical institutes usually offer only a few courses in general subjects and do not award any kind of degree. Technical institutes that offer a broader range of subjects and award degrees are usually called **technical colleges** or **technical community colleges.**

technical school A general term used to describe technical colleges, technical community colleges, and technical institutes. Compare **trade school** and **vocational school.**

technician A worker with specialized practical training in a mechanical or scientific subject who works under the supervision of scientists, engineers, or other professionals. Technicians typically receive two years of college-level education after high school.

technologist A worker in a mechanical or scientific field with more training than a technician. Technologists typically must have between two and four years of college-level education after high school.

trade An occupation that requires training and skills in working with one's hands.

trade school A public or private school that offers training in one or more of the trades (see **trade**). Compare **technical school** and **vocational school.**

undergraduate A student at a college or university who has not yet received a degree.

undergraduate degree See **bachelor's degree.**

union An organization whose members are workers in a particular industry or company. The union works to gain better wages, benefits, and working conditions for its members. Also called a *labor union* or *trade union.*

vocational school A public or private school that offers training in one or more skills or trades. Compare **technical school** and **trade school.**

wage Money that is paid in return for work done, especially money paid on the basis of the number of hours or days worked.

188